Scribners *Scribners* *Scribners*
ribners *Scribners* *Scrib*
s *Scribners* *S* *ers*
ribners *Scribner* *rib*
s *Scribners* *S* *ers*
ribners *Scribner* *Scrib*
Scribners *Scribners* *Scribners*
ribners *Scribners* *Scrib*
s *Scribners* *Scribners* *Scribners*
ribners *Scribners* *Scrib*
s *Scribners* *Scribners* *Scribners*
ribners *Scribners* *Scrib*
s *Scribners* *Scribners* *Scribners*
ribners *Scribners* *Scrib*
s *Scribners* *Scribners* *Scribners*
ribners *Scribners* *Scrib*
s *Scribners* *Scribners* *Scribners*
ribners *Scribners* *Scrib*
s *Scribners* *Scribners* *Scribners*
ribners *Scribners* *Scrib*
s *Scribners* *Scribners* *Scribners*

Scribners

THE
SCISSOR
MAN

Also by Jean Arnold

FAUSTO'S KEYHOLE

PRETTYBELLE

THE SCISSOR MAN

Jean
Arnold

Scribners

A Scribners Book

Copyright © 1990 by Jean Arnold

The right of Jean Arnold to be identified as author
of this work has been asserted.

First published in Great Britain in 1992 by Scribners
a Division of Macdonald & Co (Publishers) Ltd
London & Sydney

Published by arrangement with Doubleday
a division of Bantam Doubleday Dell Publishing Group, Inc.

A CIP catalogue record for this book is available from the British Library
ISBN 0 356 20302 6

Printed and bound in Great Britain by
Mackays of Chatham PLC, Chatham, Kent

Scribners
A Division of
Macdonald & Co (Publishers) Ltd
165 Great Dover Street
London SE1 4YA
A member of Maxwell Macmillan Publishing Corporation

With gratitude to Bill Smart and the Virginia Center for the Creative Arts, to Sandy West with fondest memories of the Ossabaw Island Project, and to my husband Jerry Wexler for his editorial skills and encouragement.

For Marita

. . . There was so much mud and swamp that we had difficulty in getting clear of it; and so many Indians attacked us, hurling their lances and shooting arrows, that it took us a long time to struggle ashore. While Cortez was fighting, he lost a sandal in the mud and could not recover it. So he landed with one bare foot. However, his sandal was later picked up, and he put it on again.

—*Bernal Díaz del Castillo,*
The Conquest of New Spain

THE
SCISSOR
MAN

1	When my brother Claude was tiny he would run out barefoot in the sandy street and teach the island children how to beg. It was an out-of-the-way place we lived in then, an island, and the people were stunted Mayan Indians, hungry and

hard-working. My brother Claude was a well-fed blue-eyed child with yellow hair, twice the size of his little friends. He told them to surround the passer-by and ask for a ten. And then, when they shyly obeyed him, little Claude with Yankee brass would shove ahead of them, hold out his own hand and shout, "Twenty! For me, a twenty!"

That amused the islanders. They rewarded him with two coins and a nickname. The Twenty, they called him. *"El Veinte."*

He was my only brother. At least, the only one who had some time to grow. I had two sisters and this one enterprising brother named for my mother's brother: Claude. The girls were Duncan, Maribel, and me, Octavia. I was the youngest. Runt of the litter, Duncan said.

El Veinte disappeared when he was seven. On our sleepy over-heated island even my doctor father couldn't keep his children alive. El Veinte disappeared of fever, and ever afterward dwelt incommunicado in a tiny house in the village cemetery, a pale blue stucco house. Like a playhouse. I used to go and visit him from time to time. Surrounded by dead people, I'd sit on his sunbaked roof and talk to him. He could hear me all right but he wouldn't answer—not out loud. He spoke through birds and insects, or the antics of the wind.

One spring some red wasps built a nest under the eaves of his faded pale blue house. When I came near they buzzed at me angrily, like guardian spirits. El Veinte was giving me a message. He didn't want his roof sat on, his privacy disturbed.

The two people my mother loved best were both named Claude. Her brother Claude, and my brother Claude. El Veinte. My mother really loved El Veinte. She didn't want three girls. She wanted that one greedy little boy. After he died, she wouldn't go to funerals and she wouldn't speak of him. You couldn't make her speak of him. Once when I was full of grievances and looking for a way to hurt, I told her that his little house was crumbling, and his skeleton soon would lie there in plain view.

She never said a word. She sent our gardener to look, and found out it wasn't true, but she never reproached me. Why did I do such a thing? I felt bad for days.

I used to think a lot about brothers, perhaps because I didn't have one. On our island, brothers were more important than they seem to be here in the States. When parents died, brothers took care of you. They sheltered and fed you, their sister. It was required. *"You can always find a husband,"* the island women said, *"but a brother is someone you can't replace."*

My mother agreed. She talked about him all the time, her brother Claude, even though she hadn't laid eyes on him since she was a girl of seventeen in Washington, D.C. She talked about him and wrote letters to him—she wrote short stories about him and submitted them to magazines back in the States. One was even published in a little magazine. I got sick of hearing about that brother of hers, but all the same I wanted one for myself. A brother would make me real. He would reflect me back and I would know there was a real person here, a visible audible person. Octavia's brother proves Octavia.

In Mother's case, this brother was her twin, and maybe that's why her attitude was so extreme. The two of them had floated together in one womb for nine long months with nothing to do but grow. Brother and sister, Claude and Catherine, all entwined together naked. I've read it's possible for boy and girl to copulate inside the womb. Do you believe that? I don't believe that. I think it's just mythology. But on the other hand it's true that newborn babies have these giant genitals. . . . Who knows? It might begin by accident, and then . . . those two, I wouldn't put it past them. They were capable of anything.

I was only six months old when El Veinte died and left me with no brothers at all, only Duncan and Maribel, these two older sisters who were nothing but misery. All through my childhood I used to think how different my life would have been if he had stayed alive. Even dead he was a pretty good companion.

When the red wasps chased me off I didn't stop visiting. I went just as often, but I kept a certain distance. I'd hang around some twenty, thirty feet away, fidgeting, yearning, not wanting to be a nuisance. I told him all the secrets he didn't really care to hear. I knew if he were alive he'd have defended me. He'd have been my friend. My sister Duncan would never have dared torment me as she did. The island children would have looked up to me. I would have been their boss. I could have ruled them with an iron hand. Some tiny stupid microbe wrecked my life.

This yearning for a brother never stopped till I was twelve, and my cousin Julian came to visit from the States.

When Julian and his father came, everything changed. Even the light changed when they came. Or so I remember. It turned sharp and pale, the color of lemons. The air was full of . . . collisions . . . impacts . . . small clicks and shocks, as if it had shattered into fragments and was running into itself. In my memory, even the sea lost its color, turned cold and gray, like a northern sea, and the people seemed to shrivel, becoming markedly smaller and darker.

I stopped thinking about El Veinte because I had so many other things to think about. A cousin can replace a brother, it seems. In some ways, a cousin is even better, though less certain. A brother you have forever—alive or dead, he's close, he's your brother—but a cousin can slip through your fingers at any time. You have to woo him and win him and then you have to hold him. A cousin keeps you hard at work. Part brother, part lover, he's beautiful trouble.

Julian and his father. They came in springtime when the fires were burning. They came for a two-week visit and stayed for seven months. Everyone loved Julian right away, but his father was another story. His father, my Uncle Claude . . . he was an unknown quantity.

For a long time I haven't thought about the island much. Lately, though, I've felt a strange pressure, a wind blowing from the past, a spanking breeze, increasing, gusting to gale force. Flags stiffly whipping. Alarm, alarm on the island. Church bell ringing and it isn't Call to Mass. It isn't *La Doctrina*. It's doomsday, a hurricane! You can hear the church bell as never before. You hear the tongue, the clapper roll around against the bronze cup, a booming, hollow sound snatched up and suffocated by the wind, drowned in wind as hard as water.

The villagers come crowding into the streets shouting and stamping, beating pots and pans. The boys are exploding firecrackers, the men shoot off their guns. . . .

No, no, no. I'm wrong.

That was the eclipse. Not the hurricane, the eclipse. Remember, Octavia? Remember the eclipse? You were so little then.

Yes, Mother, I remember the eclipse. I remember the damned eclipse.

Octavia ran out in the street just like the others. We gave her a tin bucket and a spoon so she could beat on it and frighten away the darkness. Sweetheart, you remember? Do you remember back that far?

I remember perfectly well. The bats and moths came out. The air was strange, painted with darkness. The birds went to bed. The green parrots came flying home from the mainland in midafternoon, squawking, straggling, all in disarray. Daylilies and heliotrope folded their petals, withered, died. All clocks went wild, the world was dying.

Octavia took her little tin sand bucket—

Mother, please.

I'm only telling Uncle Clo—

If El Veinte were alive today, he'd be forty-one years old. He would work on Wall Street in New York, dressed up in a thousand-dollar suit. He'd be in venture capital. He'd live in a penthouse on Central Park South with three mistresses and two wives, and every night he'd eat at Windows on the World. His nickname would be Twenty Million, because that's the smallest sum he'd bother with.

If El Veinte were alive today, he'd tell me what to do about my life, my pregnancy. He was that kind of a person. If El Veinte were alive, he'd say, "Octavia, have the kid. You'll love the kid." Or else he'd say, "Octavia, why ask for trouble? Abort the kid, come live with me." And I'd get it over with in a hurry, and fly away to Central Park South and move right in. I wouldn't have to work or anything. I'd zoom right back to childhood and I'd hunker down. El Veinte's kid sister. I'd live in a closet if I had to. His closets would be big as bedrooms anyway.

But the cold truth is he died, and having no real choice I left childhood more or less behind. I grew up, married, went to work like everybody else.

Today I live and work in Pittsburgh, Pennsylvania, teaching Spanish at the university. I'm thirty-four years old, I'm pregnant. My husband wants to have children, but I'm not sure I'm ready.

"Not ready?" says my husband. "You're thirty-four years old. When *will* you be ready?"

"When women are afraid to have babies and men are afraid to go to war, the country has come to a pretty pass."

My cousin Julian's mother said that, on her deathbed in Hershey, Pennsylvania, and Julian could never get the words out of his head. It always struck me as an unlikely remark to make on a deathbed, but she made it and very shortly afterward she died, giving it the stamp of final authority. It caused her son all kinds of trouble. In fact, it sent him to his death in Vietnam. I suppose if she had lived, she might have taken it back, or modified it, explained it, softened it, but she died, and Julian went unhappily to war rather than live with her posthumous contempt.

It bothered me as well. I haven't thought of it for quite some time, but her contempt has been there, etched in bile, on my heart.

Octavia means eight, as in octave, octet, or octopus. I was the last child, the eighth, Octavia. My mother told me I was the eighth and I took her word for it. A woman ought to know how many children she had.

Pregnancy was my mother's specialty, her field, her fate, her martyrdom. Did she want all those pregnancies? She certainly didn't want me. "I took a hot bath to make you go away," she said, and laughed, and gave me a squeeze. "But you didn't, and now of course I'm glad."

Didn't she know about birth control? A doctor's wife? My theory is, she saw her pregnancies as penance for having run away from home in Washington, D.C., to marry my father.

All during my childhood Mother put to death pregnant and female creatures, doing her bit to prevent suffering and misery. There was no Humane Society on our island, so she had to do it herself. Any pregnant or nursing animal that crossed her path she killed with all its young, using my father's medical supplies. In the early days on the island she often assisted my father in his operations, holding the flashlight and applying the chloroform, so she knew exactly what to do, and kept a special box for the purpose, an airtight box, stored in the shed behind the kitchen.

She did it from compassion. Oh yes, her compassion, especially for female animals. The sight of a pregnant cat or mother dog all skin and bones, with swollen teats, nosing for water in the dry season, aroused her, wounded her, and she would utter a special cry of affliction and pity, fluting down from A to E. Her face drew together in pain, and she put them to death.

Do I sound critical? I am not. I believe with her that death can be a gift and a blessing. But she paid a price for these acts of rescue. She dreamed of cats and kittens, grown enormous, scratching and mewing at her windows in the night, struggling for air, crying for help, imploring her with desperate eyes.

Pregnancy, a desperate state. A dangerous state. It leads to chloroform. Death is better than pregnancy.

Get in the box, Octavia.

Be grateful.

Do not mew.

2 Octavia's sister Maribel had to be kept away from the sea. She never understood about water and breathing. She thought a person could live under water. She would plunge in without the slightest fear and have to be pulled out.

Her mother let it happen once or twice. She figured: let her drown a little and learn her lesson.

When Uncle Claude came to visit on the island, Maribel was seventeen. She still had her baby teeth in front.

"There are tribes," said Uncle Claude, "where the crazy one is thought to bring good luck."

Mother protested. "She isn't crazy. She's forever a child. And now so pretty. Felipe *wants* her to be pretty—what a mistake! If we had any sense we'd shave her head and dress her in sacks. Our troubles are only beginning."

Maribel had soft black hair which Mother cut for years in the most unbecoming ways she could think of. The bangs were all right, but the rest was short and straight and shingled in the back. Later on, at her father's insistence, her hair was allowed to grow longer. Delila took to curling it, and Maribel was transformed. Everyone looked at her, and looked again.

In that same epoch she began unbuttoning her blouse. She unbuttoned twice in front of Lenin, Papa's assistant. His face turned purple but he couldn't stop smiling. And ever after that, he'd look at her, stealing looks. In Octavia's opinion she showed herself on purpose, especially to Lenin. She really liked Lenin.

Father said Maribel should lead a normal life and get married. He had his eye on Lenin as a son-in-law, and loudly said that any man would be lucky to be married to Maribel. Mother found this so preposterous she was left gasping. When she recovered she was bitter and sarcastic.

"Married," said Mother. "Oh yes, indeed. She'll make a fine efficient little housewife and mother, won't she!"

"She and her husband would live with *us.*"

"Oh, I see," said Mother. "That's the plan. So *I* can have the pleasure of raising her defective children. How delightful. Thanks very much."

"I know what we *ought* to do," Mother says to Uncle Claude, "we ought to sterilize her. If she were a boy, we could do it. But a girl—!"

"Why not a girl?"

"It's a serious operation."

"Not that serious," says Uncle Claude. "You just tie off the tubes."

"Are you sure?"

"Of course. You tie them off."

"You don't remove the womb?"

"Good lord," says her brother. "You a doctor's wife!"

Mother blushes.

"Your husband could easily do it himself," suggests Uncle Claude.

Mother gives a short laugh. "Felipe?" she says. "Never. The winds of heaven mustn't visit her face too harshly. Besides, he *wants* her to marry and have babies. Can you bear it? The man is blind. Clo, would *you* speak to him?"

"It's not my place," says Uncle Claude.

• • •

Octavia, overhearing, fails to understand. *If she were a boy, she could be sterilized?* Sterilization is what her father does to his instruments.

She now envisions a giant cauldron lying on hot coals. It is a tin tub full of steaming boiling water. Clouds of steam almost obscure the scaffolding above it. The boy Maribel struggles naked in a rope-net sling that is hanging from a winch. "Lower away!" shouts her mother, and he is lowered by a winch. Down, down, plunge! Now, up quickly. Ropes bite flesh. He is red as a lobster. Oh, he is burnt and blistered, he is screaming, no, he is unconscious, oh, he is cooked!

"A tiny surgical procedure," her mother now explains to Octavia. "You just tie off her tubes."

"Her tubes—!" says Octavia.

"To keep her eggs from descending."

"Her eggs—!"

"Of course, eggs. Every month a woman's body—"

"Maribel's *eggs*—! She has *eggs*—? I'm going to puke."

Struggling to run, Octavia scuffs through soft sand. She races where it is packed, along the sea. The sea is every shade of green and blue; she can see dolphins rolling out there; the breeze lifts her hair. She rushes the sandpipers to see them fly. They wheel and turn, alight again behind her. She squats over the tide pools to inspect the sea anemones, the baby fish. She swims in a lagoon, and under water, opens her eyes to a world of darting flashing silver, peacock blue.

Yet she has grown up with a sense that everything worthwhile took place before her birth. She lives in a melancholy and decaying time, an ebb tide pale with phosphorescent afterglow. She has missed the great storms the islanders talk about; she walks among the stranded things that have been washed ashore, beached sea-creatures, drying, drowning in air. The island is a place of relics, ruins of earlier civilizations. She is a meaningless survivor. El Veinte is dead, Maribel is damaged, Duncan has gone away. The fruit company has gone away. Beyond the blighted banana trees, the haciendas of her father's father's time are ruined and crumbling. And beyond them, scattered deep in the jungle, are the silent Mayan pyramids, some sixty or seventy of them, small in size (it is a small island), smothered with vegetation. Trees grow from their summits. They are so ancient that the people of the island note their presence with no sign of recognition, as if they had been left behind by visitors from another galaxy. The farthest back their memories and lore can reach is to the time of slaves and *hacendados,* and these are the ones they mean when they speak of *"los ancianos."*

"Worlds upon worlds, all lost," says Don Mauricio, Octavia's tutor.

She savors the melancholy sound of it: *worlds upon worlds, all lost.*

She denies that she is lonely. For her the island is home. True, she has no friends among the island children, but she has her cat and her books and the piano. She has her father and the parade of patients in the *clínica.* She has the maids, Soledad and Delila, and Domingo the gardener, and Lenin, her father's assistant, and Don Mauricio. And of course, eternally, her mother and Maribel. She has too many people. How could she be lonely?

Besides, every summer her mother takes her to Valladolid, the capital city high in the mountains of the mainland, and there for twelve weeks she attends an English-language school with other fair-haired children, to be civilized. She learns the latest slang, the latest music, the latest games and fads and crazes. She learns to read the comics and to roller skate, learns what shoes to wear and exactly the line on her knee where her skirts should reach.

Maribel used to go with them to Valladolid, to be taken to the dentist. But every time she screamed and got worse, and now she does not come any more.

Octavia likes Valladolid, but it isn't home. Isla Caracol is home. She was born here. Her umbilical cord is buried here. So is Maribel's. So is El Veinte's. (Duncan's is not; Duncan was born on the mainland. That's why Duncan is different.)

To Octavia's mother, the island is a penitentiary. With a smile that does not convince, she says: "I've done my time for any crime on the books. Even murder." (Her eyes rest briefly on her husband.) "I've paid my debt in advance and now I get to commit my crime. Watch out, all of you! Beware of Catherine!"

Maribel is playing solitaire. Her mother stands over her. Now in reality, as Octavia knows, Maribel cannot play solitaire. She makes rows of cards, she makes messy piles, puts cards on cards, picks up and puts down at random. The point is that she must *look* as though she's playing solitaire. And one day when the famous dream comes true (her mother's dream) and the famous miracle takes place (which it never will) and they are all in the United States basking in the company of the famous brother, and the long exile is over—on that great day the *gringos* can look on and say: *Why, look, there's lovely Maribel and she's playing solitaire!*

"You have no friends," Julian told Octavia when he came to the island, and it was true. But in the old days of the fruit company, Octavia had a friend. She had a best friend, Elizabeth Jane, a stocky child with carrot-colored braids. But the fruit company Americans packed up and left, taking Elizabeth Jane with them, and leaving behind hectare after hectare of stunted mottled banana trees that produced only bitter, dwarf bananas. The soil was poisoned and there was no cure. The company moved on.

Now squatters live in the abandoned rotting houses and the great concrete pier is cracked and crumbling. The islanders have been left to their ancient poverty. They fish and hunt and catch turtles, they slash and burn the jungle, and plant their corn with sticks. Coconut plantations have apathetically returned, and the sour stench of copra hangs once again around the pier.

When Elizabeth Jane left, it is possible Octavia felt lonely. Duncan had already gone away to school in the United States, leaving a pleasurable void. (Who could miss Duncan?) But when Elizabeth Jane went away, Octavia missed her more than anyone knew.

Octavia did not go to the island school. Her father wouldn't let her, because it was run by nuns. He didn't want her mind poisoned by the Church, blighted like the banana trees, as his own had been. Instead she had Don Mauricio. The life of the island children passed her by.

Octavia and Elizabeth Jane wrote to each other, and they eagerly renewed their friendship in Valladolid in the summertime. In the winter Elizabeth Jane would come to visit on the island. She would spend two weeks. But the third winter she was sick and couldn't come; and that summer, when Octavia arrived at school in Valladolid, Elizabeth Jane was in the States. By the time she finally reached the island, in December of the fourth winter, Elizabeth Jane was so changed Octavia hardly knew her.

Even her voice was different. She had braces on her teeth, and her hair was short and curly and darker. "Auburn," said Elizabeth Jane modestly, "it was always auburn. Yours is terrible, Octavia. It's a bush. Don't you ever rinse the salt out? Don't you use conditioners?"

She wasn't Elizabeth Jane at all. She was a girl who chattered about boys and clothes and hairdos, who wore a bra and kept looking at herself in the mirror. Putting on lipstick. She was not even the same shape, but taller and thinner, and her waist sank in. She didn't care to climb the guava tree. She didn't care to swim, she had the curse. She wanted to set Maribel's hair. She wanted to walk in the plaza so the boys could see her. She taught Octavia the *bugalu.* She took an insane interest in skinny, shy Lenin, Papa's assistant, stealing his hat, and making him chase her to get it back. She lay in ambush for Cano, the mayor's oldest son. Even Santiago, their ancient enemy, even Santiago, she said, was really cute.

"He likes you," she told Octavia. "Santiago has a crush on you."

A crush? Santiago? Octavia dragged along in Elizabeth Jane's wake, mystified, infantile. She found nothing to say. She only listened. At night, in bed, Elizabeth Jane talked on and on, she talked and talked into the dawn about the adorable boys she knew, not only in Valladolid, but "back home" in Charleston, South Carolina. She said the girls back home soul-kissed and went all the way. She talked about dances and parties and taffeta and net and insets of lace until Octavia's head was a stone of misery and she fell asleep in self-defense.

At the pier, when the visit was over and they were saying goodbye, Elizabeth Jane hugged Octavia and promised to write. She smelled of perfume, and had pinned a yellow hibiscus flower in her auburn hair.

"Next summer when you come to Valladolid, I'll get you a date," she said. "I know just the boy. He's not handsome but he's really nice. You'll like him. Most blind dates are awful, but not Campbell."

"Well, I don't know," said Octavia.

"He used to be crazy about me, but I liked Pepe Luis and I was going with Bob, and next best I liked Ricky, so anyway he's free. But you'll have to do something about your hair. Honestly, Octavia, it's too tacky. In Valladolid you can go to the beauty parlor. Bye, now. Don't forget to write!"

Crinkling her nose against the smell of copra *("Pee-yew,"* she said), Elizabeth Jane stepped daintily aboard the battered old

Camilio Canto, disdained the help of her maid but took instead (flashing her braces) the hand of the eager and half-naked deck boy.

"I won't forget," said Octavia.

The *Camilio Canto* wallowed out into the channel, and Octavia, left behind on the sunbaked pier, waved sadly. They who had been equals, comrades, were no longer. Somehow, while she slumbered, while she slept, Octavia had been downgraded. Without warning she found herself demoted, jettisoned. And now who was there anywhere to recognize her and respect her? All the things she was, all the things she could do, who saw them now? Octavia the bold, the swift, the nonchalant, the devil-may-care, Octavia the tease, the swimmer, runner, climber, cardplayer, puzzle-solver, adventure-proposer, Octavia the heroine—all these were now invisible. Lost. How had it happened?

She looked out to sea, at the line beyond which lay the great continent, the enormous world where Elizabeth Jane was going, where Elizabeth Jane held court. The wind nagged at her face, the sun was too bright in her eyes. The big world teemed with Elizabeth Janes and all those things she talked about.

Soul kisses. You opened your mouth and let some boy stick his tongue inside. Octavia sneered. She scratched a bite on her thigh and observed that she was wearing khaki shorts. Boys' shorts. She did not remember putting them on. She always wore them. Or else her old green bathing suit. Elizabeth Jane called them ghastly.

She turned toward home.

Next morning she woke up early and went to the cemetery to visit El Veinte. She found she had come to a decision. "I'll never go to Valladolid again," she told him.

Outside the walls a burro was braying, an awful sound, like a machine retching, a machine in mortal pain.

"And I won't go to the States either. I'm staying here with you."

Never mind that her mother was already planning next summer's trip to Valladolid. Never mind that soon—next fall, or the fall after that—she was expected to go off to Virginia to Miss Hooten's School, where Duncan had gone. Octavia did not care. Nobody could force her, nobody could pick her up and carry her. Here on this island she would stay forever, she and El Veinte, both of them would stay, exactly as they were, forever.

Don Mauricio has fat jowls and a soft fat behind, and he says to Octavia, "What kind of little girl is it who doesn't love dolls?"

Because she is small for her age, everyone calls her a little girl. It is maddening for someone nearly thirteen. At the same time, she feels a certain satisfaction.

One day, in the classroom off the *sala,* Octavia catches Don Mauricio with his hand inside Maribel's blouse. It is hard to know who is more embarrassed, Don Mauricio or Octavia. Don Mauricio pretends he did nothing. Octavia pretends she saw nothing. Maribel looks thoughtful and twists a lock of hair.

What is it about her, anyway? What is it about those breasts, that everyone wants to touch and squeeze them? If Maribel were normal, if she could talk and tell, they would not do it. As Maribel's sister and protector, Octavia should tell on Don Mauricio herself, but she knows she won't. She hasn't got the nerve. She hasn't got the nerve to do anything. Just saying the words would make her stammer and blush. Nobody would believe her anyway.

Don Mauricio wipes the sweat off his forehead. He picks up a book and adjusts his clothing. In a sullen atmosphere the algebra lesson begins.

In the back garden marvelous brownblack birds air their virtuosity. Grackles, boat-tailed grackles. They flute and whistle, cackle, twitter, chortle and cluck, peep and hoot and give advice, exclaim, question, remark, command, squawk, scold, go into conference;

they quaver pitifully, trill, buzz, vibrate—to Octavia it is obvious that boat-tailed-grackle talk is far more lively and various than any human conversation. She has spent six months in love with one special grackle—oh, this bird, this alert sharp bird, this healthy nervy bright-as-a-button flirty perky bird living it up in his own special world—his magic air-bright world of relationships, hierarchies, secret knowledge, customs, traditions, nurseries and schools and governmental institutions, kings and queens and princes (he is a prince). Octavia is dying to enter this world and know its secrets. Spread out beneath everyone's nose, nobody even sees it.

"Make the brush a little boat, over all the billows float," chants Maribel, brushing Octavia's hair. How happy she is, how busy. First she brushes and pats, brushes and pats, then with a big white comb, she rips and tears. Octavia is flushed and miserable, taking her punishment, doing penance for her crimes. Her hair is long and thick and hopelessly tangled; it is stiff and sticky with salt, from swimming in the lagoon. Maribel picks out great knots and tangles of hair from the comb and drops them on the red tile floor. Octavia was mean to her and made her cry. This is her expiation.

They are in Maribel's room, in the center of a ring of dolls. Maribel is too old for these dolls, five years older than Octavia, but she still plays with them. Octavia, sitting on a little painted stool in the center of the magic circle as Maribel bends or kneels behind her, is also a doll for Maribel, a warm one, in pain. Tears go rolling down her face. Bitterly she tastes them from her lips. Maribel neither notices nor cares. Yet she loves her sister and in her clumsy way is mothering her.

Beyond the magic circle is the bed, mosquito netting looped up high. And all around the two girls, on the walls, are Maribel's scribbles and crazy paintings. Her murals. Frescos, their father calls them. Rows and rows of people, all of them with legs, feet, and huge beetle-like torsos, but very few with arms or hands. They are surrounded by jungle. Father encourages her painting, Mother disapproves but does not forbid. As for Octavia, she hates it, she loves it.

Her scalp is on fire. Breaking her vow she cries out, "You're too rough, Maribel!"

Maribel does not see the evil in her sister's heart. By now she does not even remember today's crime—how Octavia set the blue incense burning in an unused bedroom and closed the windows, lured Maribel inside, and quickly, gleefully, locked the door behind her, locked her inside with the burning incense knowing how it frightened her, knowing she would tremble and cry and cower in the corner. Knowing all that, and doing it anyway, with a cruel, keen delight.

Octavia does these things. She swears she won't, and then she does them. Afterward, conscience falls upon her like a boa constrictor.

She has given her father a faithful promise to be kind to Maribel. He asked for her promise one night after a quarrel in the dining room. Maribel had tried to take her blouse off in front of Lenin, and Mother in a rage pounced on her, pulled the blouse together, and slapped her face. "Never do that again! You know not to do that. You *know!*" And her father snatched Maribel away and shouted at Mother, "Get out!" He took Maribel in his arms while she whimpered sloppily on his chest. Mother stood with her hands on her hips. "It's all very well for *you,*" she said. "It's all very easy and simple! You don't have her, day in and day out. You're not responsible for her training and her care!" And she marched out of the room with her mouth tight and her head high to go to her bedroom and suffer from migraine for three days.

That evening her father came to Octavia's room. He smiled and sat down and took her on his lap, but it was Maribel he wanted to talk about. Octavia must be extra nice to Maribel and not tease her, he said, because Maribel was very sad.

"But Papi, she's not sad!" Octavia protested. "She always forgets. She forgets right away. She's in there right now happy as can be with her dolls. Singing. Listen to her."

And indeed the awful sound of Maribel's singing came through the wall.

"She is sad," her father said, and the sadness in his own voice spread into Octavia's heart. "Even when she appears to forget, some part of her mind remembers. Tavvie, you have everything that she has not, and so you must be kind to her. Will you promise me?"

"I'll try." She wanted to cry at the hopeless dull grief in his voice. "I'll try, but I can't always. Papi, I just can't. She's so dumb—"

"Just promise me."

And Octavia promised.

Nobody but Octavia could recognize from the noises Maribel is making that she is chanting one of their mother's sweet-little-girl poems, the hairbrush poem.

> *Sail the rough and tangled tide*
> *Till it's smooth on every side*
> *And like other little girls*
> *You've a sea of shining curls.*

Coming from Maribel, as she happily tears out the tangles, it is no longer a sweet-little-girl poem. It is incantation.

> *Aye ha-yuh, aye ha-yuh.*

Maribel is a priestess in trance, and Octavia (wincing, flinching, crying) is the victim, a sacrifice on the altar of the hopeless love she bears her father.

> *Aye ha-yuh, aye ha-yuh.*

• • •

Now Mother bursts into Maribel's room, clutching a letter in her hands, happy to the point of tears and dancing. Her brother, oh, her brother, her brother! Her brother is coming to visit us at last, her own darling brother, her pet, her pride, her twin, whom she has not seen, has not laid eyes on since before even Duncan was born, not for twenty-four years, no, twenty-five, not since she was seventeen and he was seventeen and they lived in their parents' house in Washington, and their father wrongfully, willfully, forcibly, separated them, sent Claude away to school in secret, not even allowing them to say good-bye, and she in protest ran away from home which girls did not do in those days they simply didn't and her Aunt Lou in San Antonio took her in and it was there that she met their father, a young intern, and one thing led to another. But she never dreamed—how could she have dreamed?—that she wouldn't see him again for all these years, her brother, her own brother, her twin. She had of course been headstrong and so very young, wrapped up in her anger, foolish and willful and unthinking. You never know when your life will take a turn, and suddenly you find you can't go back. You have children, everything changes. But never mind all that—in three weeks, three short weeks, he will be here!

And he is bringing his son with him!

Octavia pricks up her ears.

"This son," says Catherine like a story-teller, "is your cousin, he is about fourteen and his name is Julian. My brother's name is Claude, but I always called him Clo. A pet name. He is a very special person. As children we were inseparable. People who have no twin can't possibly understand. One half of me has been with my brother always, all my life, wherever he went, on all his adventures.

"And such adventures! Such freedom! You can't believe the things he's done, the places he's been, all over the world. We must persuade him to tell the story of his adventures. They would fill a book. He ought to write a book. Someone could help him write it.

Perhaps I could help him. Yes, why not! What a marvelous idea. We can write a book!"

She pauses a moment, her eyes look at the ceiling, imagining the book, searching for its title. Hadn't he climbed the Andes, followed the Amazon to its source, nearly frozen to death in Tibet, been captured by Berber tribesmen in North Africa? Hadn't he been trapped between hostile armies while running along the Great Wall of China? He loves danger, seeks it out. He has been places no white man had ever seen before. . . . "Oh, Tavvie-cat" (and she hugs Octavia, who holds her backbone rigid and resistant as a stick), "the games we played as children, the times we had."

In her emotion, she fails to observe that Maribel is ripping Octavia's tangled hair out by the roots with a large white comb. She fails to observe that Maribel and Octavia are surrounded by dolls, all sitting or lying on the floor in a magic circle. She treads upon a naked celluloid baby doll and its torso goes crunch. Maribel sags. Furtively, she looks at the crushed remains. She stops combing Octavia's hair. She stands still and dark and vacant, as if waiting. She does not speak, it is the wrong phase of the moon for speaking, but she vacantly makes a face, pulling down her chin without opening her mouth.

"Don't do that, dear," says Mother absently. "Maribel? No, no."

Maribel stops making her face, and Mother starts making one herself. An awful face. Her mouth curls down, her cheeks push up, her nose pinches together. She is going to cry.

"Forgive me, girls," quavers Mother, and she bursts frankly into tears, fishing in her sleeve for a handkerchief. "It's not from sadness," she weeps. "In fact, I think it's because your mama is so happy."

Blindly, she opens her arms for Octavia, who is embarrassed and does not step into them.

"Mother, your dignity," she says.

Her mother is not usually like this. She can be loving and indulgent (as with Octavia), remote and dutiful (with Papi), preoccupied and distant (reading or writing or playing the piano), grim and tyrannical (with Maribel). With the maids and the gardener she can be patronizing and kind, or indignant and commanding. She can be nostalgic and sweetly sad about her childhood, she can be brightly determined, falsely cheerful—Octavia knows her mother in many moods, but babbling weeping happiness is not one of them. Happiness is not in her mother's repertory, as Octavia knows it.

And that has a meaning. It means that she and Maribel and Papi and the island and all their life together are not enough. Octavia looks at her mother, and in a flash she sees all the people and the things, all the texture of the life that is not enough. Above all, Papi and herself and Maribel. And so much more. The clouds and the sunsets and the green-blue sea, the tide pools in the coral rock, the sandy beaches, the lagoons and the sparkling fish that live in them, Soledad and Delila the maids, Domingo the gardener, whose head was cut off—nearly—in a machete fight, Papi's assistant Lenin (whose brother's name is Socrates), the patients in Papi's hospital, the snails, the conches, the grackles, the green parrots, the pelicans and terns that fall into the sea, the gulls, the little fishing boats, the burlap sacks of sharks' teeth, the dogs, the children, her own red cat Pablito, the mayor and the priest and the central plaza with its polluted fountains, the burros, the coconuts, the speckled bleeding life-sized Christ nailed to his cross in the village church, the guava tree, the market, the butterflies, the flowers, the vines, the jungle and its pyramids, the dead in the cemetery—El Veinte and the infant twins, Papi's mother and father and two brothers and a sister slaughtered long ago in the burned-out hacienda at the southern tip of the island—the moon and the stars, the island itself, Isla Caracol, Snail Island, Octavia's island, her world, sunbaked, windblown, moonwashed, sea-surrounded—all this, which should have been enough, was not enough.

"He's forty-two," said her mother. "Think of it."

She moves over to Maribel's mirror and gazes at herself. She touches her cheeks, her eyes, her hair, and, sucking in her breath, her waistline. She heaves a sigh and turns away, but happiness breaks through again, comes crashing down on her like surf and runs foaming and delicious up the beach wave after wave.

"I'll put him in the music room," she says. "And the boy in Duncan's room. It must be painted. Oh, so much to do! That bathroom must be repaired. Is there time for everything? You girls must cooperate. Mama will be very busy. Oh, Maribel, this room of yours—"

She is gathering up dolls and plumping them down on the shelves and furniture. "These dolls must go *up,*" she says. "In the chest, on the shelves. Why must they always be on the floor?"

Already she is getting anxious with her preparations.

"New bedspreads," she says. "New curtains. I have the material from Valladolid. Soledad's sister can run them up. The floors must be oiled and waxed. All the plants must be overhauled, and half of them repotted. The leaks—oh, why can the leaks never be fixed? In the States, who ever heard of a leaking roof? Here, no matter what you do, every rainy season . . . these walls, this room . . . oh, God, this room, what am I to do?"

"Keep the door closed, that's all," says Octavia, coolly.

"No, no, I hate closed doors. A house should be wide open." She has a vision of the house as her brother will see it: open, cool, gleaming, weathered, spotless, elegant. The sea breeze blowing through. Great pots of fern on the gleaming tile. Heavy antique furniture. And he will say, *"But, Catherine, you live like a queen!"*

"I must tell Soledad," she cries. "I must tell Felipe!"

She moves around the house, holding her letter, telling everyone.

"How long will they stay?" asks Felipe.

"He doesn't say. As long as they can. It will be so good for Maribel," she adds tactfully, knowing where his heart is most committed.

"Well, I doubt that," he says. "She doesn't thrive on change, or strangers."

"Strangers?" she says. "These are relatives. He's my twin!"

"Of course," says Felipe, and withdraws inside himself.

"You and he will have so much to talk about. You'll like that, won't you, Felipe? Another man to talk to?"

"I'm sure I will," he says formally, and examines a sheaf of papers on his desk. Catherine becomes aware of danger. She has been careless; she revealed her joy. Felipe could so easily resent him, be sarcastic and jealous.

"Of course we may not even like him," she says quickly, to undo the damage. "After so many years, he'll be changed. You're right," she says, "he'll be a stranger. I hadn't thought of that."

It works, immediately. He relaxes. He agrees with her. "Don't expect too much," he warns. "You may be disappointed."

"That's very true. I've been remembering ancient history. Well, if we don't like him, we'll hand him his hat."

And she smiles at him, allied with him against the intruder. The last thing she needs when her brother comes is Felipe glowering and disagreeable, spoiling everything. She must remember to fuss over him. Extra touches, beyond the usual. Flowers at his place.

At the table that night Catherine in an affectionate ritual turns to Octavia with a smile and extends her hand palm upward on the table.

"Put 'er thar, partner!" she says.

And Octavia is expected to put her own hand on top of her mother's for a pat and a squeeze. She doesn't even know what it means, nor does she care to know. When she was little, she accepted overtures like this, she supposes.

Octavia does not like to see her mother so happy. She would prefer to see her in bitter repentance for certain crimes and betrayals Octavia cannot name but which have, she feels, stamped and ruined her own life, making it a burden, a struggle against hopeless odds. It is as though she has been stripped of wings, then told to fly. She tries to fly, pretends she can, says she can, dreams she can, hops, swings, climbs, runs, dares all, deceives herself. But sooner or later, collapse.

And who has stripped away her rightful wings? Who but her mother, her mother whom like a fool she trusted, whom like a fool she loved. And now, this woman, this selfsame "mother," is seeking her friendship, soliciting her love, pretending an intimacy, a demeaning "partnership," that does not exist. Octavia's heart is like a stone against her. A cold hard sandy dirty miserable stone.

"Put 'er thar, pard," says her mother.

Octavia quickly slaps her hand and withdraws. Even that contact is too intimate for her. Touching her mother's skin gives her shudders.

After supper, her father gives her a book on Greek mythology with pictures that are only statues with blank white eyes. Why are these stories approved when the stories that Domingo the gardener tells are not?

"I'll tell you why," says her father irritably. "The Greeks gave us art, science, reason, philosophy. They lived at the dawn of civilization. The people on this island live at the ass end of a culture and their stories are degenerate *mierda.*"

"Felipe," says Mother, a mild reproach.

Octavia (feeling attacked) looks at the photograph of her grandfather which is hanging on the wall. She chews her pencil, strolls away. She seeks and finds her cat, and tosses him up on her shoulder in his favorite way. She takes him to the mirror so he can see how handsome he is, so she can see him twice. For there can never be enough of this marvelous purring heavy cat with golden eyes and soft thick fur and paws that open and close in happiness and prickle her shoulder.

"Ai, monster," she says. "Not so hard!"

• • •

That night the stars and planets are very large and bright and seem to be slowly, mysteriously coming closer, as if they have something in mind.

In the morning Domingo tells her about a witch who died three days ago on Isla Maria. During the funeral watch, as she was lying in her coffin, her belly began to heave, and they took out a black snake three meters long. She was a famous *bruja,* but nobody knew the source of her power. Now they know. It was the snake!

Every witch has a power source, Domingo explains. A black chicken, a black dog or goat or snake . . .

Octavia is thoughtful. "Can a person be a power source?" she asks.

Domingo stops pinching dead blooms off the climbing geraniums, raises his eyebrows, considers, but does not speak.

"Maribel? Could she be a power source?"

He evades the question, waggles his head, and returns to his geraniums.

The truth is that Soledad the cook is almost certainly using Maribel as a power source. In fact, she's in business, she's in the Maribel business, she's getting rich collecting bits and pieces of Maribel and selling them. Locks of hair, snippets of clothing, fragments of used sanitary napkins laid carefully in banana-leaf boxes.

The sanitary napkins are for burning.

Inhale the smoke, and you'll be potent in love.

3 Octavia is wearing a pair of boys' khaki shorts and a light blue shirt. Her long tangled blond hair is unlikely, a surprise, because her skin and eyes and brows are dark. She is sitting doing several things at once: eating a banana with tiny bites (aware with every swallow that her throat is sore), absently brushing her hair, and reading a book which she keeps open on the table with her elbow.

Her room is white and pure and bleak. The worn, skimpy bed cover, pale seersucker with cream and white stripes, is tucked in tightly around the mattress of her narrow monastic bed. The mosquito netting is looped up high. All books stand neatly on their shelves. All clothes have been picked up and put away. The windows, free of vines, admit a blinding light reflected by the white and sterile plastered walls. A breeze blows through.

Octavia, who goes through cycles of neatness and messiness, is in a neat phase now, which means that she is anxious about the newcomers. She is guarding herself carefully.

This is necessary because all things are lascivious and are looking at her. The spiders and the scorpions are prowlers thinking about *her*. The mosquitoes are peeping toms. What is all the curiosity about, anyhow? It centers on the place between her legs that nobody must ever see.

• • •

Sounds of splashing and wild merriment. Maribel is having her bath. Delila is laughing and singing loudly. Soledad is clapping her hands. A record is playing. Bathing Maribel is a wild disheveled undertaking when the maids are in charge. The trick is to get her clean without allowing her to be disgusting and enjoy herself. Maribel loves to be disgusting. It makes Octavia sick.

When their mother bathes Maribel it is different. She stands on guard beside the tub like a grim and stony-hearted matron in a women's prison. She becomes an ogre, a cruel stepmother, a wicked queen. She hands Maribel the cloth, the soap, and stands there, silent, stern, arms on hips. And if at any moment Maribel's consciousness begins to dim, and that certain look, as of the baby at the breast, comes over her, their mother makes a threatening step forward.

Well, it works. Kindness does not work. How else is Maribel to learn? Is she to be allowed to parade around all day with her fingers in her crotch? Is she to be allowed to undress herself at will? before anyone? and beg like a little dog for pats and strokes?

"The child must be trained," their mother says. "Every one of us has learned through early trauma what must be concealed, what may and may not be done in public. These are matters Maribel does not learn naturally. She cannot be shamed, she must be trained." Grimly, Catherine undertakes to train her.

"No, no, Maribel, no, no!"

And then, the slap. A good, sharp slap.

Delila's method is simply to distract her (which is fine, says Mother, but teaches her nothing).

Octavia is watching.

Delila sings and splashes and chatters and teases. The music is Gilbert and Sullivan. The man is singing lots of words and is funny. He is singing to an ugly old woman, and he tells her,

There's a fascination frantic
In a ruin that's romantic,
Do you think you are sufficiently decayed?

Delila, soaping Maribel, splashing, stirring the water, answers,

Jes, aseen kayam sufeesnli degay!

The bath approaches its critical moment.

"Look, Marifel," shouts Delila. "Catch the duck, Marifel! Catch the duck!"

And while Maribel splashes for the duck, Delila quickly and expertly shoves the soapy washcloth in between her legs. Maribel pauses, lifts her head as if listening.

"The duck, Marifel! Quack, quack!" shouts Delila. One, two, one, two, splash, sit, stir the water, splash again—the job is done! By the time that certain look of trance and inner attention begins to immobilize Maribel's face, Delila has already finished, has pulled out the stopper, has rinsed the cloth, and is crying, "Now, out! All done, all done! Up! Up we go!"

The chorus sings triumphantly,

If that is so, sing Derry-Down-Derry,
It's evident, very, our tastes are one!
And away we'll go and merrily marry
Nor tardily tarry till day is done!

And with a great squelching sucking noise of water, Maribel comes bursting from the tub, comes pulled and hauled out of the tub in dripping nakedness, gleaming, all breasts and pale hips, round buttocks, the body of a woman. She steps and is guided onto the bathmat, and in an instant she is toweled dry so roughly that she whimpers, she is snapped into her bra, inserted magically into her underpants leg by leg (Delila bent double), and delivered damp and bewildered in the bedroom to Soledad just as the record ends.

"*Ai cielos!*" says Delila. "All in the space of one record. Not bad, eh? I am soaked."

(Octavia bathes behind locked doors. Not even the sun must see her, not even the moon, for the sun is one eye of the sky and the moon is the other, the day's eye and the night's eye, and everything below them lies exposed and vulnerable, spread out for inspection. The island and the sea lie open and exposed. And beyond lies the mainland, the *llanos*—wet, exposed—swelling up to the highlands, and the highlands swelling to the continent, and beyond the continent the oceans and the whole wide world passive and helpless under the prurient gaze of the sky's two eyes. The sun and moon will get no thrills from Octavia.)

Sunlight filters through the nodding green leaves and blood-red blossoms of the bougainvillea at the window, falling in moving patterns on the dark tile floor. The room is a cave, a den. The vines have been allowed to flourish and to choke the windows. There is a reason for this: so Maribel cannot lean out and fall. They serve in place of bars. Domingo prunes and trims so light and air can enter, so she can see the sky and peep down into the garden, but the jungle struggles to possess the room.

In honor of the visitors who are coming from far away, a new white and yellow bedspread is on Maribel's cot, new shelves have been built to hold the dolls and toys and paints and picture books. The walls have been whitewashed, but Maribel's paintings and scribbles have not been successfully effaced, only subdued. They glimmer through the whitewash as from behind a veil.

The dolls are arranged in two long lines, facing each other, six feet apart. They simper, they look blank. Those that will sit, sit stolidly, gaze forward, do not see, see other worlds. The others are propped against one another. They all have inner secret lives. In some other world, at night perhaps when no one is looking, they are alive. Here too at any moment they may take on life, it is just a question of waiting, of catching them by surprise.

Maribel, clean and damp, stands between the lines of dolls and begins to sing (in her fashion, which is not what Octavia calls singing). She cannot carry a tune, but does not feel the lack as she rocks slowly from one foot to the other, making her neck and shoulders stiff and bending far over to the right, far over to the left.

"Ha-dee," she chants in medium voice, finding a rhythm. "Ha-dee, ha-dee. Ha-dee."

The maids dressing Maribel speak to each other in hushed voices. Delila looks eighteen but in reality is fifteen and very beautiful with fine dark eyes. Her skin is a rich tobacco color tinged with red, and her hair is worn in a fat and shining braid. Soledad is skinny and dish-faced, she is thirty-five with children of her own. Her skin is mahogany, and her hair is strained back in a bun. They step in and out of the lines of dolls, dressing Maribel to meet her uncle at the dock as they might dress the image of a saint to be carried through the streets on a fiesta day.

Delila stumbles over a doll and exclaims. Maribel turns, stricken. Delila reaches down to set it straight. Delila is vain, light-hearted, confident. She is more impatient and casual with Maribel than Soledad, whose careful attention never wavers. The two maids often speak to each other in Mayan, but to Maribel they speak in Spanish. Soledad's voice is low and solemn and monotonous; Delila's, higher and brighter, interrupts the flow.

(Catherine, when she enters, will be reminded of the murmur and response of a litany. She too will think: they are dressing the image of the saint for a procession. She will propose to herself an axiom: *That which simple peoples do not understand, they worship.* Having made this generalization, she will feel gratified and relieved, as though she had solved a problem.)

"Ha-dee, ha-dee," chants Maribel in the soft green air.

Delila sits back on her heels impatiently. "Hold still," she says sharply. "How can I fix your stocking?"

"Let her be," says Soledad. "Marifel, lift your arms."

Obediently, like a small child, Maribel lifts her arms and Soledad pulls a slip over her head.

"Ay," exclaims Delila from down below. "I forgot. Her *reglas* have begun."

Soledad glares. "And you let her bathe?" she scolds.

"I didn't notice. Not till I was drying her."

"Tonta. Now she will have cramps."

"No she won't. The water was good and hot."

Soledad goes to the wardrobe and from a shelf she takes a napkin and belt, clean underpants.

"Ha-dee."

"What can it mean, ha-dee? Is it English?"

Delila shrugs.

"Is it 'jade' she's saying? 'Jade, jade'?"

"I'll tell you what she's saying," says Delila, and she does an imitation of Maribel, partly to annoy Soledad, partly from high spirits, and partly to see how it might feel to be Maribel, to say and do whatever comes into your mind, to be waited on, and never never have to work at anything.

They support her while she lifts her foot to step into her stockings. Soledad settles the slip around her hips and straightens it.

Maribel, whimpering, touches her left breast, looks down inside the slip, inside the bra. She reaches inside and pulls it out, the big young breast. It is something to see. It protrudes now above her bra, above the neckline of her slip. It has a round pink eye with a red pupil in the center.

"Hurt," she whimpers, showing Soledad. An insect has bitten her.

As Delila combs and arranges Maribel's hair with little pats, Soledad fishes in her apron pocket and brings out a tube of ointment. Maribel is instantly quiet and passive, waiting. She presents her breast. Soledad applies the salve and gently tucks the breast away, inside its bra, inside the slip, a big soft egg in its nest. Maribel is gratified.

Now, quickly, they put her into the blouse and skirt Soledad has chosen. On her feet they slip white patent leather shoes. She is almost ready. Only one lock of hair is recalcitrant. Delila at last takes scissors and Maribel, cowering, cries out.

"Don't be afraid, Marifel. One little snip."

"No!"

"Jes!" says Delila, mockingly, in English.

"No!" wails Maribel.

"Jes! Jes!" says Delila.

"Don't tease her."

"Snip, snip!" teases Delila, and Maribel begins to shriek.

"You see?" Soledad angrily pushes Delila away.

They put a straw hat on her head, a straw purse on her arm.

"There," says Soledad. "You look beautiful."

"Beautiful? Her?" Delila snickers. She sneaks the scissors quickly and snips off the too-long strand of hair. Maribel does not react. It was too quick for her. Delila leads her to the mirror to see herself, but she does not look.

"She never looks at herself," says Delila. "Look, Marifel," she coaxes, tapping the mirror. "Look. In here. See? There's Marifel in the mirror! See how pretty? Look, Marifel. Who's that?"

But Maribel does not understand.

"She never looks, why is that?"

"Because for her," says Soledad portentously, "there is nothing there."

Delila is taken aback and thrilled. She whispers: "Nothing there?"

"She sees nothing. She sees only the room."

Delila puts her palm to her mouth. "Really? She sees nothing? She has no reflection?"

They stare at the image of Maribel, standing, swaying, with her hat on and her purse over her arm. Behind her two lines of dolls are waiting.

Soledad takes the lock of hair from Delila's hand and deposits it carefully in a small box made of banana leaves, which she then puts in her apron pocket.

"But I can see her," says Delila, marveling. "And you? Can you see her?"

Now Catherine enters the room and Soledad does not answer. Catherine is wearing a new dress, blue-green silk with daisies, and a ruffle at the neck. She is nervous but is looking incredibly pretty. The maids have never seen her so pretty. Her hair is bright and curling (for three weeks she has been rinsing it in lime juice and sitting bareheaded in the sun). Her lips are pink, her skin is glowing. Her blue-green eyes match her dress and are suddenly much bigger. The lashes and brows are dark instead of pale. In three weeks she has lost ten pounds and ten years. She smiles at the expression on their faces.

"Oh, señora! How pretty you are!" breathes Delila, astonished. "How slender, how young!"

"My brother hasn't seen me for twenty-five years. He may not even know me."

Nervously, critically, she inspects Maribel. "I told you the yellow dress. Where did you find this skirt? It's very old, it was Duncan's."

"It was in the wardrobe, señora. I thought it looked pretty with the blouse."

"Yes, but—something simpler."

"As you wish, señora."

"And stockings! In this heat?"

"Shall we change her?"

Maribel stands very still. In her mother's presence she seems almost normal.

"Let it go. Maribel, you look quite the young lady. I expect you to behave like one. You understand."

"Yes," says Maribel, rigid.

"Yes what?"

Soledad interrupts. She is uneasy, she pulls in her breath. "Señora—"

"Yes?"

"Señora, her *reglas* have begun."

"Oh no. Don't tell me that. It's early. Two days early. Are you
sure?"

Her face flushed with anger she checks a calendar on the wall
and turns on Delila. "What did you do? You used hot water in the
tub."

Delila shrinks.

"I told you to use cold water."

"She wouldn't get in."

"Then make her get in. There are two of you! Oh, I could cry. I
wanted her to be talking when my brother arrives. Can you understand that? You understand it very well."

"*Sí*, señora," whispers Delila, hanging her head.

"She is still talking, señora," says Soledad.

"Yes, and for how long?"

She scolds them bitterly. She wants to strike them, she wants to
cry.

"Are you ready to go?" she asks Soledad, sharply.

"*Sí*, señora."

"Go take off your apron. Delila, you may *not* come with us."

The maids go scuttling out, and Catherine, fragile as an egg,
inspects her daughter. So much is at stake. Not just reunion with
her brother and whether he will find her changed and old. Far
more: the value of her life, the rightness of her choice, everything
she has done for twenty-five long years. She has lived a life of
penance, spiritual death, in a landscape alien and repugnant, sustained always by one hope, that he will come. And now he is
coming! He will look at her life: her house, her children, her husband. He will ask what she has made of this. He will stand in

judgment and if she is worthy, she will be released. Oh, rescue, rescue! Life will begin again, real life.

"Maribel. This is the most important thing I have ever said to you. Listen to Mama. You must behave in front of your uncle. You must behave in front of Uncle Claude. We're going now, to meet the boat, and I expect you to remember everything. Do you understand?"

Maribel nods solemnly.

Octavia watches.

"Oh, Octavia, your hair. Sit down and let me brush it."

Octavia sits down, examines her own face in the mirror as her mother brushes her hair with long firm strokes. She asks her mother why she does not have light skin like Duncan's. If Maribel looks like Papi and Duncan looks like Catherine, who does Octavia look like?

"You're a blend," says Catherine, smiling, and brushes Octavia's bangs.

"A half breed."

"Don't say that."

"Half Indian and half white."

Catherine stops smiling. "You are *not* a half breed, and Papi is *not* Indian," she says severely. "Papi is Spanish."

"You always say so. *He* doesn't say so."

Catherine stops brushing. She hears the voice of her own father, shouting over the long-distance telephone, shouting from Washington to San Antonio. *("Go ahead and marry him," he shouts across the miles. "But remember this: Don't bring your pickaninnies home to me!")*

Determined to plague her, Octavia persists. "He always says he's Indian. *'Nosotros los Indios—'* "

"He says that to be funny. He says it to annoy me. Octavia, Mother is serious about this. It may not be important here, but in the States it's very important. I want you to understand, Papi is Spanish. Say it."

"Say it?"

"Yes, say it out loud: Papi is Spanish."

"Papi is a Welshman, Papi is a thief," says Octavia. "Do you think I'm Maribel? I'm not going to *say it.*"

Catherine, flustered, laughs. "Well, but he is, and don't forget it."

"Mmm," says Octavia, radiating doubt.

In a burst of anger, Catherine raises the brush as if to strike her, and then controls herself.

"I'm all nerves today."

She ties Octavia's hair back with a brown velvet ribbon.

"There," she cries. "Look—a princess."

Octavia looks and makes a retching noise. But she is impressed all the same. That demure and shining head in the mirror, is that Octavia?

"Come along," says her mother. "It's time to go."

4 It is spring, because the fires are burning. The air is milky and the thin line of palms which is the mainland lies invisible in a band of dusky violet. At sunset the whole world is ablaze, and at night the sky glows red and flickering and ominous. Even the sea is molten red. A landscape of hell, terrifying, nothing special.

It has been the same forever. Every year the fires are set, here and on the mainland, to clear the land. Every year the land is burned for spring planting, every year different plots of jungle trees and undergrowth are felled, slashed, burned, planted in corn and beans. (After the plots are harvested they are left alone to heal themselves in a cycle of fourteen years.) The cleared fields are far away from towns and villages; they have to be, for clearing season is also the dry season. The rains have not yet come and often the fires spread from slash to forest, and burn out of control for a time.

Faint and sweetly acrid smoke is everywhere, even the sea winds cannot disperse it. The sun burns red all day, and at night even the moon is red and swollen, hazy in the sky.

Delila explains. The moon is pregnant, ready to give birth.

"Give birth to *what*," Octavia sneers.

"*Tonta!* to more stars," says Delila. "How else do you suppose they got there, ah?"

Now it is early morning and they walk along the *malecón,* by the seawall, to meet the newcomers arriving on the *Camilio Canto*. They are a procession. Catherine and Soledad on either side of Maribel, each with an arm firmly linked in hers. Then Octavia straggling behind, resentful, yet aware of looking strange and beautiful, her hair brushed smooth, held down with its brown velvet band, her bangs waving curling in the heat, damp-looking, shiny, soft; Octavia, sullen, scuffing her feet. She does not care about the newcomers. She resents them, they bring trouble, they bring change. Behind Octavia, Lenin and Domingo trundle an empty cart with large rattling wheels, for the baggage. Catherine keeps talking in Maribel's ear, a steady hypnotic monotone to keep her attention fixed. Soledad, on the other side, is very proud of herself. The back of her head exudes self-satisfaction. She wants the world to see her fussing over Maribel. She is always fussing over Maribel, taking her for walks, taking her home to her own house. (What do they do there?)

The villagers stop what they are doing to watch the procession. They stare without self-consciousness. Women with jars of tortilla masa on their shoulders, men on their way to work, Lebanese shopkeepers sweeping the street in front of their shops. Children come running to watch, to follow. Octavia greets two girls her own age, and looks away from the boys, aware of her dress and shining hair. Boys disturb her. Girls disturb her too.

"Walking along and standing straight, going to meet the boat!" chants Catherine in Maribel's ear.

Two fishermen look up. They stare at Octavia and grin, then they see Maribel and stop smiling. She is doggedly plowing forward, head slightly thrust out, eyes down, behaving beautifully (for her). Why does everybody look? The fishermen put the bunched fingers of their right hands to their lips three times. (What does that mean?) They forget their fish and watch with intense curiosity. They call out to Soledad in Mayan, and she replies. Octavia knows only a few words of Mayan. She has grown up in a world where there are secret ways to talk. Her own secret language is English, Soledad's is Mayan.

"Smile at them," says Soledad to Maribel, "smile!" Maribel opens her mouth in an ugly way.

"Head up high and proud," says Catherine. "Maribel is a young lady, she has good manners. Maribel holds fast to her pocketbook, walks nicely, head up high. Maribel is quiet and well behaved. Her hands are quiet. Quiet hands. Her hands are ladylike. Her hands in their little white gloves are the hands of a lady. They clasp each other. They do not touch her face. They are graceful and quiet, they carry the pocketbook, they do not move."

Catherine's voice mesmerizes Octavia too, and she puts her own hands together, gracefully, quietly; she stands up straight and proud. Then catching herself, furious, she reaches down in the sandy street, picks up a chunk of broken coral rock, and with a boy's efficient pitch, she hurls it high over the wall and into the sea.

Octavia didn't want to come. She has a sore throat. It is going to get worse, she can tell. Already it hurts to swallow. It's the smoke, her mother says, but it is not the smoke. She is going to be sick in bed with a fever. Besides, her mother doesn't really want her along, she only wants to use her in some way that is not clear. Octavia has a nose for exploitation.

Furthermore, she sniffs change in the wind, a hint of carrion. Overhead green parrots are flying out to sea, squawking, conversing, a flight of noisy parrots passing overhead, heading for the mainland where they feed.

She wants me to call him uncle but I won't. She wants me to call him Uncle Claude but I won't.

To Octavia, "uncle," being English, seems intimate and secret, special and thus laudatory. She will not grant this person any laudatory "uncle." She won't call him Tío either. She won't call him anything.

Tío. Uncle. *Tío.* Uncle. Both words are ugly anyway. Uncle sounds like a grunting pig. Unkle, unkle. And *tío* sounds like the same pig squealing. *Tío, tío!* Octavia is repelled by pigs, by suckling greedy smelly pigs.

The long concrete pier, built by the fruit company, looks glaring white against the vivid blue-green sea. The *Camilio Canto* is docking. Catherine hurries up. She casts her shadow before her and to the left, under the parrots, under the great milky blue sky.

Now she drops Maribel's arm and utters a shriek, stops dead.

"I see him. Oh, I see him!"

She whirls and reaches for Octavia, uses the pet name Octavia cannot help but love.

"Oh, Tavvie-cat, do you see him? In the bow? Can that be—? Oh, I think— Let's run."

All excited and flushed, she reaches out to hug Octavia, but Octavia shakes her off. She is no longer a small child, after all. She doesn't care to drink the overflow of her mother's happiness.

"Come on, Tavvie!" coaxes her mother, pulling at her hand.

"I'll stay with Maribel."

"Come with me, Tavvie," begs her mother, full of love.

"No," says Octavia, and Catherine runs off alone, making a fool of herself, down to the end of the pier, jumping up and down like a child, clasping her hands, covering her mouth. Like a child!

Sedately walking beside Maribel, taking her mother's place, more adult than her mother, Octavia does indeed see a figure in the bow of the boat, bigger than the others. It is the uncle. She does not see the cousin, and who cares anyway? She is not thrilled by these newcomers. Let them go back home.

Tying up at the end of the dock, the fifty-foot motor sailer *Camilio Canto* is just in from Chaltún and Puerto Nuevo with a cargo of foods and medicines and dishes and bolts of cotton cloth, and yarn and thread and tools and machetes and kerosene, engines, generators, gasoline, Coca-Cola, chickens in crates, one large seasick sow, and two passengers, one seasick and the other not: Claude and his son Julian, ages forty-two and fourteen respectively.

"Clo! I can't bear it!" screams Catherine.

Octavia looks down into the water, polluted here (Papi says) but still clear enough to count the fish and the conches and the giant spiky blue-black sea urchins clustered on the sand and coral bottom ten feet down.

The man's voice behind her: "Well, Catherine!"

And her mother: "Let me look at you—I can't believe—it's been so long—Oh, Clo, such a nightmare. I'm just waking up."

The *Camilio Canto,* made fast, is being unloaded. Cartons are stacked on the dock. Storekeepers and their helpers are checking invoices and comparing lists. The chief of police smiles broadly, his belt buckle and insignia gleam, his pistol is fat on his hip. Domingo and Lenin wait discreetly, at a distance, for the emotion to run its course. A dog lifts his leg on the wheels of the cart and Lenin drives him away. Boys are fishing and swimming from the wreck of the old schooner a hundred feet offshore, even this early, with the green speckles still flashing overhead. The world starts early. Octavia has no part in it. She rejects it, and it rejects her.

From the corner of her eye she looks at her mother, embracing and welcoming that man. She looks at the man. He is tall with a scowl built between his eyes. His hair is either gray or blond, she cannot tell, and stubble of the same color smudges his cheeks and chin. He is wearing a rumpled blue and yellow shirt hanging outside his trousers. There is nothing special about him. He carries a straw hat. Her mother's brother. Her mother's *twin.*

"You've got a scowl," her mother cries. "You've got a broken nose. What did they do to your poor nose? It's very handsome," she adds quickly, "it's very manly and becoming."

He sees Octavia looking.

"Is that yours?" he asks jovially, as if she were a package.

"That's the baby, my Octavia."

Escaping from her grasp he greets Octavia, comes at her with his hands and picks her up. Actually picks her up, as if she were a child.

"She don't remember me," he says. "Can you imagine that? She don't remember me."

"Oh, Clo, she was an infant," murmurs Catherine.

And there is Octavia with her legs dangling down and her underpants showing and her dress up to her waist and his fingers and thumbs pressing hard against her ribs, for somehow his hands have gotten underneath her dress, and she is being mashed against his chest.

"Ole Missy Long-legs," he says fondly in her face as if he knew her, as if he were an old friend, and he gives her a hitch until she is sitting on his forearms, and one hand clasps her thigh and the other is still underneath her dress against her ribs.

Octavia, aged twelve, hates it.

"Why I took care of you," says this Tío Claude, chuckling, coughing, breathing out tobacco stink, putting on a phony accent, putting on this Uncle Remus talk. "I took care of this Missy when she was no bigger than a minute. Yes I did. And she was one *bad* behavin' chile!"

He staggers a little. "Still got my sea legs," he says.

"I never saw you before," says Octavia coldly, pulling away.

"You don't remember," says her mother. "You were a baby. I was in Valladolid with Maribel, and you and Papi and Duncan were here, and he just turned up, out of the blue, and then he left again and I never got to see one whisker. That was cruel."

"Gimme a kiss," he says.

"Give him a kiss," says Catherine.

Octavia (dying, dead, obligated) aims for his cheek, but he comes at her with his horrible mouth, all bristles like a hairbrush and smelling of tobacco and between the bristles, wet. He squeezes her and his thumb moves on her ribs, and she flinches because it is a kind of hard and awful tickling.

"I want to get down."

"Lord, was you a bad behaver!" he continues, fondly showing stained and yellow teeth. "Pop you into bed and what you do? You start hollerin'. Ain't nobody could keep *you* quiet. Nursie try, and Daddy try, and sister try, and they just give up and close the door and Lord have mercy, you did holler, you one world-class hollerer."

Octavia in anguish thinks: I did NOT. She thinks: Everyone is looking.

"Shuh!" he exclaims. "But old Nuncle Clo, he go tippy-toe in, yeah, *he* knows how. He the only one can hush you up! Old Nuncle Clo. Kill de mosquitoes! Whappadiddy, whap! Bad old skeeters full of baby-blood. Whap go the skeeters! Old Nuncle Clo, he jus pet you up a little bit and you go sound asleep. Jus pet you up a little bit and you go sound asleep."

His fingers on her ribs, her thigh, go creeping upward, lewdly creeping, and they carry to her heart fatality and doom. They speak of babies, bosoms, blood.

"And here is Maribel," says Catherine, tremulous with love and pride. "She's the middle daughter, Clo, she's the one we've had some trouble with. And she has her own special gift for you."

Maribel steps forward, all clean and brushed, wearing the yellow blouse Catherine embroidered with birds and vines and flowers, and a skirt that comes below her knees. Her straw hat is on straight and has a fresh stiff yellow ribbon that hangs down her back. Her face in the shadow of the hat looks pretty. Does she see him? Her big dark eyes that are Papi's eyes waver around him.

Soledad puts a bouquet of daisies and climbing geraniums, yellow and pink, in her hands and obediently she holds it out. Tío Claude puts Octavia down and accepts it. "Well, well!" he says. "Thank you very much!"

Catherine beams and Soledad beams. It is their moment of triumph. Octavia tries to escape and fails. Maribel goes into the rest of her act. She holds out her hand and twists her face. Her lips go up, her chin goes down, all right, a smile.

"How do you do, Miss Maribel?" says Tío Claude, very courtly now, taking her hand. (Octavia escapes.) He clears his throat. "Well now," he says bravely, "give me a kiss."

Maribel, rehearsed, steps up and presents her cheek.

"You're very nice, Clo," murmurs Catherine. "It's sweet of you."

"Not at all!" says Tío Claude. He takes a deep breath and pecks Maribel on the cheek, and steps back. Maribel also steps back. She puts her hands in their little white gloves behind her. Her pocketbook falls at her feet. Mother and Soledad jump to pick it up.

"What a big girl, all grown up," says Tío Claude. "How old are you?"

"How old are you, Maribel?" repeats Catherine anxiously, hoping against hope, forming the words herself, urging her on. No use. When the moon is wrong it's wrong. Maribel stands silent, blank.

"She's seventeen," says Catherine. "Was the crossing a horror?"

"We rocked a bit."

"I hope you weren't sick. I'm always sick."

"Shuh, this puddle? Why you could swim it!" cries Tío Claude. "Now I remember a typhoon in the Indian Ocean, *that* was a crossing. Overloaded freighter, precious animals caged on deck, tigers, waves sixty feet high! Even the captain had to leave the bridge or shame himself. I said, Claude my boy, if you ain't seasick now you *never* gonna be seasick."

And so he arrives, this uncle, well advertised it would seem, sunburned, tall, dressed like a tourist in his flowered blue and yellow shirt, stinking of engine fumes and copra. Who could suspect such a man? He is only Catherine's brother from the States, come for a visit, to stay perhaps two weeks, a month, six weeks at most, bringing with him his fourteen-year-old son Julian (born of a marriage that ended in divorce before its first anniversary). True, the mayor, Don Virgilio, has been warned from above to expect someone. "They say an American is coming to train the irregulars," he tells Octavia's father. "Those cretins! *Malvivientes!* Let them be trained somewhere else! What am I supposed to do?"

Her mother takes hold of him on the pier and kisses him on both cheeks, tears dripping down her face. Then she examines his forearm. She holds his wrist with one hand and with the other she goes searching for something on his left forearm, her fingers working up and down the blond hairs of his red arm.

"Where is it?" she says. "I can't find it. Clo, where has it gone?"

He withdraws his arm and his eyes sweep over the island's flat shoreline.

"I had it removed," he says.

And she freezes for an instant. Her complexion changes, her mouth falls open. "Removed! Why Clo, you devil, you bastard," she says. "All these years my only consolation has been to think, *At least I set my mark on him!* You had it *removed?*"

It seems she bit him when they were little, and left a good hard scar, her toothmarks in his forearm, a double set of toothmarks, upper and lowers, a good deep bite, a double crescent scar.

"I still have mine," she says, and shows him a certain place on her left collarbone that she was always worrying. Scratching and picking. She would rub it with her emery boards and then pick off the scabs, until the spot was white and distorted from all that molesting.

"See?" she says. "Clo, look."

"How did you come by that?" he asks politely.

"You know very well."

He thinks and frowns and shakes his head.

She prompts him. "Where we were *joined,*" she smiles.

"Where we were—?"

"We were Siamese twins, and we were joined together here."

"We were never joined together."

"What a miserable memory," she says, hugging him again, taking his face between her hands. "It was a story! Every child in school believed that we were joined. This scar was my proof! You don't remember that? Then I give up!"

But she doesn't give up.

"Oh, Clo," she says. "Twenty-five years. My mark was right *there.* Well, never mind. It's in your soul. You can't have *that* removed. Do you know, even now I can still tell how you're feeling? Whether you're well or sick? This tells me." (She taps her collarbone.) "Sometimes it aches and I say Clo's in danger! Clo is sick! And then I stop eating—I do!—until you're well again. But when it glows like a little sun, I know that Clo is happy today, wherever he is, he's happy."

Suddenly she remembers and all aglow she turns her flaming face toward the boat. "And Julian," she cries. "My nephew! Poor child, where is he? Tavvie, go find your cousin."

5 Octavia climbs on board the *Camilio Canto* to find her cousin. She picks her way around the bare-chested barefoot crew, who are trying to get an enormous seasick sow to its feet. They are small and vigorous young men in patched denim trousers stiff with salt. Merrily they pry and kick at the sow, who lies on her side, fat, panting, hoping for death. Because of their interest in the sow, they do not notice Octavia.

The *Camilio Canto* makes its fifty-mile run (down the coast from the twelve straw huts and six warehouses which are called Puerto Nuevo, and across the channel to Isla Caracol) in the middle of the night because the sea is reputed to be calmer in the dark. This choice is hard on the passengers, if any. With no horizon line to look at, no sleep to comfort them, no sun to dry their clothes (drenched by the sea), they are nearly always sick. They arrive at dawn bedraggled and exhausted.

Today in the hot dark cabin, overcome by violent motion, enveloped in the stench of moldy copra and gasoline fumes, one such passenger, a boy, lies pallid and miserable on a bunk. Octavia spots him, and now she stares from the hatchway.

Her cousin Julian. Her *primo*.

She knows his age: fourteen.

His mother is dead.

He lies on his stomach with his forehead resting on two fists.

Octavia sees his strange short bristling haircut, which dwindles to fuzz on his white neck, she sees a corner of his jaw so pale it glimmers green down there among the poisonous fumes of the engine.

His feet are large, encased in dirty sneakers. His socks have ridden down inside. His legs are long, his neck cleft down the nape. He is wearing a faded green T-shirt and wrinkled corduroy pants. A tan sweater is tied by the sleeves around his middle.

Octavia is ill at ease, seeing something she should not see, invading a privacy purchased at high price. Only souls who have abandoned hope dare enter the cabin of the *Camilio Canto*. This strange boy so chose, and must now, like a failed suicide, confront the burden of life restored.

"It smells bad in here," she says at last. "Come look at the pig. It's seasick too."

Instinct tells her that this boy, like other boys, will relish the distress of that female pig. Basely she betrays its suffering to coax him out. (Why does she do this?)

Julian, hearing himself addressed, turns his head. Octavia can see one lackluster eye looking at her. It is a small intelligent light eye fringed with black lashes and roofed by a thick black eyebrow.

"I'll be there," he says huskily and clears his throat. "I'm coming," he says, making an effort.

Hearing his voice, Octavia knows immediately. His reply, if thick, is courteous and strangely accented (he has lived in Hershey, Pennsylvania, among the Pennsylvania Dutch). It is not the voice of a child. Although it is still light and unsteady, it has nevertheless definitely *changed*. Octavia knows immediately that she is dealing with a person of experience. The glamour of travel radiates from him, knowledge of far-off places, of the States, of American television and football, talk shows, and skiing in the snow. His sweater is worldly, his haircut elegant, his wrinkled corduroys, to her, exotic.

Octavia (once worldly-wise herself until worked over by Elizabeth Jane) stands small and timid in the hatchway, bitterly aware of her isolation, her ignorance. She is humble. She needs this boy. She wants to learn from him, to follow him, to copy him, to worship him as she once copied and worshiped Duncan. She feels it physically, this need, an aching in the throat and chest like thirst. Even his name is beautiful: Julian!

Will he like her? She is instantly in love.

In the dark cabin, Julian sits up.

"I'll get my things," he says.

His face is pale with dark circles under the eyes. His hair stands on end, his eyebrows arch with exhaustion, he looks like Laurel, waiting for Hardy, but beautiful all the same—elegant, cosmopolitan. He does not complain. She will never hear him complain. On the pier he will make an effort to be sociable, to do the right thing, to greet, touch, join, to embrace her mother. He will always make these efforts, so gravely, and he will always have to make them, for nothing will come to him naturally and easily. He is too much aware of the loneliness inside his skull, the privacy there, the imprisonment. He lives inside his skull, crouched there in darkness with two holes to see through, two holes to listen through, and his unprotected body inexplicably outside.

From the deck a shout of laughter. In the bright sunlight the roped pig lies on her side near the rail breathing heavily with her mouth open and her round snout twisted to one side. She waves her delicate stiff little feet, she retches, she will not stand up. She is an enormous and very sick pig, a great red sow with a white belt around her shoulders, and she is willing to endure a great deal rather than get to her feet.

One of the crew—barefoot, with rolled-up trousers—is wedging a dirty canvas sling under her belly. Two others are shoving her from behind. Her eyes are shut. She will not budge.

The laughter is at the expense of Manuel Vasquez (once a patient in the doctor's clinic with a gunshot wound in the leg). The sow has fouled the deck during her ordeal, and Manuel, hauling on her rope, slips in brown mush and falls flat on his bare brown back. Everybody cheers.

Not Octavia. Octavia hates to see this female pig so sick and self-abandoned in front of everyone.

"Daughter of a whore," says Manuel. He rises, grinning and swearing, and kicks the pig. He summons his father and his brother Rafael, the new owners of the pig. Together they sweat to get the pig on her feet. They speak to her and kick her. All the dockworkers and fishermen have gathered now. On the dock Octavia's mother is clinging to Tío Claude's arm, talking away, and Tío Claude is watching the pig and laughing. Octavia can hear his wheezing rattling laughter, which rises in a series of whoops and dissolves in a spasm of coughing.

"Amigos!" he calls out to them. "Why not eat her here?"

Manuel, letting go his rope, helps wedge the canvas sling under the pig's side, and his father and brother, pulling on her legs, manage to roll her over on her back. Quickly they fasten the sling and attach it to a winch. The pig opens its eyes (surprisingly intelligent), and with great convulsive jerks scrambles to its feet, utters a piercing cry, and is hoisted into the air.

Shouts, cries.

She is hoisted wrong. She is dangling from her hindquarters, she is upside down. The rope breaks. The pig plunges screaming into the sea. There is a great, resounding splash.

(This is what it means to be *lost,* Octavia is thinking. This gross and horribly enchanted being, imprisoned in its flesh, abandoned and sickened in its suffocating flesh, is lost.)

And there is the pig in the sea! There is the great pig-body with clear green water closing over it. A mermaid pig.

Julian stands beside Octavia with his packages.

The pig emerges from the depths, breaking water, clean in the water, concentrated, struggling, but clean now in the bright translucent water, almost handsome, feces and vomit washed away.

She swims!

"Ole!"

She swims away from the boat, her snout and eyes above water, snorting, puffing, churning her feet.

"Grab her at the beach!"

She clears the boat, she hesitates. She eyes the shore, the dock, she appears to take thought, and then decisively—oh, there is no doubt, she has made her choice—she heads out to sea.

"Ai caray!"

Julian watches passively as in a dream. He follows his new cousin up the plank from boat to dock.

The pig swims slowly, steadily, straight out to sea. To turn her back, they throw things at her, shells, empty cans, anything they can find. Most miss, some hit. Manuel is going to jump in and swim after her, but his father prevents him. "Take a boat," orders his father. "If you struggle with her in the water she could drown."

On the pier Catherine cries out, "Is that Julian? That grown-up boy?"

She embraces him wholeheartedly, considering that he is redolent of copra and has been seasick all night long.

"How handsome he is!" she exclaims.

The luggage is piled on the cart (scuffed leather suitcases ragged with travel stickers, a duffle bag, four cardboard cartons strapped with rope). Julian will carry his own small suitcase—but Catherine insists, and it is piled on top. The procession starts for home.

But the pig! thinks Octavia.

Along the malecón they go, and everybody looking.

"Pigs!" says Tío Claude. "They're quite intelligent, did you know that? You can teach them tricks, did you know that? You can teach them simple tricks."

Catherine has one arm linked in his, and the other reaching out for Julian, seeking to hug Julian, to pull him close.

"I saw a trained pig in a circus once," Tío Claude goes on. "They're not as stupid as they look. Nor dirty either. Man makes them dirty. A pig in the wild is clean. A very useful animal. Man makes the dirt. Did you know in parts of China they use pigs for plowing? And to pull carts? Yes, sir! I've ridden in many a pig cart. I've always liked the pig. I've seen plows drawn by a woman and a hog, harnessed side by side. Side by side, what do you think of that? A woman and a hog!"

He emits a burst of laughter. He slaps his thigh.

Octavia walks beside Julian, proudly. He is hers, her cousin. He is carrying a neat packet of comic books tied with string. Octavia looks at them. Later she will learn them by heart, all of them, including the ads. Soft dry paper, crumbling at the edges, stamped with adventure.

"There's wonderful fishing here," says Catherine, turning to Julian. "Do you like to fish?"

"Not really."

"And boating. You'll like that. And swimming—you'll have a wonderful time. You'll be brown as a berry. Octavia will show you everything."

Julian does not respond. She smiles at him, pats the side of his head, and turns her attention back to Tío Claude.

The wind is blowing from the sea, gusty, coquettish. The sun is gathering its heat, beaming it down. Octavia dares to steal a glance: he is incredibly white.

Julian has spotted the naked boys diving off the old wrecked sloop aground on its side offshore.

"How did they get there?" he asks suddenly. "Did they swim out?"

"Yes," says Octavia. She is very shy, trying to think of something to say, trying to think of something to do.

"Are there sharks?"

"Only at night."

She can see he would like to be swimming with those boys.

"We can go out there if you like, we can swim out. I'll take you out there after lunch." She has never dared swim out to the wreck. Not from fear of sharks, but from fear of the boys who would tease and jeer at her. But now she has her tall cousin for company, everything has changed. They wouldn't dare!

"You have to be careful not to step on the sea urchins, that's all."

Julian looks at Octavia from the corner of his eye without enthusiasm.

"Does everybody here speak Spanish? I mean, only Spanish?"

"They speak Mayan."

"Nobody speaks English? I mean, the kids?"

Octavia shakes her head. "I do," she says.

"Well I know that," says Julian.

Silence. Octavia feels the heavy weight of being a girl.

"There used to be kids who spoke English. The company kids, but they're gone."

"What company?"

"The fruit company."

"What fruit company?"

"I don't know," says Octavia, feeling weak. "They just call it the company."

"How long does it take to learn Spanish?"

"I can teach you. It's easy."

Again the cautious sideways look.

She is casual. "I'm older than I look," she says. "I'll be thirteen in November."

"I'll get a tutor," he says.

She runs in front of everyone and scrambles up on top of the seawall. She walks on top of it, as bold and brave as any boy.

"Now you be careful, Missy, don't you fall," says Tío Claude, interrupting the stream of talk about people Octavia didn't know or care about, the friends and relatives in Washington. He has brought gifts and a rare, precious letter from Duncan, who has a job now with the State Department.

Missy? Why does he call her that? She hates it.

"Octavia, get down," says Catherine.

On top of the seawall she is aware of her audience. "Hey, Julian," she shouts. "Tide's out, want to look at tide pools?"

"Not now," says Catherine. "Let Julian get home and clean up and rest."

She turns to her brother and touches her forehead to his shoulder. She wipes her eyes. "I can't believe you're here," she says.

Octavia is jealous, for her father's sake. Why should this man mean so much? Doesn't she have Papi? And herself, and even Maribel, who is being so good and quiet, clumping along in her hat? Why is she always sighing and unhappy and complaining about the island?

She remembers now that Julian's mother is dead, died just a month ago, and hastily amends her thinking. Never never criticize your mother, for what if she should die?

Julian plods along, impassive, carrying his comic books. His mother is dead.

How can you live, exactly, if your mother is dead?

Tío Claude is speaking very loud.

"Do you know in Yucatán they're dredging up old bones from the pool at Chichén? Human bones, young Mayan girls, you know, young virgins, thrown in as sacrifices to the rain god. They always chose the prettiest, you know, pretty and well born, the best, and always very young. About like you were when I saw you last." He winks slyly at Catherine and digs her with his elbow. He looks up at Octavia.

"Very young virgins," he says. "Just like this Missy here. She looks like you, Catherine. The way you used to look. How would you like to be thrown in a well, Missy Long-legs?"

He makes a grab for her but she skips forward out of reach. A virgin, is that what she is, a virgin?

"They'd have taken one look at Missy Long-legs, those old priests, and they'd have tossed her right in the well. Best place for her, too. Don't you fall, now."

As if she were a baby who would fall.

And then suddenly there is Santiago her enemy in his father's sombrero, Santiago carrying a machete and two bloody dead iguanas slung at his belt, dangling against his legs, Santiago who has just come home from working at his father's *milpa* (he is so dirty), Santiago looking at her, grinning at her, saluting her from the street.

She shakes her hair in the wind, she stands up tall.

"Gringa!" says Santiago, without sound, and makes a sign.

Her foot lands on a part of the wall that is crumbling, a section of bleached pink stucco comes loose, gives way, she loses her balance, tries to regain it, fails, and down she goes, sliding and slipping down the sea side of the wall, scraping her thigh, landing on the narrow wet beach, on sand and coral and old broken shells, conch shells, landing on sharp coral with her knee.

She sits on the sand with one leg buckled underneath her and looks out to sea. Who is to blame? Santiago is to blame.

Her knee is cut open, and she holds it, but she is unconcerned and does not cry. Three white faces look at her, over the wall, three Humpty-Dumpties, and then a fourth one, darker, farther along, the face of her enemy. Her knee stings like a hornet bite. She shrugs. It's nothing.

"Oh no," moans her mother. "Not on the coral, Octavia. Not a coral cut."

Tío Claude swings his legs over the wall and slides down. He kneels beside her in the wet sand.

Her mother is complaining up above. "Another infected knee. I've *told* you not to walk up there. You're too old for that."

Octavia feels all undone.

"The wall gave way," she says. "It's not my fault."

Julian is looking at her intently, the first time he has looked at her with any interest, the first time she has looked directly in his eyes. They are guardedly curious. At least he isn't laughing. The blood is oozing from her knee in a crossed crescent, a decent-sized cut, a really pretty good-sized cut. She is gratified.

"We'll fix this Missy up," says Tío Claude, and takes out his handkerchief.

"Don't use sea water, Clo," says her mother. "It's contaminated here."

"We'll just fix her up," says her uncle. He takes a knife from his pocket, opens it, and stabs himself in the butt of his thumb. His own red blood comes out. He squeezes and it comes running out.

"Clo!" says Catherine.

And he claps his bloody thumb against Octavia's knee, wound to wound, so that their mingled blood runs up her thigh.

"What are you doing?" says shocked Catherine.

"Indian trick," he says. "Old Indian trick I learned in the desert. Urine's better, tell you the truth."

He squeezes his cut again, and squeezes Octavia's, and presses them both together once again.

"Got no water, wash it with piss. Got no piss, use blood."

"You're a savage."

"That feels better now," he tells Octavia.

No, she wants to answer, it does *not.*

On the top of his head his hair is thin and grayish blond. In the center of his left ear, hairs grow out of a round red lump. He talks to her as if she were six years old, an imbecile like Maribel.

And now she hears his voice, very low, just for her, a whispery, breathy voice, saying: *"That's a bond now, Missy. You and me, we got a blood bond now."*

6 When I was seven, long before my cousin and my uncle came to visit, Mother gave me a solemn, thrilling lecture about boys and men. Thrilling because it meant (or seemed to mean) that she was giving my safety in the world some thought. Boys and men were dangerous, she indicated. Precautions must be taken.

I was impressed, because Mother was hardly a worrier, not about me. Danger to Octavia was not a subject that came up often. Even when I was little, swimming in the lagoon, with the barracuda following me, eyeing me thoughtfully, working their jaws, curious as a pack of dogs, Mother was unconcerned. She sat on the bank, embroidering. She laid down no rules. I could go alone into the jungle any time I chose. Once I toddled a mile into the jungle to visit the pyramids and the cenote, and toddled more than a mile back—having lost myself. But when I recounted this adventure, Mother gave me an absentminded pat on the head. For her the jungle was "the woods"—like the woods of Rock Creek Park back home in Washington, where the only danger then was poison ivy. And the sea, after all, was the same one she had known as a child at Rehobeth Beach.

"I never worry about Octavia," my mother said. "It's the other one that must be watched, every blessed minute of the day."

In the years when Elizabeth Jane lived on the island, her

mother wouldn't allow her even to leave their compound unless some grown-up was along. She couldn't swim in the lagoon because of the barracuda, or visit the cemetery because of "the germs." Even accompanied by a maid, she couldn't set foot in the jungle because of . . . God knows what. The unknown.

I was proud of my freedom. But all the same—people clearly cared about Elizabeth Jane.

Then at the age of seven, I discovered this one thing that deeply upset my mother. Soledad our cook (scandalized) told her I had been out fishing all day long on the sailboat *Pájaro Verde,* out of sight of land, with only Fortunado and his brother and his sons for company.

She called me into her bedroom, made me sit down beside her on the bed, took my hand, looked in my eyes and told me gravely that I must *never* go fishing with Fortunado or anybody else, unless a woman was along.

Further, I must never let myself be coaxed indoors or on a boat or other private place by any man or boy who offered fruit, candy, or presents.

The blinds were down and sunlight striped her like a cat. I squirmed and looked at my knees. Thrilled as I was, some inner demon made me challenge her.

"Why not?"

"Because, I am sorry to say—there are bad men who do bad things to little girls."

"What things?"

"Things they shouldn't."

"Make them pregnant?"

"Little girls don't get pregnant."

She wasn't up to giving the details, and I pretended to be mystified. The truth was I knew very well what she meant. She meant Soledad's old grandfather, who called me around to the side of their house one day and opened up his trousers to show me what was living there inside. He had not offered me candy but a look at some baby pigs. I was instinctively wary, even then, and what he showed me was no baby pig. It was a remarkable item. I had seen the little ones before, plenty of them, nubbins, on baby boys, but I had never laid eyes on one like that, so dark, so lumpy, so big. I ran away.

I was also well aware, had somehow thoroughly learned, that there were boys and men possessed to look at me between my legs, and I knew that, to my mother, boys-and-men were an inflammatory subject—but always in connection with Maribel, not me.

Now she was warning *me*. Seriously. Directly. Protecting *me!* I was overcome.

Aged seven, awed by the importance of it all, I gave her my solemn promise: no man or boy would *ever* catch me unawares. Mother and I, together, side by side, would stand foursquare against the world of men.

Yes, on that occasion she really seemed to care about me. But except for that one time, all through my childhood, until I was twelve, I didn't think much of her as a mother. All in all she didn't give a damn, in my opinion. She never took her eyes off Maribel. I could stop eating for days at a time and she'd hardly even notice.

"If you don't eat, you won't grow," she'd say, if it came to her attention. "Do you want to stay a little child forever?"

I decided she wasn't my true mother anyway. My true mother (the original—powerful, magical, dedicated to *me)* had faded away, and even though I looked and looked for her, and went from pillar to post, she was nowhere to be found. Instead this substitute was there, this impostor, and "Mother" was the name I had to use. Sometimes it gagged me coming out like a finger down the throat. "Mother." When Duncan tickled and tormented me and I ran to complain, she only laughed in an absentminded way. Is that a mother? A mother protects. Same features that woman had, same voice, same hair, but she was only the shell of my true mother, not the meat.

• • •

Now that I'm pregnant, I think about the island more and more, I can't get rid of it. Even at work, standing in the classroom, my mind goes wandering. How far can I trust my memories? Isn't the witness tainted? Hasn't she been reached? Isn't it possible that childhood's villain, seen through adult eyes, might be . . . pathetic? And its hero commonplace?

My childhood is nagging, plaguing me, it's like a searchlight in the eyes, a signal light across dark water, beamed right at me. It blinks and blinks. Long, short. Dah, dit. Is there a code to break?

7 "Can you feel it?" he breathed into her ear. "Can you feel that blood of mine just whizzing through your veins, all over your body, everywhere?" He had caught her in the gallery that same day, arrival day, and gripped her arm.

"No," said Octavia, scornfully.

But in reality, she *could* feel it. As soon as he mentioned it, she could feel it, this alien unwanted uncle-blood, streaming in her veins like a bright acid, spreading through her body, everywhere, mixing itself with her own blood, merging with her own to form a new entity, a strange new blood that was not hers not his, but all the same was passing at this very minute through the valves of her heart.

"I do mean everywhere," he said.

Her head got dizzy and the light changed, and she saw her mother and a pig harnessed together to a burro cart where Tío Claude and Maribel were riding on a load of fish and green papayas, and he was laughing and breathing with a whistle sound, and he thrust his hand out to her, and said, *Climb aboard.*

And she said, *No!* and shrank away.

• • •

In the *sala* waiting for midday dinner to be served, drinking sherry, her mother still can't take her eyes off him. She can't contain her joy, she can't sit still, she is giddy, like a child.

"But you're a total stranger!" she carols. Reaching out she hugs him, smooths his hair. "How handsome you are!"

And Octavia sourly thinks, Handsome? Him? She studies the silvery blond hair, the frown line deep between his eyebrows, the pale blue eyes that do not look at anyone.

"You're an impostor," teases her mother. "You had that scar removed?—a likely story. I don't believe you're my brother at all. Let me see your port wine mark."

And there in front of everyone (Papi, Julian, Lenin) she unbuttons his shirt and pulls up the undershirt. "Excuse me, old gentleman! Can you be Clo? Let's see—right side, third rib from the bottom, one two three—" Her fingers walk up his chest.

"Mother, what are you doing!" says Octavia, shocked by the unseemliness.

"By George, it's there," she cries. "But so faded! And bigger than it used to be." She rests her amber head against his chest. "Do you know what it means to me, your being here?" She puts his clothing back together. "Felipe knows. Octavia knows." She turns to Octavia. "Don't I talk about him all the time?"

Sourly, Octavia nods. She knows all the stories by heart, the travels, the adventures. Angola, Peru, the War. She wants no part of her mother's giddy display of intimacy. The uncle doesn't want it either, she observes. His laugh is wooden.

"Do you know how old we are? We're forty-two, nearly forty-three! Can you believe Catherine and Clo are forty-two? Did you recognize me? Have I changed so much? Am I ugly, Clo? Thick in the waist, this tired face, my hair so much darker—oh, never mind, never mind!"

On and on she gushes. Do you remember this? Old snapshots, old pets. Their parrot that sang "Margie." The plays they put on in the garden. Mother, Father, Jenny. The house, the attic where the devil hid. Dessie the maid. School, the beach. Do you remember—?

Octavia, studying their faces, thinks, They are so white, all white, pure pearly white. They are Cortez. Maribel is Doña Marina, the Indian princess who rode with Cortez, and she herself, who is she? Who is Octavia? She has blond hair, but it is not smooth or silken like her mother's hair, or Duncan's. It is strong and harsh and curly, unmanageable, and it sits incongruously on a dark-skinned face. Her blondness is a freak of pigmentation. She is both the darkest and the lightest of the sisters.

Her mother and this man are twins. Octavia can find no resemblance between them. For nine months they lived together, naked and entwined, in her grandmother's stomach. Looking at them, Octavia can't believe it happened. These two people? naked together in someone's womb?

Her mother's eyes are pink again with tears. "Sometimes I think my whole life here with Felipe has been lived just for you. Subject matter for my letters! Everything that happens, I think, Here's something I can write to Clo! And now you're here, and I'm all disoriented. We've changed, we've grown apart. Oh, Clo, we have to find each other! We have to bring it back."

Octavia grinds her teeth. How can Papi bear this? How can he sit there with that smile on his face? What is Julian thinking? He thinks she's a fool.

Once they are in the dining room her mother changes. The flush in her cheeks may be intensified, but she is elegant and correct, the gracious hostess. Perhaps she senses she has gone too far too fast. Perhaps she sees from his face he cannot match her emotion. Now she is showing off. She wants to impress him. Everything in her life must be perfect for this brother of hers. Let him send word home to Washington, the word that will justify her choice, her life, her children.

Over the soup he says, "Well, Catherine, you're very well appointed here." She can barely conceal her pride.

"You thought I'd be living in a grass hut?" she smiles.

And when he says to Felipe, "You speak English very well," she cries, "Did you think I married an aborigine? Felipe's family is the finest in Valladolid. His uncle was president!"

"President pro tem," Felipe corrects her. "He lasted for three months."

But nothing stops her. She brags about the island, the house, the servants, even about Maribel. "I worked so hard with her," she tells him. "Everyone said it was hopeless, but I kept on and on, and oh, my dear! the change! Today she is a perfect little lady—I could take her anywhere. I could take her to Washington! You and I, in Washington, Clo, we could take her anywhere, we wouldn't have to be ashamed."

Uncle Claude has brought presents for everyone. For Maribel and Octavia sweaters and jigsaw puzzles. For Father French brandy and for Mother a blue silk blouse.

"What on earth's in those two huge crates?" asks Mother. "Lenin and Domingo stacked them in the *bodega.*"

"Those crates?" Across the table he winks at Octavia solemnly. "Ah, those crates! Now that's very interesting. In those crates is . . . diving equipment!"

"You're going to dive?" asks Felipe.

"Well, sir, I'll tell you," says Tío Claude, leaning back, expanding his chest. "This area of yours, this sea, is full of wrecks. The currents are deceptive here, and those old ships, in a blow, they'd be driven on the reefs. Right offshore, on the south side of your island, near the lighthouse, in 1683 two ships ran afoul of a reef and sank. I have the spot pinpointed on my maps."

"What kind of ship?" asks Catherine.

"Pirates!" he says.

There is a pause. "Pirates," says Catherine. "Oh no. Not . . . treasure-hunting, Clo."

"You can bet on it!" cries Uncle Claude. "This island of yours was a pirate station. They would lie in ambush for the Spanish galleons beating up the coast to Cuba, laden down with gold from Peru."

There is another awkward pause. Octavia is reluctantly intrigued. Julian is glum.

"You'd do better with the Spanish payroll ships," says Felipe, prosaically. "They were forever going down."

"Aha! They went down because the pirates sank them! And first they were relieved of their valuables."

"So you didn't come to visit *me* after all," says Catherine, smiling brilliantly.

Uncle Claude laughs. "Two birds," he says. "Two birds, one stone, Catherine."

She laughs politely. She doesn't want to talk of pirate gold. "You'll never guess what we have for dessert," she says.

"Tell me."

"It's—apple pie!"

Uncle Claude blinks and looks disconcerted. "Splendid," he says, and exchanges a glance with Felipe.

And Catherine must explain in some detail the thought and labor expended to make this pie for him, a simple apple pie but his remembered favorite. Apples are almost unknown here, she explains; these were a special order from Ciudad de las Flores on the mainland. Imported from the north of Mexico, and worth their weight in gold. "Soledad, our cook, has never even heard of apples! Down here they think Eve tempted Adam with a banana."

She has made a joke but no one smiles. Her husband considers it in doubtful taste, and Tío Claude does not seem to hear.

"In the jungles of Java," he says to Felipe, "dinosaurs still exist, did you know that? Gigantic lizards, big as a boat. Their appetite is for monkeys."

Octavia, looking up, is caught by that phrase. *An appetite for monkeys.*

"If a monkey ventures down from his tree, and goes out into an open field, the lizard will catch it in his jaws. He doesn't kill it right away. He takes the arm in his jaws, and walks with that damned monkey into the jungle. They walk together. The monkey doesn't struggle! The two of them just walk together into the jungle like a pair of lovers."

"Why, Clo, how fascinating!" Catherine, doting, turns to Felipe. "He has the most amazing fund of information." All the same she is waiting her chance to turn the conversation back to topics of greater interest.

"Like lovers!" Tío Claude continues. "It's a form of hypnosis. Nature's anesthesia. The monkey goes right into trance. Of course, once safely in the jungle, the lizard eats him, but the natives say they make love first. Can you believe it? They swear it happens. Some form of sexual activity—before lunch, so to speak. Ha, ha."

Father glances at Octavia to see if she has noticed the use of a certain indelicate word.

"All love is hypnosis, anyway," says Catherine.

"Ha, ha, that's very good," says Tío Claude. "Love is hypnosis."

"And like all lovers, ultimately they devour one another," says Father dryly.

Catherine looks at him. *"One* devours the *other,"* she says, correcting him.

"I see," says Felipe, inclining his head. "Love is a contest then. Who eats whom."

Tío Claude takes him literally. "Oh no. The lizard always eats the monkey."

"Might makes right," smiles Catherine with a sigh.

"Doesn't the monkey *ever* eat the lizard?" demands Octavia. "What if you have a big monkey and a very small lizard? A sick lizard?"

The adults titter in a bored way. Octavia feels they have missed her point.

• • •

Julian is sitting next to her. Throughout the meal he is glum and unhappy. His father eats heartily, but Julian stares suspiciously at his plate.

"What is this?" he says to Octavia.

"Conch."

"What?"

"Pickled conch."

Pickled conch in a green tomato sauce? Black mashed beans sprinkled with something yellow, and turkey in a bitter chocolate sauce—*chocolate?*—so hot it set his mouth on fire? Julian has no appetite for such things. Besides, the stench of the *Camilio Canto* still hangs in his nose. The floor and the chair heave underneath him when he moves.

He is the first to see Maribel standing in the doorway. He recognizes her, the crazy daughter who was with them at the pier, a dark pretty girl with a strange off-center look on her face. Nobody but Julian notices what she is doing: she is unbuttoning her yellow blouse.

Oh, she is taking out one breast! She pops it out over the top of her slip. Wonder and delight! Her blouse is open down the front, and cupped in her two hands she holds this breast, her own bared breast, as if especially for him. It is the first breast Julian has seen outside of the movies, and his ears begin to throb. Big and bare and soft, an incredibly interesting thing. Bare!

Maribel advances on the table. Her breast has a red spot on it, she is wounded. She steps right up to her father and puts it near his face.

She makes a sound that may or may not be, "Hurt."

Julian glances quickly round the table for reactions. They are all worthy of attention, but the most dramatic is Catherine's.

"Oh no, oh *no,*" she says in a rage, and jumping up she seizes the dark girl by the arm, standing so that Julian's view is totally obstructed, and pulls her quickly from the room.

Julian feels he has been waiting a long, long time for this

occasion. A great tension within him relaxes. He wants to laugh. He has passed a milestone, he has seen a living breast.

The girl cousin sitting next to him is dying of embarrassment, red in the face and gleaming with perspiration. The doctor looks ruefully amused. The doctor's assistant sits rigid, his eyes on his fork. Julian's own father is unmoved, finishing his dinner.

"Like a child," says the doctor, with an indulgent smile.

From beyond the door, there is the sound of whimpering and a sharp slap. The doctor throws down his napkin. "Excuse me." He hurries from the room.

It is fifteen minutes before the two of them come back, the doctor and his wife. He is genial, talkative, as though nothing has happened, only breathing a little fast. She has obviously just recovered from her tears.

"Come," she says brightly to the visitors. "Let's have our coffee in the patio. Julian! Do help me finish off this pie."

Julian, no longer seasick, feels his appetite stir and accepts a second piece of pie. His father declines. In fact, his father has barely touched the celebrated apple pie.

Church bells are tolling as they leave the dining room. They are tolling for the mayor's youngest son, who was killed yesterday celebrating a fiesta. Four other fiesta victims are in Felipe's *sanatorio*— one gunshot and three machete wounds—and he feels obliged to go to the funeral, for political reasons.

Tío Claude says, "I'll go with you," and Octavia's mother immediately intervenes. "Clo, you're tired. You don't have to go."

He turns his blank face toward her. Octavia observes once more that he looks past her, not at her. Why is that? If by mistake his eyes alight on her, he withdraws them hastily.

"Funeral customs, I collect them," he says. "Judge a people by their funeral customs."

She lets him go with a smile. "I've waited twenty-five years—I can wait an hour more."

Octavia asks Julian, "Do you want to go? You can see the bricking in."

"The what?"

"You watch the mason."

"Doing what?"

"He sets the bricks, and slaps the cement on, and writes the person's name there with a stick."

"You simply stand on one foot and the other, watching this person work," her mother finishes. "I'm glad to miss it. I've had enough of funerals."

Julian, looking at his feet, says, "I'd like to go upstairs."

Now Catherine remembers, and puts her arm around him. "I'll come up with you. How wonderful to have a boy in the family, and such a big nice boy!"

Octavia also remembers with a shock what she keeps forgetting: that Julian's mother is so newly dead.

She follows them upstairs.

Next day, although her throat is sore and swollen, she camps outside his door. Timidly she knocks.

"Want to play checkers?"

He opens the door a crack and shakes his head.

"Don't you like checkers?"

"It isn't that," he says mournfully. He is trying to get rid of Octavia as politely as possible. "I'm just not used to people younger than myself. I've never been too fond of girls."

Octavia's ears ring. She wants to say that she is different, but for some reason, in the face of his melancholy, the words don't come out. She is aware he isn't trying to hurt her, he is only stating a simple miserable fact.

All she can find to say is another simple miserable fact.

"But I'm all there is."

"I know."

Dolefully he sighs and says, "Excuse me." He closes the door, and will not emerge for all the inviting thumps and whistles and animal noises that Octavia makes outside his door.

All morning she waits there hopefully, clearing her throat and coughing, jumping up and down to make noise with her feet.

"Let him alone," says her mother. "He's tired out."

"But he's awake. I can hear him in there."

"Leave him alone."

"I just wanted to borrow a comic book."

Perhaps it is this vigil that sets the pattern for their relationship, this camping at his doorstep, listening, hoping.

She loves him. She wants to study him, observe him. Already she is copying the way he eats (head down over the chicken leg), the way he holds his head (cocked to one side), the way he walks (a rangy lope), his turns of phrase, the lilt of Pennsylvania Dutch in his voice.

"Do tell," he said at the table.

"Do tell," she whispers now, practicing.

She brings her jacks and plays, not silently. She brings a ball and plays One, Two, Three, O'Leary.

"Octavia," says her mother, "are you still there? Run outside and play."

But she does not. Her throat is hurting. She drags back to her own room and reads *The Princess and Curdie* for the hundredth time. It is her mother's book, from her mother's childhood. Julian is Curdie, cool and resourceful. Not yet, however, is he devoted. She collects a pile of books and brings them to his door. She starts to knock and does not dare. She leaves them outside on the floor.

She plays with her cat, snuggles her cat, and is consoled for a long time. Love fills her heart, overflows. She cannot hug her cat enough, she is insatiable in her love for him; it suddenly changes to a desire to squeeze him hard, too hard. She shudders with horror. *Pablito, I never would.* But the truth is that she could. She could cut off his foot, she could set his fur on fire. She could do this to her dearest friend, her cat who loves her and trusts her, who purrs and makes bread in her neck, and eats her hair and spits it out.

She does not squeeze him too tight, her love is stronger. But her teeth go click-click and her body trembles as the temptation goes through her and then ebbs away. Pablito is her prey, all unbeknownst to him. He is at her mercy. She could kill, torture, eat him.

How can that be, when she would die for him? She feels a deep strain of evil in her heart.

She goes out into the hall, the gallery, and stands in front of Julian's door. Silence. She bumps into the door with her shoulder as if by sheerest accident. Silence. She whispers, "Julian, Julian, Julian." Silence. She scratches at the door like a little rat. She hears a sound inside and runs away—but not so far that she can't see if he opens his door and looks out.

The door stays shut.

Julian hadn't wanted to come at all, she found out later. His father had descended on him in Hershey, Pennsylvania, arriving suddenly, and scooped him out of school with remarks to the principal about the educational value of foreign travel. His mother had been dead only two weeks and he was living miserably with an aunt. At least he knew the aunt. His father he scarcely knew at all. He was sunk in a profound melancholy which gave his body a sad slow dignity, as though he were exhausted after a hard day's work.

He wanted to be let alone to dwell on his grief. He was not interested in this girl cousin. Was he expected to entertain her? This little kid? He sighed heavily. What could he say to her? What could they do together? On the walk to the house he had noticed with relief that there were plenty of boys on the island. The boy with the dead lizards seemed okay—for a foreigner. But they were all foreigners, they didn't even speak English. He'd never be able to make friends with them, what was the use?

Imagine eating a lizard. Those lizards. Eating them.

Even in this house they had strange customs. Midday dinner they called lunch. The food was strange. A lot of fish. He didn't care for fish.

"You'll like *this* fish," said his new aunt, his father's sister. "Just try it."

To be polite he tried it, and through the sour bile of his prejudice he knew it really was good and she was right, but all the same he didn't care for it. He didn't want anything new, he didn't want so much change, everything changing at once. It was disloyal to eat this fish. With his mother, he always refused. His eyes suddenly stung and he feared he might cry for his loss but he controlled it. He hadn't cried, not even at the funeral, and when they buried her (that was the worst), he had only felt this aching hole inside, this sudden expanding hole of black pain. His insides were nothing but this hole. He had known she was probably dying, she'd been sick so long, and he could hear her groaning, and then for days she didn't even know him. And when she finally died, they told him . . . they told him he should be glad. *You should be glad,* they said. *She's been released.* And they buried her in the barely thawed ground where soon the worms and insects would be crawling, where there was no air, no air to breathe, but of course she didn't need it, she was dead.

Octavia lays siege to her cousin, plans her campaign. She will be inventive, boylike, daring. She will entice him with games. She will find something to offer him, some treasured possession that will augment her value in his eyes.

What has she got? She searches her room. Books, arrowheads, one spearhead, two tiny female figures, *ídolos,* found near the mounds and the cenote in the jungle, gold cuff links in the shape of tiny frogs which belonged to her father but which he never wore and had not missed, a seated Buddha which had belonged to her mother's mother, a safety razor, a knife. In truth, her dearest and best possession is her cat, but she knows from experience that people do not understand the miracle of cats. Presumably Julian will not either. He may even regard cat worship as a weak and girlish thing. She will offer Pablito cautiously, without much hope, to be admired.

No, her real hope lies in a special stolen treasure that lies hidden away at the bottom of her carved sea chest, in the secret drawer, below the blankets and bedspreads. She has never used it, she just likes to think about it. She likes to know that it is there, heavy with power.

Before daring to take it from her parents' bedroom, Octavia made an experiment to determine the risk she would run. She pulled out a hair from her head and glued the ends over the drawer of her father's bed table in such a way that the hair or the glue must give way if the drawer were opened. For a whole month the hair was undisturbed and she felt safe. She convinced herself, perhaps in error, that for her father it was an unwanted and uninteresting object like the cuff links, and one morning she smuggled it out, hidden in the folds of a sweater. Along with a tiny box of its bullets.

She gloats. She is a fisherman, and this will be her bait. What boy can resist a gun?

At the same time, her throat is sore and seems to be getting worse. She plays with the bullets in her bed and becomes aware her head is burning. Each swallow is a spasm of pain. Two o'clock comes, time for the main meal of the day. Julian will be there.

She tries to get up and discovers she cannot. Her body will not support itself. She is feeling miserable.

She is sick.

8 Octavia is in bed in her monastic little room, so different from her sister's room. She is sick with tonsillitis. To swallow is like an explosion. She lies on her bed in a thin cotton nightgown. It is twilight, and she has let down the mosquito netting.

Someone appears in the doorway, a man.

A man is standing in the doorway.

He stands there in the shadows, in the doorway of her room, looking at her. Well, Missy, he says. You're a bad girl to be sick.

She is twelve years old and small for her age.

He stands in the shadows, leaning against the door, and looks at her. Let's see what we can do. He pulls up a chair and sits beside her bed.

The room grows dark. Palm fronds are tossing, rustling outside the window, scraping, brushing against the window.

I wouldn't do this for everyone, he says. But you and me, we've got that blood bond now, my blood inside you, running all around. So let's just see what we can do.

A breathing sound. The smell of tobacco.

His hands are touching her.

• • •

May the sharks devour him, may the little jungle men dismember him. May the siren Xtabai sweet-sing him to her cave and torture him and chew his bones.

I know you, old man, old man with a withered leg. I know you old man my uncle, I know your brown leg bone, your dried and twisted grapevine leg, I know it, because I gave it to you, I wished it upon you, I have withered you and cursed you. I have bent you and maimed you. Unto eternity forever may you twist in pain.

"Mother," says Octavia, "that uncle came into my room."

"I know," says her mother.

"He had this stick of purple light. He rubbed it on me."

"Did it help?"

"He rubbed me . . . everywhere . . ."

It hurts to talk and she can't get started. Her mother cannot seem to hear. Something happened, serious, difficult to grasp. She is at a loss, but this much she knows—there was a breach of faith. Defenses were bypassed, the line was crossed, an enemy masqueraded as a friend. Now steps must be taken, her mother must act, her mother must be horrified, outraged.

"It's something new they're using in the States," her mother says. "He told me about it. Ultraviolet radiation to kill the germs. And look! It's working! By tomorrow you're going to be all well!"

Her mother doesn't understand. "He touched me, there."

"Oh, nonsense, Tavvie."

"Well he did."

"Where do you get these ideas?"

"He did."

She sits up sternly. "Octavia, you have a fever and you're being foolish. It was very kind of Uncle Clo to visit you."

"I don't want him coming in here any more."

"All right, all right," says her mother, irritated. "It's nonsense. Try to sleep."

"Tell him."

"I certainly will *not*. You're dreaming things."

"You always said . . . you always said I should—"

"What? I can't understand you."

Octavia has to swallow. Her throat is killing her. "You always said I should tell you—"

"Honey, you're not well. Your little mind is all confused."

"I'm *not* confused." It hurts too much to argue. Octavia falls back on her pillow.

"The best thing you can do is sleep."

Nothing she can say will make it clear.

Her mother rearranges the mosquito netting. "Hush now, you'll be better soon. Soledad will bring you up some soup."

Octavia gets through the day. It threatens rain and she is not better. Her father looks inside her mouth with a flashlight and prescribes antibiotics. Her mother puts hot and cold compresses on her throat and says, "Julian is sick too. Tummy trouble."

Octavia lies blinking in a stupor. She has failed to get her message across. She is adrift, she is somewhere she has never been before.

9 I had a brother older than El Veinte but one night, long before I was born, he was flushed away at sea, down the toilet into the Bay of Campeche. You wouldn't think I'd worry about *him,* a foetus, but I do. He's in my thoughts a lot. Mother was on shipboard at the time; it was, in fact, her honeymoon. She was on deck when the cramps and pain began. It was night, dark night, and Father was somewhere else. She went down to her cabin and something happened, she knew something had happened, and when she looked down she could see it, there it was, a small white form in the toilet bowl.

She looked at it a while, appalled. What should she do? What does a person do? Nothing she had ever learned in all her life could guide her. A ritual, a prayer at least, seemed indicated. She sank down on her knees, but divine instruction did not come. She turned off the lights. Darkness, she hoped, would make it easier. Instead, a miracle took place. The water in the toilet bowl was all aglow with flashing points of light! Seawater, full of microscopic phosphorescent creatures.

"I am the Resurrection and the Life," she quavered, and pulled the chain.

A rush of waters upon the deep. A mighty spiral of glittering light . . . the tiny almost-human thing, homunculus, whirls round and vanishes, sucked down into a black hole.

• • •

"The basic form of the universe is a spiral," my mother used to say. "A spiral of flashing light." Was she thinking of the toilet bowl in the Bay of Campeche?

This morning in Pittsburgh I awoke before dawn. The streetlights fell on my walls like whitewash from a failing moon. Inside my head a dog began to bark, a rooster crowed, the breath of the sea caressed my face and I was once again on Caracol, my island. Caracol where I was born, an eight months' baby covered with hair and possessed of eleven fingers, one of which the midwife pared off immediately with a fish scaler. The scar's still there, a dimple just above the thumb. (My husband Justin likes to kiss it, sentimentally. I laugh, of course. What else? I could never tell him what it really is, because, being Justin, being impossible, and thinking the way he thinks, he would never believe me. What a fantasy! he'd say. Born with a little penis, were you? Poor baby, and they cut it off?)

Isla Caracol. Flat, hot, humid, measuring no more than fourteen by seven miles, edged with jagged coral shores, tufted with scrubby "jungle," it is a green wart on the warm blue skin of the sea. It stands twelve miles off the Central American coast and suffers from banana blight. Do you know what happens in banana blight? The sensitive young trees grow just so far, then wither. The fruit is bitter and stunted, no bigger than a child's finger.

Caracol. Also known as Isla de los Indios, because, unlike the other offshore islands which are now populated chiefly by blacks, ours is an enclave of Mayan Indians, the original inhabitants. Caracol. Tropical, but hardly paradise . . . except to me. I loved it; it was home. It was also home to uncounted billions of amoebas, biting flies, rats, cockroaches, sand fleas, buzzards, ticks, microbes, viruses, dogs, lizards, spiders, witches, and anopheles mosquitoes.

Children withered and died there like banana trees. True there were no poisonous snakes, but that just proved, I suppose, it was not paradise.

Once a penal colony of sorts, it became a hideout for fugitives and a place of exile—an Elba—for personages politically embarrassing to the government but too highly placed to murder without risk.

One of these personages was my father, long ago. Mother, pregnant then with Duncan, already miserable, already longing for home, longing for her twin, came with him from Valladolid where they had been living for two years. I don't mean to imply my father was in prison or under guard. No, he was quite free. He became the island doctor, he visited the other islands, now and then even touched in at Ciudad de las Flores (pop 45,000) on the mainland for supplies and medicines. But the message from the capital city was clear: We give you your life. Return, and you vanish.

That was the message. The expectation was that he, like most of his predecessors, would not return. Would, in fact, like them, die naturally of fever within a year in that sleepy plague-ridden beautiful hellhole which was Isla Caracol.

My husband Justin doesn't know a thing about death. He never fought in any war. His parents and two brothers are still living. Nobody in his family ever died, not really *died,* not in full view. His grandparents disappeared before he was born, leaving behind four stones in two green fields. Once he attended the funeral of an eleven-year-old girl cousin who died of kidney disease, and she was on view, and he looked at her, but she lay there in her pink-padded coffin as pretty as a waxworks doll, with pink cheeks and pink lips and curly hair and lilies of the valley in her palely pious, slender, elegantly modeled hands.

What does Justin know?

He says my Dead are consuming me. Not just Mother, all of

them. He wants me to face them, look them in their jellied eyes, exorcise them once and for all and get on with the business of living, which to him means having this child I'm pregnant with.

Perhaps he is right and I am obsessed with my Dead. There are so many.

Maribel is dead, El Veinte is dead. Father is dead, and now my mother too. Everyone in my immediate blood family is dead except for Duncan, my oldest sister Duncan, who escaped the island early and has managed to thrive in McLean, Virginia, married to a rich man who actually plays polo—polo!—when he isn't fiddling with futures.

Death is everywhere, of course, but somehow on my island there was more of it. You can't have anything to do with Indo-America without finding yourself awash in blood and death. The very soil stinks of blood and torture, betrayal and death. That's what my father used to say, and he was right.

That's why we left the island, my mother and my cousin and I, when I was twelve. Death and betrayal. Betrayal and death.

My father had a fine, soft, drooping mustache and molten mournful eyes. He wore white trousers, a white loose Yucatecan shirt, and cowboy boots when he did not wear the white jacket of his profession. It was no wonder that Mother fell in love with him when she met him as an intern in San Antonio. She had run away from home in a rage at being separated from her twin, and was staying with her aunt and uncle (also a doctor) in Texas. They met and fell in love and since her father was passionately opposed to the match—a Latin-American being scarcely better than a Negro in his mind— she let herself get pregnant and was obliged to marry him.

I have no photograph of my father, but when I think of him, he always has a mournful look on his face, and he is tall and sad and beautiful. Although Mother insists (it is important to her, at this time) that his blood is Spanish, there is Indian in the flare of his nostril and the curve of his lip. His face has a ruddy glow (except when he suffers a malaria attack, and then it fades to a pale and eerie green). And I am languishing for love of him, knowing that his heart belongs to Maribel. I see him as he stands beside her bed —full of love and pain, blaming himself, torturing himself. More and more he lives as lover and protector of this child. Always in his mind is the image of her as she was before her illness. He looks at grown-up Maribel and sees the little girl who rode on his shoulders and sang the *"Mañanitas."* She has the dark hair and eyes of his mother, he says. She has his mother's nose and mouth.

He is a man of many contradictions. As a doctor he is clever and conscientious and dedicated, but with the passage of years he becomes increasingly curt and short-tempered with his patients. They ignore his advice, he says. They neglect to take his medicines, they disobey his orders, they do not boil the water that they drink. He scolds and berates them, adults and children alike. He puts more and more work on Lenin and Sara Valdés, the nurse. Often at night he sits in his office across the patio and drinks *aguardiente.*

Then on his way to bed he stops in to look at Maribel asleep, touching her hair, weeping, for in her sleep she is normal again, she is well and beautiful, his angel. With tears still wet on his cheeks he gets heavily into bed and wakes up my mother to make love. (She is responsive as a stick, he growls. A handsome woman still, but cold. And why does she flinch and jump at his touch, as if he were going to hit her?)

The compassion that once flowed for the sick children of the island now flows only for Maribel.

He is the one doctor for seven islands, and he goes from one to the other, hitching regular rides on the government patrol launch. (The very government that has exiled him.) No one has assigned him this territory, and he certainly makes no money from his work. It is even doubtful that all of his patients welcome his attention. Yet he persists, battling for clean water and a better diet, battling to halt the use of human manure on the fields, battling the witches and the *curanderos.*

As a proud atheist, he also—along the way—does his best to insult and undermine the Church, and boasts that his is the only doctor's office south of the Rio Grande that does not have a crucifix on the wall. No crucifix, and no Madonna! That is his boast.

As I look back, I'm not so sure. On the whitewashed walls of his office hang reproductions of paintings, and all of them—except for Botticelli's *Spring*—all of them show blood and torture and martyrdom. They are the work of the great Mexican muralists. Indian faces with mournful eyes look out of them, and the faces (at least in my memory) belong to bodies that are being roasted, boiled, carved, cracked, trampled.

No Virgin and no Christ, he says?

Who is that in Botticelli's *Spring* if not the Virgin? And don't those tortured Indians stand in for Christ?

Our big two-story house, built in town by my grandfather in the days of slaves and haciendas, is a hollow square. The patio in the center is open to the sky. Around it run open galleries on both floors, from which the rooms are entered. The entire northern side of the house has been turned into my father's clinic. Doors and windows opening on the patio from that side have been bricked in, except for one high quatrefoil window that gives light and ventilation to his examining room. Patients enter from the street and do not disrupt the life of the household.

In his office are a large worn mahogany desk, innumerable filing cabinets, and a round table covered with green felt where once or twice a week he drinks and plays cards with the judge and the mayor and the captain of the port, with Don Emilio the agent, and sometimes Don Carlos or Don Doroteo the planters, or even two of the Lebanese brothers.

The islanders do not know what to make of my father.

What do you make of a man who comes back to the island where his parents, two brothers and a sister were slaughtered, comes back with a *gringa* wife—not for revenge but to rebuild the decayed town house of his parents (the hacienda being in burned-out ruins) and set up a medical practice? Why has he done this? What is behind it?

Even when the government changes hands and the name of Sandoval is honored once again in Valladolid, he stays on.

Are his medicines poison? Is he a devil, killing off the children? Why did he pick Lenin Dominguez, of all people, to be his aide? Lenin Dominguez, son of the man who led the raid on the hacienda?

The truth, which they do not know, and would not believe, is very simple. He is paying with his own devotion for the crimes of his father. He has a thesis to prove: *Disinterested benevolence does exist. Human beings are capable of it.*

The person he hopes to convince is himself.

"Pablo!" Octavia, sick with tonsillitis, scolds her cat. "Where have you been?"

He sits in the middle of her bed, unafraid, all needs attended to, protected, stretching, yawning, luxuriating, washing himself elaborately. His innocent self-love is the measure of her success as cat-mother. Watching her cat is the deepest satisfaction she knows.

Yet he goes out, away from her, putting himself in danger where she cannot stand guard, looking for female cats, making kittens and more kittens that nobody will feed, that will starve and suffer and die. It weighs her down, but she does not have the heart to curtail his freedom. He does what he has to do. He is forced to do it, betrayed by nature, by something within. It is sex. What is this sex? It is everywhere.

My mother had a superstitious side to her nature, and a mystical side too, which was probably transmitted from her own mother, a fragile handsome woman who became an ardent practicing Buddhist even though she was married to an officer in the U.S. Navy and lived a busy social life in Washington, D.C. So ardent was her Buddhism that she died of it in 1927.

Mother always said she died of joy.

Needless to say, no one believed her. Who could die of joy? To die of grief may be possible. Grief turns flesh to lard. But dying of joy is not possible. Joy irradiates the being, like love. It energizes, it gives life. Nobody dies of it.

Since no one else would listen, I was the one she told. I was too young to argue, and I loved a story.

"Grandmother died of joy in Washington," my mother said. "She ran out in the snow in her nightgown. She played in the snow like a child. She was thirty-seven years old and terribly beautiful. It was a kind of bliss—it was enlightenment."

Most of the things my mother told me in childhood weren't worth a buzzard's drip. This about my grandmother capering in the snow in her nightgown was the first she passed along of any value. (Later she told me it was really Abel who slew Cain, which was also interesting.)

It was nighttime and the sky was the color of peaches, the dark skin of peaches that are overripe. The city was closed inside a marvelous hush. No traffic, no car tracks on the street. Snow was swarming like bees around the streetlights, it was thick and deep on the lawn. My grandmother ran out of the house, laughing and crying, and she picked up the snow and tossed it into the air. The family followed, helpless and amazed—my grandfather, my aunt Jenny, my mother and Uncle Clo (aged six). My grandfather (unenlightened) wrung his hands and sent my mother inside to fetch a cape at least. He was a captain in the U.S. Navy and his wife was a big embarrassment. When he put the cape over her shoulders, instead of warming herself she laughed and lifted her arms at the beauty all around her and threw it off. It lay there on the snow like a huge black bird that had fallen from the sky.

Soon thereafter she died, maybe from excitement, maybe from a chill. Maybe when her ego popped, her life drained out.

I think of my grandmother's cape lying crumpled in the snow so many years ago. I think of it falling, falling, a great black bird shot out of the sky.

"Tell me about the snow," I said to my mother. Snow . . . it was cold but was not ice. It was soft but was not feathers. It was white but was not a sheet. It fell in the movies, it covered the earth in picture books. An impressive fly-specked mural in our bakery (La Coronación de la Virgen was its name) showed Mary and Joseph on a burro riding through deep snow to Bethlehem. Under sparkling stars they struggled through snowdrifts that Jesus might be born.

"I'm telling you about your grandmother, Octavia, not about snow."

My father was one of those who refused to listen. To him Buddhism was just a sillier form of Christianity, and Christianity was a priests' plot to enslave the populace. He was exquisitely bored by my mother's mother and her Buddhist joy.

"She was brought up in China," my mother protested. "Her parents were missionaries, Christians of course, but still she was exposed to Buddhism at an early age and it intrigued her from the start. A perfectly normal faith for her to embrace, a woman of her background. Nothing strange about it, nothing exotic."

My father coughed and fidgeted, his mind wandered, his eyes glazed over, and he remembered he had left the sterilizer boiling in the clinic. He excused himself.

His boredom was not directed at mothers in and of themselves. On the contrary he had a Latin reverence for mothers. The memory of his own mother obsessed him, made him tremble, darkened his life. Or rather, lit it up, for almost every night in his sleep, or half-sleep, the old hacienda at the southern tip of the island went up once more in flames that stank of kerosene. Over and over his mother begged for mercy on her knees and the machetes rose and fell, the black blood spurted against the flames and smoke. Almost every night in bed his heart went into spasm, his muscles twitched, he panted, sweated, he raced to save her. I'm coming, Mother, wait!

"Felipe, you're dreaming again," my mother would say, and for a time he would stare at her without recognition, drenched in sweat, until at last he came to himself and rose in silence to pace the gallery outside their bedroom, up and down, up and down, smoking his cigar, until the screaming and the flames faded away.

So it was not mothers in general, or even women, that he disdained. It was specifically his wife's mother, and more specifically her Buddhism, her joy, her snow. *Ai caray!* What a subject on which to waste one's time!

Today, when I know all I care to about snow, I lie here in Pittsburgh reading books on Buddhism, trying to be like my mother's mother, trying to understand birth and death and enlightenment.

What is enlightenment?

"Not this," I read. *"Not that."*

I read that the founder of Zen sat facing the wall of a Chinese cave for eleven years until some small boys came in and hit him on the head with a stone, whereupon he was immediately enlightened and broke into peals of laughter.

To become enlightened what you must do, it seems, is maul and macerate your ego, puncture your ego like a balloon, and then, suddenly—wham, pow, bliss!—everything there is to know, you know.

"Everything suffers," I read.
"The iron rooster lays an egg," I read. *"Dust rises from the sea."*

Sometimes in my morbid fantasy I wonder if this growing blob inside of me, this small invader that is changing everything about my body and my life, might not be someone that I know. Maribel for instance. Or Mother, Mother herself!

What if the Buddhists are right? What if my mother has cleverly planned that I should be the vehicle of her rebirth? Has she somehow wormed her way inside my belly—little bitty Mom all young again, curled up, taking a swim, taking her ease, filing her nails, preparing to be born again, all thanks to me? Octavia's baby.

My mother liked to think that way, liked to turn things inside out. She and her brother, in Sunday school when they were children, played a secret game they called "Reversals." In this game, it was Abel, really, who killed Cain. Adam who tempted Eve. Goliath who slew David, the lions who ate Daniel, and Isaac who raised the knife while Abraham was crying, *"Izzy, Izzy, where's the lamb?"*

They also made up verses on the model of the one their Sunday school teacher taught them:

> *In Adam's fall*
> *We sinned all.*

Catherine wrote:

> *In Cain's red eyes*
> *Is a big surprise.*

On our island, when a woman gave birth they always said, "She bought a baby." They said this to be delicate about it.

"Bought it? Did she really? Where do you buy babies?"

"Tonta! *In Paris! Where else?" Delila said.*

Soledad confirmed that babies were bought in Paris. Everyone agreed. Buying your baby in Paris lent a touch of class to the proceedings. It also implied control. *I'll take that one. . . . On second thought, no, I'll take that one over there. . . . Or perhaps, after all, I won't take any. No, not today.*

I wouldn't mind buying a baby if I could pick it out. I'd pick out Julian in miniature. But as it is, I've got a pig in a poke. Suppose it turns out to be my Uncle Clo! Can I return it? Listen, I'm a consumer. I want a written guarantee.

And how did I get pregnant anyway? With all the precautions I took, it should have been impossible.

The night it happened, sound asleep in the middle of the night, I heard a voice. I'd swear it was my mother's voice.

And when I opened my eyes I saw the whole room, our bedroom here in Pittsburgh, Pennsylvania, filled with flickering light, an aurora borealis pulsing in rhythm with a sound that came from everywhere at once, a beating sound, like a great engine, as if I were aboard an airplane or a ship. Blinking and alarmed, I was up and out of bed before I knew what I was doing, groping around in that strange light that flickered like feathers on my skin.

Somebody seemed to be there.

"Who is it?" I whispered, and stumbled against the chair. Suddenly I smelled the sea, and heard the slosh and movement of waves, I had a feeling of sunlight, bright air, and a green tropical sea. Birds crying. The beating of that powerful engine, and a voice.

"Octavia."

My hair prickled. I leaped back into bed, burrowed under the covers, and pressed myself against Justin's sleeping back.

The engines faded away.

My eyes were wide open to the shadow pattern of bare

branches, cast by the streetlights shining through the trees. My ears were open to the muted sounds of Pittsburgh late at night, city sounds. A siren in the distance.

Whatever was there had gone. Trembling and sweaty, I shook Justin by the shoulder, I woke him up, I couldn't help myself.

"Justin, please, something happened, I'm sorry to wake you, but there's been this terrible . . ." I didn't know what to call it— nightmare? vision? "There's been this terrible *event.*"

He mumbled and moaned, slowly regained consciousness. When I told him what had happened he was not impressed.

"Event," he muttered. "What is this Mickey Mouse event? It was a dream, that's all. You want an event? Feel this."

I felt it, and jumped. It was a big warm erection.

Now that I'm pregnant I stay awake all night licking my dry lips. My heart makes the bed springs squeak. I think of my cousin Julian, who faced his fears and got killed for his trouble. I think of Maribel. I think of the dogs and cats my mother chloroformed, and by dawn I can smell on myself a strange skunklike odor, the odor of fear.

For twenty-two years I've tried not to think of my sister. I locked her out of my life and only now she's wormed her way back in. Maribel and Mother, they know I'm pregnant and they're claiming me. They crawl, they swarm all over me. They lie on top of me and hold me down. They'll give me no peace until I make up my mind.

Shortly before my cousin and my uncle came to the island, I saw something I'd rather not have seen. I saw my parents in a sexual act.

They really loved each other, my parents. At least, they loved each other at one time. But what I saw that morning didn't look like love.

I was snooping in their bedroom when I heard them at the door and jumped to hide, crouching down between the bureau and the wall, behind a screen. They came in together. My father closed the shutters and began.

I saw it, and when I closed my eyes, I heard it.

He seemed to be angry. He made her kneel down, opened his pants, and stuck his penis in her face. I was staggered at its size. He whacked her cheeks and made her grab for it as if she were bobbing for apples. He called her a bitch. Afterward they both cried, from emotions that were obscure to me.

Father was the first to cry; he cried and said he loved her. He said, "What has happened?" She didn't cry then, she cried later, after he left the room, great horrible sobs.

Maybe I'm wrong and she cried when he called her a bitch. I think it's very possible she did, but if she did, it was not loud crying (how could she sob, with that thing rammed in her throat?), it was just tears running down her face.

Mother. As I look back, I see that all her life she was looking for answers, haunted by her mother in the snow. She sought an answer in each and every birth. Maybe that explains why she didn't use a diaphragm or anything. Maybe every time she lay beneath my father's pounding cock, she hoped awakening would come to her. She was brought up a Protestant, but never could forget her mother's joy while playing in the snow in her nightgown.

I didn't want to see what I saw that morning. I thought my father was trying to kill her. I wanted to cry out, *Stop, stop!* I had come in their bedroom looking for something. Whatever I was looking for, it was something I wasn't supposed to have. It was not enlightenment. In fact, it was my father's gun.

10

The moon has a bridal veil flung across its face, streaming out on each side in long wings of luminous cloud, thin as chiffon. A ring is also visible, a rainbow ring around the moon, and furthermore, an ominous indigo darkness pushes up from below. What is this darkness? Clouds? Sky? Other? What does it portend?

Octavia, nearly recovered from her illness, goes downstairs, and Domingo, cutting the grass in the patio with two machetes, gives her the answer. The darkness pushing up against the moon last night was none other than the demon-goddess Xtabai.

Xtabai, half human and half beast, on moonlight nights goes hunting for her prey, her human prey, deep in the jungle. Her victims are hunters, lost and drunken hunters. She beguiles them with her beauty and then wraps them in darkness.

Octavia, old enough to scoff, prefers to believe (or half-believe) in Xtabai.

"If she's half beast—what kind of beast?"

"A terrible beast."

Standing half in moonlight, half in shadow, she calls the hunters sweetly. Her monster-part is concealed in darkness, and the woman-part stands naked in the moonlight. Her black hair streams over her pale skin. She calls to them mournfully, and if they do not approach, she weeps. At last they always come to her. And *zas!* She leaps! Roar, struggle! She drags them to her cave and devours them.

Octavia thinks about the hunters who cannot resist. Why can they not resist? It's sex again. Always sex.

She imagines Xtabai's life in the jungle. How does someone get to be half person and half beast? Was the father a *tigre* and her mother a beautiful lady? Or was the father a handsome hunter caught by a giant female iguana who dragged him to her cave, and had sex with him before she ate him? Like the lizards of Java with the monkeys? And then nine months later lying on her side she gave birth to their monstrous child and called it Xtabai.

"What was she like when she was little?"

"Just like *you!*" says Domingo.

Octavia is disturbed by this answer. It may be a joke but she does not smile. She has always felt something is wrong. Perhaps she *is* half beast. Is Maribel half beast? Is her mother?

"I am not half beast," she stiffly says.

Domingo, squatting, trims the grass with his two machetes, one in each hand, snip snap, like giant scissors.

"The beast emerges when you come of age," he informs her, and finishing one patch he combs the grass with his fingers and waddles forward to begin another.

"Did you ever see her?"

"Me?" says Domingo. "I certainly did." (He pauses in his work.) "One night hunting fox. What a struggle! I seized her, I wounded her, I had her down, and I was choking her, so, when she found my machete on the ground—*zas!*—she gave me this."

He pats the terrible scar that winds across the left side of his neck and face, puckered and indented like a river at the bottom of a canyon.

"Xtabai gave you that?"

"Who else?"

Octavia, in possession of the facts, says scornfully, "A *chiclero* on the mainland gave you that."

All the same, she sees the struggle clearly. She sees Domingo's blood spurt black in the moonlight, and Xtabai go running—hobbling, dragging herself, for how could she run very well with one human leg and one beast leg?—deep into the black and yellow jungle. Running to the safety of her cave piled deep with human bones. There to weep and grieve and nurse herself.

"You hurt her?"

"Clearly I did. After fighting with me, she didn't take a hunter for three years. She was wounded. Here, I'll prove it to you."

He pulls up his shirt, and there, just below the ribs, is a purple stain.

"Her blood," says Domingo, awed. *"Ya ves?"*

Later on, while he is pruning roses, Octavia sneaks up behind him silently with Maribel, and with a shout she pushes Maribel against him. Wiry, tough Domingo is afraid of Maribel! He winces and pulls away, he dodges here and there, and Octavia pursues, yanking Maribel, holding Maribel's arm outstretched, trying to touch Domingo with Maribel's hand. Maribel just stumbles along, confused, incompetent, letting herself be pulled and hauled.

"Stop that," cries Soledad, coming out of the kitchen. "What are you doing?"

"I'm not hurting her," protests Octavia. "It's just a game."

Soledad takes Maribel by the hand and scolds Domingo in a burst of Mayan. He squats down, pulling weeds from flower beds.

As soon as Soledad disappears, he finds three fat snails and lines them up on a tile. He looks at Octavia, grins, and slowly, almost lovingly, he lowers his foot so that it is touching all three at once. Octavia holds her ears and closes her eyes. She hates the suspense, the pressure building, and then the awful crunch as one by one the thin shells give way and the soft slimy bodies with their delicate soft horns are mashed beneath his sandal.

Domingo's revenge.

Octavia knocks at Julian's door but there is no answer. She goes back to bed. Her fever has gone up again.

Octavia's bed stands at an awkward angle to the wall. Not parallel, not square, but on a slant. Soledad the cook is responsible for this, and she does it out of love. All beds in this house head east, and their feet point west, and since the walls run otherwise, the bedrooms have a sloppy, seasick look.

Octavia's mother has fought a losing battle over these beds. Every morning at nine-thirty and again in the evening, Soledad abandons her other duties, abandons her kitchen, abandons even Maribel, long enough to check and align the beds. Delila has been known to be careless, and the doctor and his wife cannot be expected to understand. Their minds are alien and deeply confused. The señora is even more stubborn than the doctor, being a *gringa*— and a Protestant, God save us, which means she serves the devil, even without knowing it.

Soledad labors patiently on behalf of this fine house and her *patrones*. She keeps the devil at bay.

Octavia, indifferent to the fact that her bed heads east, opens the secret drawer in her sea chest and takes out her treasure.

Her father's gun. She fondles it and dreams.

"What is this?" exclaims Catherine, shocked. "What on earth is this? Octavia! Your father's gun?"

Ordinarily she knocks, believing strongly in the right to privacy, even for a child, but today she has absentmindedly walked right in. And finds this child, this baby daughter, playing with a gun, a pistol! Lying in bed with a book and her cat, and a pistol big as life lying on her belly!

Octavia turns pale but tries to carry it off.

"I've had it for ages," she says. "It's just for target practice. Papi said it was all right. Long ago. He may not remember now—" (she suavely says) "but he did say so."

"I don't believe you, Octavia, for one minute," she says severely. "Children should never play with guns. A gun is not a toy."

"Oh, Mother, I know that. I'm not a fool. Do you really think that I don't *know* a gun is not a toy?"

"Give it to me."

Octavia makes a bored face and hands it over. "Take it. I don't care."

That night—remembering what the child might have seen in the bedroom, remembering how, after Felipe went back to the clinic, a tiny flicker in the corner caught her eye and there behind the wicker screen, all folded up, was Octavia, her little face striped dark and light from the shutters, staring wide-eyed like a frightened animal, hiding something in the pocket of her shorts (the gun?)— Catherine comes back to Octavia's room and stands beside her bed. She doesn't put the light on. Darkness will be easier for both of them, she thinks. But it isn't. Fires on the mainland have turned the moonlight red, like an infection.

Inside the mosquito netting, Octavia is motionless, perhaps asleep.

"Tavvie, listen," Catherine says. "Tavvie, married people some-times seem to be . . . fighting, or doing strange things . . . when really . . . Tavvie, that morning, what you saw . . . was nothing, nothing bad. Your father and I . . . we weren't fighting . . . You'll understand when you grow up." Is she making it worse?

"Tavvie? Are you listening?"

And then there is a silence, and finally Catherine hears her daughter's voice, that tight cold little voice, in full denial:

"I don't know what you're talking about, Mother. I didn't see anything."

And she holds to that, and holds, until Catherine begins almost to believe the child is telling the truth and has simply wiped the whole painful scene out of her mind. Forgotten it.

Sighing, Catherine is tempted to forget it too. Perhaps the child saw nothing, hidden there behind the screen.

11   Octavia, stronger now, recovered, lies in wait for Julian.

"I have a gun," she tells him.

And that wakes him up. He is surprised, because she is a girl. "You? You have a gun?"

"We could take it into the woods and shoot it." She's not about to tell him that her mother took the gun away. This afternoon she'll search for it. She'll find it, all right; it will be there, somewhere in the bedroom.

"What kind of a gun? An air rifle?"

"It's a Smith and Wesson .38."

"No kidding." He is impressed.

"We could shoot tin cans. We could make a target."

"Let's see it," he says.

"Okay," she says, "but not right now."

"Why not?"

"I lent it to somebody."

His glance flicks past her. "You haven't got a gun," he says mournfully.

"I do! When I get it back we'll go in the jungle, okay?"

"What's in the jungle?"

"Trees and birds."

"You shoot at birds?"

Guardedly, she says, "I could."

"Where's the jungle?"

Where's the jungle, what a question. "Everywhere," she says. "Everywhere that isn't beach or town, that's jungle."

"You mean those woods? That's a jungle?"

"I shouldn't let you touch my gun," she says, "because nobody is allowed to touch it except me. I only lent it out this once, to a grown-up person. When I get it back I'll let you see it."

"Well, okay. I wouldn't mind."

He starts back into his room.

"Why don't you stay out here?" she says. "What do you do in there?"

"Read."

"You could read outside. And I'll read too. I like to read. I'd like to read your books. You can read mine."

"Maybe sometime," he says. "I spend a lot of time by myself. I like to be by myself. I don't hang out with girls too much."

She stands alone, disconsolate, outside his door.

In the garden she drags a string for her red cat to play with. She doesn't hear Tío Claude come up behind her.

"Have you ever eaten cat?" he says.

Is he joking? Are there people who eat cats?

"It's delicious, cat meat," he says. "You take a young cat and slit its throat, letting it bleed to death."

Octavia shrinks away.

"Oh, it doesn't hurt them," he says. "Bleeding to death is an easy way to die. Then you cut its head off, and bury the head exactly five hundred paces from your house. That's important. Five hundred paces, and by moonlight, to lay the ghost."

Now Mother appears. She has come looking for him. "He's joking," she says to Octavia. "He's teasing you."

As they stroll away Tío Claude is telling her, "No, I have the recipe, from a medieval cookbook." He glances back at Octavia. "You simmer them slowly, with herbs—"

"Clo, for heaven's sake, now don't torment the child," laughs Mother.

Julian is doing card tricks in the back garden by the kitchen. He can do fascinating and mystifying card tricks.

"Pick a card."

She picks a card (the ten of clubs) and puts it back. He flips cards over in front of her, spelling as he goes. "T-E-N O-F C-L-U-B-S," he says, and on the letter S, the card he turns over is the ten of clubs, her card! Not possible!

"Where do you go to school?" asks Julian, shuffling the deck.

"I don't."

"You don't go to school?"

"Not here. Papi won't let me, it's run by the nuns."

"He's not religious?"

She shakes her head. "He hates religion. Are you religious?"

He shrugs.

"Do you think your mother went to heaven?"

Julian digs at a root. "No," he says at last. "She didn't go anywhere. She's just dead."

His dead mother is always there between them.

"Sometimes I dream she's still alive," he says. "And then I wake up. You know?"

"Do you like your father?" It's a nervy question but she has to ask it. "I mean, do you like him very much?"

Julian sighs and starts to speak, then turns away and shrugs.

"Well, you know," he says, rubbing his lip, looking at the trees. "They got divorced before I was even born."

• • •

"My favorite smell of all is gardenias," Octavia tells Julian.

In the back garden a large ugly gardenia bush is blooming. Domingo has neglected to water it and the leaves curl dry and yellow along thick stems. Still, it is blooming. The smell in the air is so good you could eat it, you could roll in it, rub it all over, everywhere.

Julian gravely sniffs, and nods his head. But what he says is: "Don't they have cars on this island? I never heard of a place without any cars. It's really primitive around here. They don't even have window glass."

"*We* do," boasts Octavia. "And we have electricity. Our own generator."

"Weird things to be proud of," he says, "electricity and window glass!"

"I don't hang out with boys too much," she tells her cousin. "There's one particular boy, Santiago, and I hate him."

"How old is he?"

Catching the scent of danger, she says, "You wouldn't like him. He's stupid." (If Santiago and Julian get together, go off without her, laugh at her, gang up on her, she will die.)

"I'm not like other girls," she quickly says. "All they want to do is play with dolls and sew and cook. I hate all that. I can beat Santiago. I fought him, and I won."

Julian's eyes shift, but he does not look at her or show that he is impressed.

Perhaps he did not understand? "We had this fight," she says, "I beat him up. I won."

"He let you win."

"Let me win!" she cries. "*Let* me win!" Should she offer to fight Julian? Can she win? He's a good head taller. How can she fight without being angry? How can she fight without hating him?

"I can run fast," she says. "I'll beat you to that tree." And she sets off with fantastic speed. He doesn't follow, just continues plodding along. She reaches the tree and looks back. He isn't even looking. She comes back and falls in beside him. She can't think of anything else to say.

But today she is walking with him through the plaza and the streets of the village, showing him off, her tall young cousin from the States. How suave he is, how handsome, how calm and civilized. The village children stop their work, set down their burdens, to stare at him. She shares the glory because he is hers, her cousin, her possession, proof of her uniqueness. She yearns to abandon her flesh and enter his. *This is Julian and he walks with me!*

She entertains him as they go. She is a traveling sideshow. She runs, prances, dances, dawdles, balances, jumps, struts, climbs, zigzags; she makes jokes and faces. She tells stories about everyone they pass, she proposes acts of crime—spying, entering, theft. Cleopatra lurks in her heart. Keep him guessing, keep him entertained! She must cement him to her with her infinite variety. Fiercely possessive, she snubs all the staring children and tells her cousin they are enemies. She wants his eyes on *her*. The world is a great trap.

She seizes his arm and points. "That is Rafael. He is as old as you are, and look how little he is. Those are his brothers and I spit on all of them! They are no good. They smile, but they do terrible things."

"Like what," says Julian.

"They eat spiders. Fried spiders. They eat caca. They can't read or write, and they don't even bathe."

She looks to see if Julian is impressed. He is looking at Rafael, silent and perplexed. Rafael looks back. An electric current crackles between them. They are dogs sniffing each other. Soon a tail will wag, and then a playful lunge. . . .

"Is Spanish hard to learn?" he asks.

She tells him Spanish is very hard to learn. She tells him the boys speak only Mayan. She intends to keep him isolated. She intends to be all things to him. Santiago is looking out the doorway of his house. Octavia does not acknowledge him.

"Let's go home," she says. "I'm not *afraid*—who could be afraid of *them?* But they're savages and it's a hundred of them and only two of us."

Julian obliges but he scuffs his feet in the sandy street, and glances over his shoulder.

She knows what he's thinking. He is planning his infidelities.

The dog pack is running in the streets when Octavia awakes. The moon astonishes her face, and the dogs are running, barking in the sandy streets. It must be late. Dogs are a late sound. A rooster crows but that does not mean dawn. From midnight on, they crow, each in his own yard, hurling challenges.

She is curled in the bottom of her wardrobe and her own shoes are sticking in her back. The doors have swung open. She is miserably uncomfortable, despite her sweaters, which she uses as mattress and pillow. She yearns for her bed but is afraid to be there. What if her uncle comes?

Julian says that if the moon shines too long on your sleeping face you become a lunatic. *Luna, lunatic.* The moon rays enter your brain. You change. Your face changes. You become a fiend.

She feels her face with her fingers. Has it changed? She can't tell. The teeth, are they sharper? Have the eyes turned mean and cruel? How can you tell without looking, and she is afraid of the mirror, afraid to look. Suppose she saw the fiend there, looking back at her?

Then she would scream, and he would scream back, the fiend, and she would run and run, but how could she ever escape? Even swimming and swimming in the sea, he would be with her, until she drowned him in the depths, and floating downward past the swaying trees, before her eyes he would turn into Octavia—Octavia! her hair all green, her face all pale and dead.

Her uncle is hanging from a beam, from a rope, by his neck. If he is not dead already, he is very close.

Nevertheless, holding her pistol in both hands, Octavia takes aim and fires. At the last minute she shuts her eyes, but hits her target anyway. The bullet tears into her uncle's left chest and his dangling body jumps and rocks. It begins to revolve slowly in a silent little jiggling dance, looking quite merry.

The body rocks on a horizontal axis. Its feet jog north while its head nods south. It keeps on bowing and ducking back. It is also spinning slowly, winding up. Soon it will wind slowly down.

The closing of her eyes is not due to feminine squeamishness. She is trying to unite two worlds. She has to shoot him in both places—inside her head and out of it. She is trying to set things right. The bullet tears into his left chest, but in fact, she aimed for his stomach and hit him in the chest, by accident, high up, near the shoulder.

There is no question that murder is her intent, but death must come slowly. Even a shoulder wound can kill under the right circumstances. It can cause fatal bleeding, or shock, or lead to uncontrollable infection and gangrene. Shoulder wounds are not to be despised.

She feels the kick from the pistol run up her arm like an electric thrill. It jars her neckbones. She shoots the body of her uncle, who is hanging from a beam by his neck. Why he is hanging there, the reason for it, how it came about, she does not specify. He is deformed and withered, eaten by disease.

With a gun you can shoot what is stronger than you are. If you are a slave, you can shoot your master. If you are a very young girl, a child, you can shoot your uncle, it is definitely possible. Octavia would have attacked her uncle with a heavy stone or bludgeon, had that been necessary. She would have caught him in his bed asleep. She would have hit his head repeatedly, as hard as she could, using her stone.

However, stones are risky.

A gun is better. A gun equalizes. A woman is equal to a man, a child to an adult. A cat with a gun is equal to a dog. Cuautémoc could have killed Cortez. Christ with a submachine gun could have blasted his way down from the cross. The alligator could get Tarzan. Teeth and claws and horns aren't in it with a gun, which is why all animals are in such a sorry way. Let the bull run into the ring and shoot the matador, it's another story. Give them guns enough, the meek will do all right.

The world is made of victims and tormentors.

Guns were invented for the helpless.

At the moment she pulls the trigger Octavia knows the victim, it is she! Later, she is not so sure. A victim with a gun resembles a tormentor. Who is who? Objective standards must be found.

Octavia does not care to find them, not right now. She has her work to do.

She is still twelve years old. Close to thirteen but not there. The problem is to get there. She cannot do it while her uncle lives unpunished.

Who will punish him for her? No one, evidently.

Whatever falleth to thy hand to do, do it with thy might.

She fires again and hits him in the thigh.

The rope gives way, he falls to the floor, he is swarming with maggots. Several jump on her. (They look like silverfish.) She screams in horror and tries to brush them off. One runs up her arm and down into her clothes. She searches frantically, it is somewhere in her body. She cannot find it.

It has entered her.

• • •

The moon is a crippled sun, says Domingo the gardener.

Long ago, says Domingo, the sun and the moon were equals. They were married, he and she, two suns.

But one day the moon fell in love. She fell so much in love with the planet we call Venus (a very macho planet, not female at all) that she was careless and the sun caught her, *flagrante delicto.* In his fury he scorched the earth, created hurricanes and droughts. Inventing Night, he exiled the moon, he banished her and all her million children and decreed that she should suffer and be feeble, she should wax and wane, her eye should be blinded every month so she would never again forget who was boss. And not only that. He decreed that she should never touch her lover again—and that is why you see them reaching out for one another, yearning, coming close, so close, but never able to touch.

And so she languishes—the moon, this fallen sun. But every so often she gathers up her strength and rises in rage against him. Eclipse! The world quakes in terror of the darkness. She humiliates him, puts out his light. They wrestle together until her strength begins to ebb, and he emerges again, victorious, his blinded eye restored, more cruel and bright than ever.

He gives her menstrual periods, to keep her good and weak.

"Don't *pester* him, Octavia!" says her mother.

At first, when Julian arrived, everyone was relieved that Octavia had someone to play with like a normal girl. For years they had nagged her to go and play with *somebody.* For years they complained that she was an antisocial tomboy, a *macha.* But now, now that she's interested, now that she acts the way they said she ought to act, they go the other way and complain again. Especially her mother, who says she is *too* friendly, she pesters him.

"He doesn't want you hanging on him all the time," says her mother. "For heaven's sake, Octavia. Don't follow him around like a little dog!"

She runs to her room. A dog! She is a dog? She follows him around like a little dog?

"I don't!" she cries out. "I do not!" She screams and kicks the bed. They hate her. They pick on her. They ruin everything. Nothing she ever does is right!

It was my cousin Julian who caught me not even knowing how many brothers and sisters I had, dumb as Maribel, my brains all melted out.

12 We were walking along the path that skirts the jungle, between the jungle and the fields, and the dogs were following. He had just arrived and I was showing him around the island. I was taking him to the cemetery to see the graves.

The weather was so dry that everywhere the leaves of the oranges and limes were curling, ready to fall. The corn drooped, stunted, the soil turned to sand. We were dying for want of water, yet glittering all around us was the watery sea. We passed Filomena's house, neat oval walls made of stakes placed side by side in the ground. No windows, one low door that locked with a string, a thatched roof, tall and tidy.

He asked me where I got a name like Octavia, and I explained. I was the eighth.

"Octavia means eighth. It's like October, the eighth month."

We walked along. "Who are the eight?" he said.

Immediately I began to panic. I knew something was wrong. "Well," I said, "there's Maribel and Duncan and me, we're the ones still living."

"That's three," said my cousin sadly. His thoughts were somewhere else.

"And the twins and my brother are in the cemetery."

"That's six."

My heart clamped all its valves. A person twelve years old who'd never added three and three? He didn't say it to be mean. He was only pointing out a sad and quiet truth. I felt my brain become the brain of Maribel, a kind of whirling vacuum. Duncan was right, she was always right, I was a fool.

The walls of the cemetery were made of concrete blocks that were mostly sand and shells. They made a giant box filled halfway up with sand and earth so people could be buried for a while. You couldn't just dig down, on our island. You hit the coral rock too soon. And so the walls bulged out, from the weight of earth, from the pressure of dead people packed inside, shoving to get free. They bulged and crumbled, held together by vines.

The big front gate at the top of the stairs was padlocked so I took him around back where I knew a wide crack and a twisted tree with heavy vines would help us climb.

"Come on," I said. "Watch out for thorns." And I went up the tree as fast as a lizard so he wouldn't notice that his question went unanswered. He swung up after me and we sat balanced on the top of the wall for a while before dropping down inside. He looked down at the cemetery, I looked at him. His eyes were clear and solemn, good gray eyes with straight black brows. I loved his eyes, my cousin's honest eyes.

But all the while I was thinking, *Who are the other two? Why have I always thought there were eight when there aren't eight?*

Down below us were weeds and grass and rotted wooden crosses sagging at different angles, and all the gaudy little multicolored tombs like playhouses. It wasn't far to jump, because the ground was higher inside than out.

A dank odor like mushrooms came up to meet us.

My cousin Julian's mouth fell open.

"I don't like this place," he said, but I was already in the air and down, and he had to follow. I led the way over the weeds. The footing was soft from tangled weeds or maybe from the rotting coffins down below, and we sank down with every step until we reached a path.

"The other two died on the mainland," I told him casually. "They're buried in a cemetery there, they're buried in Valladolid."

I waited for him to jeer, but he didn't. Julian never jeered at anyone.

"Jeez," he said. "Only three alive out of eight."

As we walked the thorn branches grabbed his ankles and stuck on his trousers, and he stopped to pull them off.

To do this, he leaned against a tomb until he saw the skeleton inside. The roof of the little house was intact, but the brick sides had collapsed with age and weather, and lying there inside was the small delicate skeleton of an eight- or ten-year-old child, without the skull. This didn't bother me. I was used to seeing human bones, and neither did it bother me that red wasps had built their nest in the rib cage of that skeleton and were busy flying in and out.

But Julian was definitely bothered, and watching him I felt delightfully kind and superior. My self-confidence returned in a rush. I was Octavia the fearless, the bold, and I would guide my cousin through death valley. I would not jeer at him (as I would have jeered at anybody else). He was my cousin, intelligent and sad. I loved him.

"Don't be afraid," I said, and pulled him away.

"Where's the . . . head?" His face looked sick.

"It's around here somewhere. Come on."

But ten feet further along he saw something else and stopped again, ashen and transfixed. In a sandy patch to one side of the path lay a human jawbone. It had six teeth, three molars on each side. He stared at it.

"What's *that?*"

"It's just a bone," I said kindly. "They're all over. There's a pile of them in the corner."

And to show him it was just a bone, I reached down to pick it up, but his shock had reached me, and my hand stopped short about a foot away. It seemed to have struck an invisible protective shield.

The air was humming. I pushed through the shield and picked up the jawbone.

The six teeth were loose and rattly. And at the very moment I straightened up with the jawbone in my hand, an ant bit me like fire, in the wrist. I screamed and flung the bone away. Julian flinched back so violently he stumbled and sat down. For a minute there the bone was taking its revenge. The sunlight turned to violet and all colors were wrong. The bone was chattering and crying out and scolding us. All the dead in the cemetery reached up for us, their bony fingers plucked our clothes and pinched our feet and ankles.

"It's nothing," I said. "An ant bit me."

Julian got up. "At home the cemeteries are like parks," he said. "They have trees and green grass, like a park. They don't have bones lying around. People bring flowers—"

"Here too." I pointed to the tin cans with the withered geraniums, the brown wreaths with rotten ribbons. But he was heavy, full of gloom. I took him to visit his dead cousins. First the playhouse where the infant twins were hiding. It was very small, its yellow paint all streaked and faded. I thought about the two tiny skeletons inside, entwined in each other's arms. They were named after my father's grandfather and my mother's mother. Ernesto and Emma were their names. They died when they were two weeks old.

El Veinte's playhouse was bigger and painted blue.

"He died when he was seven," I told Julian. "The same fever that hurt Maribel killed him. My mother loved him best. She wishes Maribel had died instead of him. She never says his name, it makes her cry."

His name was written there in bronze. Mother's maiden name came last, as maiden names always do in Latin countries. *Claude Sandoval Fisherwood,* it read.

"That's almost the same as my father's name," said Julian. "Claude Fisherwood. It's weird to see my father's name on a grave."

"He'd be nineteen. His nickname was El Veinte. Do you believe in heaven?" I asked. It was a question I'd asked before, maybe two or three times. What was wrong with me? I kept forgetting that his mother was dead. His mother was only two months' dead, and I talk about heaven, I bring him to a cemetery to look at graves?

His hands dangled at his sides. "I'd like to go back to the house now," he said.

We climbed up the wall and down the vine and scuffed along toward home. High in the sky the *zopilotes* were wheeling and sailing, but I didn't point them out to Julian because they too were fixed on death. He plodded along with his eyes on the ground.

"At least you have your father," I said politely. His father who wasn't anything like Mother said. He was no hero, soldier or world traveler. He was icky Uncle Clo.

Julian showed no enthusiasm. As we walked along he turned his head and looked at me.

"How old are you?" he asked.

"Almost thirteen. I'm small for my age."

But after that we walked in silence. His bleakness made my legs drag. (How can a person live without his mother?) I ached with love for him, my melancholy cousin from Hershey, Pennsylvania. He was my first love and he left his mark on me.

When we reached the house, he went straight to his room. But just before he closed the door he turned and blankly said, "You've got it wrong, you know. October's not the eighth month. It's the tenth."

And he was right. October *is* the tenth month. Named for number eight, it nevertheless is number ten. I counted again and again and it was stubbornly the tenth. Twice in one day I'd been an idiot in front of my cousin. He could never like me now, and I knew whose fault that was. In a steaming fury I searched out my mother.

She was at the desk in the living room writing a letter.

"Mother," I said, standing before her in all my outrage.

"I'm just finishing a letter to Aunt Jenny."

"Why do you always say you had eight children!" I cried out.

She put down her pen and looked at me. I suppose she was holding back her laughter.

"Julian thinks I'm an idiot who can't count."

And that was when, in simple words as though I knew nothing at all, she explained to me that two babies were lost "very early, before they were able to be properly born."

"Those were miscarriages!" I hotly said. I knew about miscarriages. Soledad had one. "They don't count!"

"I count them."

"Where are they then? Where are they buried? Did you put them in little coffins? Did you have a funeral?"

She was silent. I had her.

"And October isn't the eighth month. It's the tenth!"

Her lips twitched and she covered her eyes with her hand.

"It isn't funny, Mother."

"Did I say it was the eighth?"

" 'Octavia means the eighth, like octave, like October.' That's what you *always* say."

"But it *is* the eighth month. And September is the seventh. *Sept* means seven, and *oct* means eight. An octogenarian is a man of eighty. From the Latin. November is the ninth month, *nove,* and December the tenth. *Dec* means ten. Decade, decimal. December the tenth month—"

She stopped.

"Oh? December is the tenth month, is it?" I said bitterly.

"But . . . it has to be. *Siete, ocho, nueve, diez.* Seven, eight, nine, ten . . ."

She stopped again. Counted on her fingers.

"How absolutely baffling," she said in distress. "I hate these damned surprises."

I stood there hot-eyed, tight-lipped, burning in my grievances.

"We'll look it up," she said, but before she could even pick up the dictionary, she lifted her head, listening. She heard her brother's voice.

"There's Clo," she said. Her eyes were soft and happy. She couldn't help smiling. "He's back." And without another thought she went out joyfully to meet him.

That night at supper my cousin Julian didn't look at me once. He put food in his mouth as though it were an unpleasant duty. I didn't eat at all. I kept my hands in my lap and didn't take one single bite of anything, and she never noticed. Papi noticed, and said, "What's the matter, Tavia?" and I shrugged and said, "I'm not hungry," and looked at my mother and she never even heard me say it. She just kept chattering away about old times, leaning toward her brother, touching his arm. She was looking back in time, her eyes were looking at some precious pictures in her head. "Remember? Oh my god, remember?"

And sure enough, the next day my cousin got a book, *Beginning Spanish,* from Don Mauricio. Father helped him. By the time I found him in the *sala* he had already memorized what he wanted to say to the boys.

"*Sí, quiero jugar fútbol con Ustedes. En mi país este juego no se llama fútbol, se llama soccer. Pero sí, sé jugar.*"

The words were stiff and clumsy in his mouth, all mispronounced. I didn't laugh.

13 In town the houses are white plaster washed with white sun, sun so powerful and stern the sky is bleached by it, the blue cannot survive such sun. On the walls cling tiny lizards, delicate and young, with pink translucent hands and feet. The tips of their tails are also pink, translucent. The roofs of the houses are palm thatch, loved by rats, iguanas, cockroaches, Octavia. Viewed from the street, the thatch is shaggy and unkempt, but from inside the stems make patterns that are neat and elegant. Hammocks are looped up during the day, coiled and hung on iron hooks. Food dangles in baskets from the beams; but clever rats sometimes run down the string.

In the bleached sky buzzards go soaring, effortless, free, without desire, untainted by death. They are dream birds, riding the trade winds, soaring, sinking, balancing on strong wide wings. Never mind their nasty habits here on earth. In the sky they are dreaming angels, beloved of God. Perhaps all angels have two faces.

And the dogs, the dog packs run in the streets, they scavenge and fight and mount one another. The guinea fowl peck in the dirt. Their long red necks look sore and featherless. Who has plucked them in advance of slaughter?

At the bakery shop Octavia sniffs the rolls, a little stale now, pasty-smelling. It is dark inside the bakery. After the brilliance of the street she can hardly make out the rolls in their big baskets, the heavy larded cookies set in pans on the shelves.

The name of the bakery is *The Coronation of the Virgin*. Octavia loves that name. The scruffy little grocery shop down at the corner also has a name that pleases her: Pearl of the Caribbean. All the shops and taverns and tiny restaurants have names: the Green Bird, the Golden Anchor, the Sultan's Wife, the Black Snail, the Hidden Waterhole. But her favorite is this one, this bakery: *La Coronación de la Virgen!*

Soledad comes to work with her face all swollen and her lip cut, but it wasn't her rival Filomena who did it. Soledad's own husband Gerardo got drunk and beat her up. So much for the power of witches, if they can't stop their own husbands from beating them!

"Punish him!" Octavia urges Soledad. "Make him sorry, make him suffer, make him sick." But Soledad only shrugs, and looks in the oven. Her eyes are half-shut. Her lip is so swollen she can hardly eat. She drinks *atole* mixed with mashed papaya. Witchcraft doesn't extend to husbands, it would seem.

Octavia consoles herself with thoughts of Xtabai, against whom all men are helpless. Octavia distinctly sees Julian and Santiago being caught by Xtabai. Santiago is eaten in slow bites but Julian escapes. Xtabai has a soft spot in her heart for Julian.

What is her power, what is her secret? Okay, it is sex. She lures them with sex. All those hunters and fishermen, they think they've found themselves another Maribel. They go crazy wanting to feel her breasts and stick their big things in between her legs. They think they'll get away with it.

She calls them, she invites them. But the minute they get close, *pow, bam, crunch!* Ha, ha!

• • •

Aided by Don Mauricio, Octavia solves the mystery about October. Long ago, Julius and Augustus Caesar shoved their way into the calendar and screwed up the rest of the year. A month named July for Julius and a month named August for Augustus were just wedged in. Nobody gave a damn about October, the month called Eight, which was now the tenth. Nor did they give a damn about September, November, or December. Nobody could add, back then. Nobody gave a damn for logical consistency.

This explanation, while it relieves her mind, does not cause Octavia to forgive her mother. Her mother should have known. Mothers are supposed to figure these things out. If her mother had cared, she would have foreseen the pain and suffering this error caused her daughter. She would have taken clear protective steps.

To her cousin she says, "I'm October anyway. And you're July."

He does not respond.

In the kitchen Octavia likes to look at food but not to eat it. When Soledad makes cookies and offers her the bowl to lick, she refuses. Her mother finds this incomprehensible. "Clo and I always licked the bowl," she says. "We were always hungry. We never got enough to eat—especially sweets."

"Why? Were you so poor?" asks Octavia coldly.

"You know we weren't poor. Papi was a naval officer and we lived very well."

"Then why were you so hungry?"

"We just had healthy appetites. Not like you—pick, pick, pick at everything. How do you expect to grow?"

Octavia, wedded to childhood, does not want to grow. She watches Soledad's little boy Porfirio scoop out the batter with his finger and suck it off. He is wearing a shirt and nothing else. His fat little stomach does not hide the bunch between his legs.

"Well, you'll change. When the time comes, you'll find your appetite."

Oh, will I? thinks Octavia. "Mother, make Porfirio keep his pants on. It's disgusting for him to go around like that."

"He's just a baby. Don't be such a prude."

"I'm not a prude. It isn't sanitary," says Octavia, hot and bothered. (What would Julian think? No wonder he hid out in his room with the door closed.) "He'll make a mess on the floor and Soledad will clean it up and it will get all mixed up in the dinner. And you'll say, 'What's the matter with this soup—it has a very funny smell, what herb is *that?'* and it will be Porfirio's disgusting caca. Caca soup, is that what you want? Well, go ahead, eat caca soup. But don't expect me to eat it."

She runs upstairs in outrage, unable to bear her mother's odious good nature, well aware she's been a fool.

With the nail of her forefinger, Octavia molests an ant on her windowsill. She watches it race about and finally, in a blind rush, drop over the edge and fall. That is panic, she thinks. The ant is in a panic.

Everything feels fear.

Later, in the back garden, Julian is there! She hangs back, aloof. She is no little dog, barking and fawning. She is a comrade, a philosopher.

"You know the difference between plants and animals?" she says. "Plants don't panic. They have no emotions. That's the difference."

She waits as Julian gravely considers.

"Yeah," he finally says, but his tone is tentative. Will he approve? "But you don't really know what they feel," he says. "All you know is, they don't express it."

The lime tree spreads its foliage. Does it feel? There is the sturdy trunk, the branches twisting upward, dividing into smaller branches, twigs, and then the silent burst of leaves. Among the leaves, a hundred green marbles, solitary and in clusters, the ripening limes.

"If they don't express it," she says, "they don't feel it. Not the same way. They couldn't."

Julian ponders. "Yeah," he says.

She feels a gush of gratitude that makes her eyes prickle with tears. He listened! He agreed!

14 "Papi," says Octavia.

"Yes, pretty." He is preparing his valise for a trip to the other islands.

"Tío Claude . . ."

"Eh?"

"Tío Claude, he chased me in the garden."

"Eh? Well, did he catch you?"

"Papi . . ."

"Yes, *güerita.*"

"When I was sick, he came into my room."

"That's nice."

"And more times after that . . ." She can't say it. No use, she can't, she can't. She is too ashamed.

"And where is Julian today?" her father asks indulgently.

"He went out."

"You didn't want to go along?"

"He went with Santiago and the boys."

"They didn't ask you to come?"

"No." (Which isn't true. Santiago said, "Come on," but Julian looked so glum at the idea that she lifted her chin and picked up her cat and turned away without a word.)

Her father smiles and puts his arm around her. "Poor *güerita,*" he says. "Does it make you sad?"

"No, why should it, I don't care," lies Octavia.

"Boys *need* to play with other boys. And you should play with other girls." (He thinks of his sister Nicola, in the old days in Valladolid, always surrounded by a knot of *compañeras,* chattering girls in their blue and white school uniforms.) "We must find you some girls to play with."

"I've never been too fond of girls," says Octavia, wanly. She remembers Elizabeth Jane, but Elizabeth Jane is gone.

Maribel is in the *sala* for her eating lesson. The heavy door is pushed open and Delila comes in, carrying food on a red and black lacquered tray. A glass of milk, a plate with sliced chicken and peas. Maribel will have to cut the chicken. She will have to switch the fork from hand to hand. She will have to balance the peas on the fork. She will have to use her napkin.

Above all, she will have to drink that milk without spilling it.

Maribel glances furtively at the tray. She wriggles, a minor spasm. Her eyes dart about, hoping for rescue or escape, hoping for Papi and failing to find him.

"Sit quietly, sit straight," chants their mother. "Don't pick at your face, Maribel. Breathe through your nose."

"She'll ruin that new dress," volunteers Octavia. "She'll spill milk all over it."

"No, she won't. Watch and see. She's vastly improved. Today is our graduation ceremony! She understands very well."

"All right," says Octavia. "But she'll spill it."

(Octavia hopes she'll spill it.)

"Show Tavvie, Maribel," says their mother. "Now! We're in Washington with Uncle Claude and we're sitting at a table in a restaurant—all of us, Tavvie and Mama and Uncle Claude—"

(Not me, thinks Octavia. *I* won't be there.)

"—and Maribel is there too because she is a big girl and eats very carefully. She concentrates. She remembers. She is wearing her beautiful new red dress. There is no towel to protect her because she's out in company. Shoulders back, head up, Maribel. Now. A sip of milk."

Octavia and Delila watch in frozen attention.

Cautiously, tremulously, breathing through her nose, Maribel reaches out for the glass. It is full, almost to the top.

"Slowly," says Mother. "One hand. You can do it."

Octavia and Delila hold their breath. Their mouths are open, to help. The milk travels slowly through the air, wavering slightly. Maribel is breathing through her mouth now, but their mother does not correct her. Nearer, nearer, the glass arrives safely at her lips. She takes a sip, and slowly, decorously, wonder of wonders, guides it back to the table, sets it down.

Mother, beaming, cries out in triumph. Delila claps her hands. Octavia shrugs and returns to the pack of old snapshots she has found in a desk drawer. But even she feels proud, and can't help smiling.

"Did you see?" crows Mother in Spanish to Delila. "She does learn. Remember how it used to be when you first came? What a difference, no? All these years of work are worth the trouble. They are bearing fruit. Octavia? Did you see?"

"What a marvel!" exclaims Delila. "She eats like an angel. How pretty she looks. A señorita! Who can believe it?"

Wiping her perspiring hands, Maribel doggedly picks up the knife and fork. Octavia studies the snapshots, one by one.

There on the beach, not wearing a stitch, lies Octavia on a blanket. Exposed. For all the world to see. To laugh at and deride. Who put her in such a position? Mother. Who else?

Baby Octavia on the beach (goo-goo ga-ga), a naked shameless suckling pig. And big Octavia (studying the snapshot) can't even remember. Unfair! Unfair to have lived so long unconscious, like an animal, exposed to ridicule and shame. Exposed to the lascivious eyes of boys and men. Duncan has told her about Baby Octavia.

Duncan delights in telling her—over and over—every miserable detail. The diapers, for instance, the smelly diapers. The nakedness. And here is the snapshot to prove it. Naked, naked, naked on a rug and unashamed! As bad as Maribel.

"You wore diapers," fiendish Duncan tells her on a thousand occasions, holding her down, forcing her to hear. "You made big gooey smelly messes in them. You had to be cleaned. Everybody saw it. Everybody."

"They did not," cries Octavia.

"People stood around and watched. Don Carlos saw it, and Don Virgilio the mayor saw it and the priest, Domingo and Lenin, all the children in school . . . Santiago saw it. You were naked and covered with smelly bubbly brown mess."

"No!"

"And everybody held his nose. Ick, ick, ick. And after we cleaned you, we held you up by the heels. Like this. And put powder on you, and everybody got another good long look. You were just like Maribel. You were worse than Maribel."

It is true. Octavia knows it is true.

Shame, disease, decay. Subtle and sickening, a weakening of every fiber in the body.

"You sucked your thumb," says Duncan, holding Octavia down. "Like this."

She pops her eyes and makes piglike smacking suckling noises. "Even Maribel never did that."

Octavia (worse than Maribel) wants to die. She struggles to free herself but cannot, held by iron hands.

"Dis-*gusting,*" says Duncan, her favorite word. "Disgusting! Mother would pull your thumb out and you just put it back. It was wet and slimy and repulsive. Like a slug."

"It was not!"

"Uck! So do you know what we did? We tied your hands. We

tied them to the sides of your crib, one to the left and one to the right, and you had to lie there with your arms sticking out all night, just twisting and screaming. You drove us crazy. All night long, screaming."

"I didn't!"

"But it broke you. The second night you didn't cry as much and the third night broke you. That broke you all right. That broke you good."

As Octavia writhes, Duncan puts her fiendish face two inches from Octavia's and recites a nursery rhyme, her favorite:

> *"The dreadful scissor man will come*
> *To naughty little suck-a-thumb!"*

"Well, he didn't come," cries Octavia. "He never came!"

"Don't bet on it," says Duncan. "He'll come. He never forgets. You're on his list. It could be tonight. When it's all dark he'll come sneaking in with his scissors . . . snip, snap! Shriek, scream! And there your icky thumbs are, lying on the floor, your slimy bloody icky thumbs!"

Big Octavia, aged twelve, thinks of Duncan, now twenty-two and working at a job in Washington, and hates her still, will hate her forever. And yet part of Octavia, a slavish, abject part, worships her sister Duncan, lies in hopeless bondage, asks nothing better than to be her favorite dog, to follow her around like a dog. And why not? Duncan rode Papi's horse (Octavia was not allowed), she swam faster than any boy, she ran like the wind, she was taller by far than any woman on the island, taller than most of the men, and she was beautiful. There was nothing that she could not do! Her breasts clung close to her rib cage, small and taut, not soft and repulsive like Maribel's. Oh, if you can't be Cortez, next best is surely to be

Duncan. If you must be female, then be Duncan as she gallops by, long-legged and strong and tanned by the sun, teeth flashing, blond hair whipping in the wind. Duncan is not really, not seriously, female. She is a predator, a tawny silky puma. Cruelly, she holds Octavia down and tickles her until she sobs and screams. It is a form of torture, the worst form. And yet . . .

When Duncan left the island, Octavia celebrated. She hates her sister. At the same time, she is bound, enthralled.

"Nasty, Maribel!"

How many thousands of times has her mother said that? How many times has she said, *We keep our clothes on, Maribel, we never parade naked before anyone.* And slap scold punish, year in, year out, the entire household organized to put down and keep down Maribel's female body.

Maribel learns very little, but Octavia learns all of it. *Look at me, Mother. I don't do that. I don't touch myself, Mother. I don't undress. Mother, look at me.*

She has learned to bathe without the slightest awareness of her torso, as though even her own eyes must not look. Arms and legs she can admire (strong and straight, nothing hidden, folded, pink, or moist), but her torso she washes (if at all) in a trance of inattention and distaste.

And her mother still insists there is nothing shameful about Octavia's body, that it is *sweet* and *pretty!* Her mother tells this lie out of mindless good will, to make Octavia regard herself with pride as "feminine" and "attractive."

Attractive to whom? The sun, the moon, the selfsame leering, sneering boys and men she has been warned against? Only a fool could fail to see the fraudulence, the duplicity, in her mother's position. How can Octavia respond except with rage? Her mother lies.

● ● ●

(Duncan does not lie. Duncan, cruel, tells the truth: Octavia wore diapers. She lay in her own shit.)

"Tavvie, every baby in the world wears diapers," her mother says. "What is this nonsense about diapers? Duncan wore diapers."

"Duncan?"

"Yes, Duncan! Of course she did. She sucked her thumb, she dirtied her diapers just like every other baby in the world."

Can that be true? Duncan? It is not true. Duncan is smooth and clean between her legs, skin-covered. She possibly has two small holes but nothing more. She is invulnerable and perfect. She never sucked her thumb. Duncan.

At the table Maribel is slapping away at the pictures in the book. "A horse, a pig, a cow," she says, slapping each one in turn, and turns the page. It is the first quarter of her moon and she is talking. Catherine hopes that today she will read. There is always a chance. Nothing is hopeless.

"A man, a woman, a sun, a moon."

"The sun, *the* moon, Maribel. There's only one sun, one moon."

"The sun, the moon," says Maribel, and keeps on going. "A hammer, a nail. A plate, a cup." She turns another page.

Catherine, sighing, glances away from the book toward her youngest daughter lying on the couch, and shakes her head. Such dignity (she thinks), such scowling dignity. Look at her legs, a woman's legs on a child's body.

At that moment, Octavia glances up from her snapshots, catches her mother's eyes upon her, and looks away as though scalded.

Catherine's smile fades. This life we lead (thinks Catherine), oh, this unnatural life.

"A, apple, B, boy, C, cat," drones Maribel, slapping the pages.

And in another world, unremembered, sunlit, black and white, Octavia is playing with a certain boy, a certain recognizable boy, one Santiago. Today he is her mortal enemy, second only to her uncle. But in this other world (so they have told her, and here is the photograph to bear them out), long before Elizabeth Jane, he was her dearest closest friend.

She frowns over the snapshots in which the loathed Santiago, with the backward sweep of time, is transformed into a friend. Not just one, a dozen photos of the two of them.

Octavia squats with Santiago on the beach. She is very little, so is he. They are looking at something, a sea creature. Santiago has reached out his hand to touch. Octavia squats, absorbed, her two fists cradling her chin. Their heads are nearly touching, his black one and her blond. Their hair intermingles. How much paler her body is than his! And on the back of the snapshot her mother's hand has written:

Adam and Eve.

Octavia's lip curls as Duncan's lip would curl. Her nostrils open in disdain, as Duncan's nostrils would have opened.

Now, in photo after photo, her enemy intrudes himself. And Octavia cannot remember. Here he brandishes a wooden sword, threatening a dog who only laughs at him. Octavia too is laughing and she claps her hands.

Here he dives into the sea; Octavia is following. Here she climbs a tree, and Santiago, grinning, is right behind her. And here, in the back garden, where the roses are now (and in the background is the guava tree, grown smaller), they pose together for the camera. Santiago is solemn, even scowling. He holds his cap over his heart. His ribs are showing, and his knobbly knees. The noon sun gives him a big triangular white nose; his black straight hair falls over his fore-head. Octavia is smiling a new-moon smile, an idiot smile, a simple-ton's smile, a Maribel smile. Bashfully, she spreads her skirt out at the sides in her two hands, trying to look pretty for the camera. (Octavia grinds her teeth; she could throw up, she could puke.) Her eyes are shut, they have caught her blinking. Who is this simple simpering Octavia?

On the back, her mother again has written something unforgiv-able.

Los Novios. The Sweethearts.

She can't remember. And yet the places are the same—the sea-wall, the lighthouse, the sailboat *Pájaro Verde*—these she knows. The tide pools, the waves, the lagoon where she swims, the Mayan stone in the patio, the guava tree—these she remembers. But San-tiago's place is blank, a cut-out space. She never did these happy childish things with him. The snapshots are a lie.

As she puts them face down on the floor a gull is laughing in a demented way. It is Duncan laughing.

Or perhaps it is Santiago laughing, for there is one memory of him that she has kept, the father of all memories, and Santiago has kept it too, treasuring it, storing it up against her, clasping it to him like an amulet to keep her small and weak forever.

He is hiding behind the bougainvillea.

And she—oh, little girl, unwarned and ignorant, squatting by a tree, alone, absorbed, can't you see your danger? Poor trusting sim-pleton, oh, idiot, beware, beware! Wake up!

The warning comes too late. In the bushes Santiago lurks un-seen. Unconscious Eve in all her simple innocence pulls off her bathing suit. The moment is at hand. No photographs of this, but memory begins right here.

Now it happens, now. Santiago bursts out from his hiding place, yes, memory is born. He laughs and crows, he points. Eve awakens with a shock. She is conscious, she is ashamed. She is naked, she has sinned.

Santiago laughs and pirouettes. Octavia screams at him and throws a stone. She covers her caca with sand, she pulls on her suit, she runs away forever.

Octavia and Julian are going swimming. She observes that his arms and legs and chest are tan all over now. At first she was amazed to see how white he was, electric white, attracting every barracuda on the northern shore. They walk up the beach toward the path that leads to the lagoon. He is carrying an empty wine bottle.

Before they left the house, Julian made marks on a piece of paper, folded it, and pushed it in this bottle. Now, as they walk in the sand, he twists a cork in tight and hurls it out to sea, high over the surf, as far as he can. It lands without a splash and bobbles around in the blue-green water.

"The world is waiting for that message," he says.

"What does it say?"

He shrugs. "I don't know."

"What language was it?"

"How should I know?"

"If you don't know, it doesn't say anything."

"That's what you think," says Julian. "It's a message in an unknown tongue. I didn't write it, you know. Something was using my hand. An alien force."

The idea gives Octavia goosebumps.

"Somebody will find it, and preserve it, and one day five hundred years from now, they'll translate it."

The bottle and its message are drifting languidly with the off-shore current. Octavia watches, thrilled. What can it say?

"Maybe it says, Help!" she offers.

"You don't understand. It's something really important, like . . . when the world is going to end."

"Or what happens after you die."

"Or how many planets are inhabited."

"Or what religion is the real true one."

They look at the bottle.

"Well, we'll never know," says Julian calmly. "Maybe it says, the writer of this message is an idiot."

They leave the bottle floating around and wander up the beach toward the path of the lagoon. Are they friends? Their conversations are brief and tend to be heavily philosophical. She tells him again that she is not like other girls. Her tastes are different. She will never get married and be someone's wife. She will never have children. The thought of giving birth disgusts Octavia. And besides, it's wrong.

"Bringing a child into the world is condemning it to die," she informs her cousin. "People never even think of that. A baby has to die, right? I mean, someday. If it wasn't born, it wouldn't die, right? So, if a person has a baby, she's bringing death to that baby. She's a murderer. That's why I'll never have one."

Julian glances at her from the corner of his eye.

"You're just afraid," he says.

Octavia? Afraid?

15

"Where did you bury my cord, Filomena?"
"Who could remember, after all these years?"
"No, tell me. Where did you bury it?"
"Who says I buried it? I threw it in the sea."
"You wouldn't. Why would you do that?"

"Because you are a gringa, and the cord of a gringa is not buried but is thrown into the sea."

"You are teasing me, Filomena. Did you really? The sharks would eat it. You didn't. I am not a gringa. My mother is, not me. I am not my mother! Tell me truly, where did you bury it?"

"It's in the tree."

"What tree? Which tree, Filomena. Tell me!"

"The umbilical tree."

"That tree is just for boys."

"There is a tree for boys and a tree for girls. That's where I put your cord. I threw it high up in the tree for girls."

On my island, the fate of umbilical cords was important. They had a lot to do with your future, which was likely to be grindingly unpleasant unless, when you grew up, you could somehow find your cord and burn it. Burning your cord set you free. The standard expression for a stroke of good luck was, *"Híjole,* he found his cord!"

When I was born, gap-toothed Doña Filomena, the midwife, delivered me, spanked me, bathed me, put a red button around my ankle as she did for all girl babies on the island. Then, at Mother's request, she took a good sharp knife, a fish scaler, and (as I have said) pared off that extra finger on the left hand. After that, she washed my mother, massaged her belly, and trotted off into the jungle to dispose of my umbilical cord, wrapped in a banana leaf.

How she disposed of it I never knew. Most people said the cords of boys were tossed high up in the branches of a certain tree, the umbilical tree, and the cords of girls were buried in a damp and secret spot deep in the jungle. Domingo, however, disagreed. He said girls' cords were thrown up in the same tree as the boys', but the girls' were thrown higher up, and were guarded by a flock of angry birds with sharp beaks.

If your cord was up a tree, you could hope to find that tree, climb up and retrieve it, burn it, and enjoy a wonderful life. But if your cord was buried, forget it. Buried cords would rot and disintegrate, could never be found, could never be burned.

One of the reasons I hated being a girl was the business about cords. Females were condemned in advance to unhappiness. It wasn't fair! Boys' cords dangling bravely in the breeze like ribbons, while girls' lay rotting in some dank bad-smelling soft spot on the forest floor.

Even in Domingo's version, girls' cords were higher up and harder to reach. Girls got the shitty end of everything.

When Julian came to the island, and we walked in the jungle, we always kept an eye open for the umbilical tree. In the schoolroom we drew pictures of it, festooned with cords and guarded by ferocious umbilical-birds, some of whom built their nests out of the cords, while others, always hungry, quarreled and tugged at them, as if they were worms.

My mother used Filomena at the birth of all her children except Duncan (for whom she made a special trip to Valladolid). With her Victorian sense of modesty, she didn't want her husband watching while she sweated and grunted and pushed like an animal. She didn't want him looking at her private places with a cold and clinical eye. She wouldn't have minded another, unknown, doctor. It was specifically her husband, Don Felipe, she objected to. In front of him she chose to remain ineffable, her feminine mysteries intact.

Papi said she was worse than the cloistered nuns. He had a lot of trouble with the cloistered nuns. For years, in attendance on the cloistered nuns, he had to conduct his examinations through the mother superior.

"Press sister *here*"—he would say, pressing himself—"and ask her if it hurts." One day, at the end of his patience, he went on strike and refused to attend them at all. At last a compromise was reached. He was permitted his examinations, he could even lift the sheet and palpate the trembling flesh, but afterward the guilty sister fasted and atoned for her sin, she whipped herself and crawled three times around the church on hands and knees.

So Papi won his struggle with the cloistered nuns, but not with Mother, who managed matters so that labor was induced while he was away on his monthly visit to the other islands. She was placid about it. Of course she would call her husband if anything went wrong. But her births were normal, and Filomena was perfectly competent and clean (she scrubbed, and rinsed her hands in alcohol).

That's why it was Filomena, not my father, who spanked me at my birth and put a red button on a string around my ankle, and disposed in fateful manner of my cord.

• • •

Born early, I had hair growing on my body like an animal's. This did not disturb Filomena one bit, for unlike most Maya, she had hair growing on her body too, especially on her cheeks and chin. (It was said she had Italian blood.) But it did disturb my mother Catherine, who had never heard of such a thing. The hair dropped off within three weeks, however, and I was bald as an egg for half a year.

This in turn astounded Filomena, and the other islanders as well. They crowded around to have a look. But Catherine was placid. Bald babies ran in her family and always turned out adequately haired.

"The hair is fine," Filomena said when I was eight. "It's the soul that has a warp."

Me? My soul? It was Maribel's soul that had the warp, not mine.

Soledad was interested in that scrap of conversation, even way back then. She stopped stirring beans and squeezed my arm.

"Is that what Filomena said? That Marifel's soul has a warp?"

"No. She said *my* soul has a warp."

"That one," said Soledad. "That witch. She asked about Marifel, eh?"

"I don't remember."

"Try to remember."

"No, she didn't."

"Listen, you must never talk about Marifel with her. Understand? Stay away from her, she's no good, she's a witch."

"So are you. That's what I hear."

"Did she say that?"

"No."

"You love to tease. But this is serious. She's no good."

"Mother doesn't think so."

"Pues . . . your mother. Your mother is a foreigner, isn't she? How can she judge? Ask your father, he'll tell you. Listen, that lady goes to the *Pántheon* at night. After midnight, when the bells are striking very little hours. People have seen her, there in the cemetery. Now why would she do that, eh? Why?"

Morning.

Octavia is awakened by the maids from a dream of Cortez the Conqueror.

During the night, in and out of dreams, her breasts have grown .03 centimeters, and three new pubic hairs have formed, but Octavia does not know this. If told, she would refuse to believe it. She refuses her body. It is a foreign government that she won't recognize. Tossing under the mosquito netting, she dreams of Cortez and his friends. She is one of them. She gallops at his side, a sword clanking against her thigh, and a falcon (hooded, malevolent) upon her wrist.

Forward, she cries, spurring her horse. To the attack! Kill or be killed!

The maids see upon the tumbled narrow bed a girl of twelve, wearing a skimpy thin white cotton nightgown. Her soft thin face, burned almost as dark as their own, is topped by its mass of sun-bleached hair, perpetually damp about her face, either from heat or from seawater. Small curling wisps stick to her forehead and her cheeks. They see her clothes thrown on the floor (inviting scorpions), half a dozen books on and off the bed, and on the cool tile, in defiance of her mother, a saucer of food set down for her red cat. It is in process of being devoured by a swarm of miniature ants, ants so tiny they can barely be distinguished.

"Wake up," says Delila.

"Wake up," says Soledad, and taps Octavia's shoulder.

Octavia frowns and turns. She does not choose to wake up. Her dream was so comfortable. No, she remembers now: it was horrible. Oh, horrible. She and Cortez, and the others, the *conquistadores* (and she one of them), all of them (with their armor and their swords) in a schoolroom, like the island school, no, like the abandoned school at the banana plantation, they are playing kick-the-ball. A small black ball, misshapen. Taking turns, they kick it under desks and under chairs; they find it and kick it out again. And Octavia must kick. She must. She is expected to. If she does not, she will be exposed as a fraud, an impostor.

The ball is crinkled, black. It is forbidden, something repulsive, a horror that will drive you mad. Is it a head? A shriveled wrinkled human head, moist and decaying? Is it a baby dead at birth? Pressure builds. She must kick it. Must! Must look at it! Cannot. And now she realizes it is something familiar, something that she knows but dares not see, something of Maribel's? Something *of her own?*

And then the maids awaken her, and you would think she might be grateful, released from such a dream. Not at all. Octavia deals in horrors. She is a specialist in suffering. She is a maiden drifting on a dark and burning lake, trailing fingers from her canoe, afloat between flame and fetid slime, preferring these to shore.

As she sinks away once more, Soledad scoops up the cat from the chair beside the bed where he is curled and sleeping. She dumps him on Octavia's back. It is a trick to get her wide awake, but Octavia doesn't care. She turns over in sleepy delight to greet and stroke her cat, red cat with golden eyes. He smells like talcum powder. She nuzzles him. The softness of his fur, the purring! Oh, the love!

She goes to the market with Delila, who is fifteen and beautiful. They each carry sisal shopping bags. At the stand of Burro León the egg basket is empty.

"What!" exclaims Delila. "You have no eggs?"

Burro says: "How do I not have eggs?—I have two of them and

they are beauties. For you, precious Delila, it would be my pleasure to have three, or four."

Delila claps her fingers to her mouth and turns away in confusion. But she soon recovers herself, and boldly says:

"I need more than that."

"I bet you do," says Burro Leon.

Delila gives advice: To avoid witchcraft, be inconspicuous and polite. Don't show off. If you've already been bewitched, act brave and try to frighten the witch. (But never, never *kill* a witch—whoever kills a witch assumes all the witch's sins.)

Delila's younger brother Doroteo was bewitched, and vomited white worms.

On the way home they pass the dock and watch the fishermen. Along comes Octavia's enemy Santiago with no shirt on. His ribs stick out as usual. His collarbones, his shoulder blades stick out. Santiago is made of bones. He has been clearing land all day for his father and his face is filthy, his trousers stiff and wrinkled with dirt. The only things clean about him are his gleaming almond eyes.

A baby barracuda is gasping its last upon the dock and Octavia kicks it in Santiago's direction.

"Go sleep with pigs!" she says.

The baby barracuda is dying but it explodes when kicked. Its sharp young teeth go SNAP as if she has triggered a gun. Octavia jumps in surprise, but Santiago is not disturbed. He laughs at her silently and bends his knees—the start of a certain mocking infamous gesture. She whirls away, on fire, puts her nose in the air.

It is late afternoon and a flight of green parrots with red in their wings is returning from the mainland. They flap heavily overhead with raucous greetings.

• • •

Santiago, hanging around Julian (like a little dog), bursts a balloon in Octavia's face. Octavia hates balloons. She hates the bang. She hates the boys who like to break them in her ear (not Julian, he never would). She hates the boastful satisfaction of their fat, inflated shape. She hates the wrinkled dwindling of a second-day balloon. She hates the damp creased rubber rag that's left when a balloon has popped. Balloons in every aspect, every phase, she finds despicable—reminders, somehow, of her fallen and deprived estate as a princess who commands and is not answered, whose vassals have run off, proclaiming her to be an ordinary child. One day they'll find out. One day the world that has betrayed its rightful queen will know her vengeance. Heaps of smoking and dismembered bodies everywhere.

Octavia's red cat is playing with a beetle on the rug. He bounds and cavorts like a kitten, he gallops by, puts on the brakes, and pounces with both front paws. Oh, he is very fierce, his ears laid back, his tail lashing, his hair on end!

Octavia, doting, beams on him.

Now he attacks a snapshot fallen on the floor, he settles down to chew it, spitting out bits of paper, shaking his head. When Octavia rescues it (and there is Papi with Maribel on his lap, Maribel at three), he jumps on the bed and sits on all the snapshots, sits very primly, his front feet close together, prim and tidy, his face blank and innocent, round-eyed. Octavia laughs. If she were lying reading now, he would balance on her stomach, he would sit on the page, he would lie on the book and fold his paws and purr. O marvelous cat.

She gathers him up against her neck, smoothing his fur. Busily, he starts to eat her hair. Much chewing and rejecting, sounds of disgust amid the purring. Spitting out, purring, chewing again.

Octavia holds him as he burrows and chews. She loves the tiny tugs on her hair, one strand after another. She loves him, heavy and satisfying in her arms, this big cat who is forever a kitten. He is funny, clumsy, perfect. She can watch him forever.

This is what true mothers feel. True mothers guard to the death. True mothers watch in endless delight. True mothers are in love like this, they burn, they are transfixed with love.

Fiesta! Octavia is three. Fireworks. A white dress, and much praise because her hair is yellow. For the first time she is aware that she is different. She is special. (Can that be true?) Dancing, costumes, music, incense, flowers and applause, masks and devils, running, exploding! Someone breaks an eggshell on Maribel's head. It has been sucked dry and filled with flour. Octavia is afraid of the noise and yet she wants this to go on forever. Confetti, streamers. She sits on her father's shoulder. The dogs are terrified. What does it all mean? Everything bursting into light!

Uncle Claude in the patio glances at her cat and rolls his eyes. He says, "Did you know, if you hold them up by the tail their eyes drop out?"

16

Uncle Claude has a camera and takes photographs of the island and its people. He walks into the jungle and photographs the ruined pyramids. He rents a boat and photographs the coastline all around. He rents an airplane from the mainland and photographs the island from above. He also photographs Octavia, against her will.

She finds the gun again—just as she knew she would. It is wrapped in a towel and hidden behind the books on the top shelf of the bookcase in the *sala*. She smuggles it up to her room, puts it under her pillow, hard and cold and dangerous.

"Get out," she will say. "Get out of my room. I'm warning you." And he won't believe her, and she'll shoot. She'll pull the trigger fifty times until he is nothing but ground meat.

Murder. You go to jail.

But if you're a child? If you say it was an accident?

Smeared with mosquito repellent, Julian and Octavia take the gun into the jungle and fire at the blossoms on the trees. They love the jungle. The ocean is closed away as if forever; the village is gone, the sky is broken in a million parts, the birds live here.

It is a tame domesticated jungle, compared with the jungle on the mainland. Wind and drought have tamed it, but in the jungle there is a hush you never hear in town or on the shore. The wind is missing. You are enclosed. The jungle is a million rooms within one giant endless room. You smell the trees and the decaying ground, and pass from room to room. The jungle is a cemetery for another race of beings, who do not order things the way we do. The vines are their inscriptions, their tombstones are the living trees. Their great decaying corpses are everywhere you step, they underlie the world.

Crossed by many paths of the *antiguos,* worn in places down to the coral rock, the fringes of the jungle are benign. The farther in you go, the more large life presses in, none of it human. The trees are breathing. They are conscious. They are waiting. Are they waiting to attack? In the jungle you glance behind you as you walk. It's not a person you're afraid of, it's a stealthy rearrangement of the trees.

Julian and Octavia fire at leaves or at a bird. They are relieved that they have never actually hit a bird.

"All the people who have died on this island, where are they?" asks Julian. "They can't all be in that little cemetery."

"In the old days everyone was buried in the jungle," Octavia says, as if she knows. "That's what made the jungle. Dead people are good fertilizer. Trees love dead people."

Every tree and every flower grows from the belly button of a corpse. Can you grasp such a world?

Eight or twelve persons are cut in two. Then the halves are sewn together in a crazy way. The top half of one is sewn to the bottom half of another!

They show each other their scars, great angry red scars that loop diagonally around each body, high in front and low in back.

Uncle Claude's top half has been sewn onto a pair of skinny little legs, the little modest legs of a young nun! He tries to stand up but the legs keep kneeling down in prayer!

And when he urges them up, they just flop down again! Octavia laughs out loud. It puts her in a good mood all day long, this dream.

She offers to take Julian to see the market, and he agrees to go. So many varieties of mangoes, of *zapotes,* of chilies. And beans, so many beans.

"Which beans do you like best?" she asks him. "I like *canarios.*"

And Julian, to whom beans are beans, remembers how his mother floated thin slices of lemon in Campbell's black bean soup, and how, with a drop of sherry, she served it even for company in delicate thin china, and says, "Black beans, I guess." On second thought, "Pork and beans."

"Which chilies do you like?"

"I don't like any of them."

"These are *lloronas,* because you cry when you eat them. And these yellow ones you cut up very fine and use for *chilaquiles,* and these are *poblanos,* for stuffed chilies. I like them. And these, you cry if you even smell them. Papi can eat them whole. Touch one— and then touch your lips."

He touches one, gingerly, and touches his lip, and feels the sting begin.

They pass a row of women seated on the ground with pots of cooked food.

"That smells good," says Julian. "What's that?"

The woman, smiling, scoops out some of the steaming stuff with her forefinger and holds it out to him.

"Pruebalo," she says. Julian shies away.

Octavia ordinarily does not go to the market for fear of seeing sick and starving cats and dogs—fly-ridden puppies and shivering huddled kittens, dry as crusts of bread. Even today, showing her cousin around, she practices selective vision and keeps her sight-line high.

"What did that woman say?" asks Julian.

"What woman?"

"That woman."

"She said, 'Taste it.' "

"Does she expect me to lick it off her finger?"

"Sure. Why not?"

"You didn't do it."

"My Papi does not permit me," Octavia says offhandedly.

And Julian looks at her with curiosity, thinking how every now and then she turns into a foreigner. She calls her father "Poppy." *My Poppy does not permit me.* Permit? "Poppy?" Who at home would say that? Nobody. She also says things like, *To where are you going?*

"It's funny, an American who's never been to America," he says.

"This *is* America," she replies, wounded. "Central America is still America."

On the way home they pass shark meat drying over coral rocks; it looks like dirty linen, like a baby's gray diaper. Nearby is a burlap sack full of teeth, teeth of innumerable sharks, clean and white.

Octavia plunges her bare arm deep into sharks' teeth. They are smooth and cool. Deeper, to the shoulder. She squeezes the smooth cool teeth between her fingers, she scoops them up and pours them from one hand to the other, like a miser counting gold. She wants to bathe in them, to rub them on her neck, let them slide down her back.

The fisherman laughs at her, rinses his mouth, and spits, Maya-fashion, in the sand.

"May I take some?"

"Take," he shrugs.

She fills her pocket, a modest quantity (despite her greed) for manners' sake.

"Him too," says the fisherman, grinning. "Take."

And Julian takes a fistful of white teeth.

On the beach, Julian is building a fort out of conch shells. Octavia is helping him.

Not fifty feet away, on the hard sand by the running surf, two men with great knives in their hands, machetes, begin to fight; they are the color of mahogany, their feet are bare, their long black hair falls into their eyes.

The fight is silent, deadly. They circle each other and feint, slicing the air in short arcs. The younger man crouches, showing his teeth. Now incredibly, a blade flashes out and his head is cut almost in half. For an instant the wound shows white, then blood comes prickling, blood comes pouring. From the back of his neck into his mouth the cut is spurting blood; you can see his jawbone—it is pink; you can see his teeth—they are laid bare. Mother is pulling Octavia and Julian away.

Men have caught the assailant, the victim is still staggering about; he will not sit down, he will not fall down. He turns around and around, he heads for the water, into the sea he splashes and flounders. A cloud of red in the green water. They pull him out. Julian and Octavia are taken away and see no more.

Soledad the cook says the fish will smell his blood. Tonight, she says, five hundred sharks will swim in close to shore in a blood frenzy, looking for him.

Domingo the gardener says the men are gatherers of *chicle* on the mainland. Long ago when he was a young man, Domingo was a *chiclero* himself, gathering the sticky sap that makes chewing gum for all the world, and he has a horrendous scar from a machete fight just like this one. *Chicleros* are low-life murderers and thieves, he says. They are criminals who have no law. Domingo's scar also runs from the back of his neck to his mouth, but it is old and white and puckered. His jawbone saved him. If the knife hadn't hit his jawbone, it would have cut his head clean off.

The wounded man is taken to Papi's clinic. Will he live? Domingo shrugs and spreads his hands.

Octavia and her cousin choose hushed places. They love the hushed underwater world of the lagoon, where they swim using the snorkels and masks that Tío Claude brought with him.

They do not loll on the beach because the sand fleas are biting. But they like tide pools, and once on the coral rock they find and remove thirty-seven strange and living creatures from a tide pool no bigger than a broad-brimmed hat. Many more they do not catch. Removing them is difficult. Some bite, some sting, some turn to jelly, some to paste, some seem to melt into the coral rock, some flash away. Most remain affixed, capable of instant shrivel. With patient labor and persistence, Octavia and Julian capture them, pry them loose from their home, that warm clear underwater scene. Baby conches no bigger than a fingernail. Baby starfish, infant sea urchins of several varieties, and others, many others, with no name.

Drying on the rock, the captives are not impressive. Julian and Octavia put them back. Maimed and torn, the desiccated tide-pool creatures go back into their watery world, too late.

Santiago is sharpening his knife on a stone near the kitchen door. Lately, everywhere she looks he is there. He is always hanging around. Why? What does he want? He wants Julian, he says. He wants Julian to play soccer.

Under the guava tree the trap she once made to catch a grackle is lying on its side. That was long ago, six months. It seems forever.

"My cousin is busy. He can't play with you."

Santiago does not leave, he hangs around. He shows her a tiny idol he found near the pyramids. He is carrying it in his pocket. She frowns at it and pets her cat. Santiago wants to be friends but she is not deceived. Let him go home. Any minute he will make the gesture that she dreads, and she will die of embarrassment. Her heart will be filled with the black and smoky flames of murder.

But he is busy hunting scorpions. He knows where they hide, these big eight-legged insects with claws in front and a stinging upcurled tail behind. Beneath the vines and under every flowerpot there is a coiling scorpion, and Santiago with his clever quick brown fingers catches two, the fattest and shiniest, one for each hand.

Scorpions are deaf and almost blind (as a result of having stung the moon-goddess) and are therefore fairly easy to catch. Some are black and some are the color of straw. Santiago is good at catching them. With a fiendish grin he nips them just back of the head and runs at Octavia to frighten her, while she shrieks and scolds and chatters like a monkey. Sometimes he throws them at her, aiming short or wide. But as he holds them he is careful. If their barbed tails ever reach his hands he would get desperately sick. He could even die.

Today he doesn't try to frighten her—not yet. "Look," he says. He sets them down on a patch of sand and slams the grackle trap over them so they can't escape.

"Hey, look," he says.

She doesn't want to look but she can't help it. He pokes a stick through the screening and sets them to fighting each other as if they were cocks at a cockfight. They are fat and black and shiny, and he teases them until they are aroused and fighting in earnest. With their pincer claws they clinch and loosen grips. Their tails whip in and out, loaded with creamy poison.

At last one reaches the other, and injects death. The victim curls and staggers, lurches away to die.

Santiago is proud and pleased with the show he has provided. He lifts the trap and grabs the victor.

"Shall I eat him? Want to see me eat him?"

"No," says Octavia coldly. She is holding Pablito in her arms, rubbing his head with her nose, inhaling the clean smell of his fur. He'll throw it at me, she thinks, her skin all itchy. If I walk away he'll throw that scorpion on my back. Nevertheless she insolently turns and strolls away, her back all nerves. He doesn't throw it.

On the garden bench she settles with her cat beside her and begins to whistle the *Mañanitas*. She does this for a purpose: to show off Pablito's trick. Whenever she whistles he comes running, jumps on her lap, and pats her cheek to make her stop.

Santiago watches, holding his scorpion.

"Look," he says. "I'm going to eat him. Hey, Tavia, look! *Mira qué lo voy a comer!*"

Octavia's indifference is unblemished. Putting Pablito on the ground she coaxes him with a feather in the grass to see if he wants to play. He pounces and pursues the feather, overruns it, leaps in the air, lays back his ears, crouches in the grass wriggling his hindquarters, and then explodes in a charge.

"Want your ball?" says Octavia to her cat. From her pocket she brings out a small soft rubber ball and throws it past his nose. It bounces across the grass. "Get it!"

And he does. Runs madly twenty feet, catches it in his claws, lashes his tail, picks up the ball like a mouse in his mouth, and brings it back to Octavia and drops it at her feet. O special cat! Retrieving cat!

Santiago steps in front of her with the big squirming insect still in his hand.

"I'll eat him," he brags. "Want to see me eat him? I'll eat him if you give me something."

"I won't give you anything," she says.

Under her baleful haughty gaze, he eats it anyway. He plucks the barb from the upcurled tail, pinches it off, and tosses the scorpion, alive and wiggling, into his mouth. He chews in an exaggerated way, with his eyes popping open, and then swallows in a great gulp. When he chews, the scorpion crunches like a dried-up husk. But inside the husk, she knows, is a vile yellow cream. How can he do it?

"Qué rico!" he says, smacking his lips.

Octavia is supposed to scream and faint, she is supposed to be overcome with admiration for his daring. "Disgusting," she says, looking bored. "Dirty. Go take a bath." This is unfair because the Maya are obsessed with cleanliness and bathe three times a day. She doesn't care.

She remembers Elizabeth Jane, who thought Santiago was cute. She hears her saying, *"He has a crush on you."* Elizabeth Jane was crazy.

"They're females, you know," says Santiago, meanly.

She denies it, but she knows it is true: the big ones are the females. She has seen them with twenty babies on their backs.

To put Santiago in his proper (ignored) place, she picks up her cat, inspects his fur, and holding him against her shoulder marches indoors without a backward glance.

"I'll eat another one," offers Santiago.

She does not stop.

In her bedroom she remembers how in the snapshots Octavia and Santiago squatted together long ago (in the unremembered world) to inspect a tide pool on the coral shore, their heads close together, his dark head, her light one.

He has a crush on you.

She remembers him as he was the day her cousin arrived on the *Camilio Canto*—dirty, exhausted from three days spent away from home with his father clearing a field in the jungle, his face smudged with ashes, dark with smoke, only his eyes clean, gleaming like precious stones. Two bloody iguanas dangled beside the machete at his belt. He would eat those iguanas later. (What would he not eat?) He and his mother and father, his brothers and sisters, his grandmother, his aunts and uncles and cousins, would eat iguana stew with carrots, potatoes, onions, chilies, and a thin green sauce.

She realizes that today Santiago is wearing a freshly ironed shirt, he is spectacularly neat and well combed, as if he were going to Mass. From her bedroom window she peeks down at the garden.

He has a crush on you.

He is standing still, doing nothing, the scorpion eater. He is staring at the door through which she has just passed.

Years later remembering Santiago and the scorpions I am sentimental and shed tears. I think, If only he could stand before me now with a wriggling scorpion in each hand, how I would scream and faint for him.

Santiago, my old enemy.

17 "Show me your sore place, Maribel."

Maribel shows a small spot on the bulging mound of her breast. Octavia stares and studies. The point of the mound is round and pink and slightly bulbous. When a breeze comes in the window, the nipple changes before her eyes. It erects. Octavia will lose her lunch. Too horrible to be believed.

"Get on the bed, Maribel. Show me down there."

Maribel does not obey. She looks at the door thinking of their mother.

"Mother says to do it," says Octavia sternly. "I have to look at you, I have to see if you're clean. Mother says lie down and show Octavia. Take off your underpants."

Uneasily, Maribel lies down and tries to show Octavia.

"Wider. Spread your legs out wider. Like *this.*"

She pushes her sister's legs as far apart as they will go. Shivering, she reaches out a finger and touches it (the place). But still she cannot really *see,* and she must see it all. Lightly she grips the hair on either side and holds it open wide, and there it is, laid out before her. Ugh beyond belief! This then is the female. This. Incredible ugh! Are all of them like this? Her mother's? Duncan's? Her own? Or is each one different? Octavia stares. For the first time a fuzzy thought arises: she could look at herself. She could take a hand mirror and inspect herself. The idea makes her faint with disgust.

She will never do that, never. She will sublimely ignore herself. She is not like Maribel!

Maribel is getting dreamy. She lifts her head and tries to look down there herself. Her body heaves, her arm begins to move, her hand reaches out—but Octavia slaps it smartly.

"Cover up!" she says, and pushes one knee against the other. "That's enough. Don't show me any more. Get up!"

Next day, while Maribel is in the kitchen, Octavia and Julian pile all her dolls in her battered old wardrobe and lock it with the big iron key. Octavia lights a bowl of incense, sets it on the floor, and they go downstairs to fetch Maribel. They pull her into her room and then run out and lock the door behind them. Inside, they hear her noises, like a rooting pig. Noises of alarm, whimpering, calling sounds, and crying. They laugh. At least Octavia laughs. She laughs so hard that even Julian snickers.

And at his snicker a revolution takes place in Octavia. She looks on Julian with eyes of anger. She pushes him. Why is she here with the enemy, torturing her own kind, her very self? "It isn't funny," she says, and unlocks the door.

"It wasn't *my* idea," he reasonably says.

"I'm her sister, it's all right for me," says Octavia and shuts the door against him. She and Maribel are one person. She is the brains of this person and Maribel is the body. What is to be done?

She tries to comfort her sister. She sits on a painted stool and offers her the brush and comb.

"It's very tiny," he said the last time, the uncle. "You must have been a bad bad girl. What did you do that was so bad? Stop that! Hold still! You want me to tell on you? Tell what you do? Looking at your sister, I saw that. You want me to tell? You better hold still.

Besides, you want it to get bigger, don't you? This will make it bigger. Wait and see."

She does not speak to him. She has never spoken to him. She is tongue-tied. The thing that happens seems to happen in another world, a secret twilight nightmare world where she can't speak or run, and she is not herself at all. She is a monkey, that monkey, the paralyzed monkey who walked arm in arm into the woods with the lizard.

Last time when he finished and was ready to leave, he said, "If you're not nice to me, I'm never coming in to visit you again. I know another little girl who's nicer than you are. You better be good, and if you're good I won't tell on you. But if you're bad, then everybody's going to know, because I'll tell them everything."

As he went out, she touched the pistol under her pillow. All she had to do was shoot and he would die, the hated sharer of these underwater scenes of intimacy. But she didn't shoot.

Instead, when he shut the door behind him she exploded into helpless rage. She leaped out of bed, turned on the lights, put the useless gun on the windowsill, and slammed herself around the room. She pulled out all her bureau drawers and emptied them onto the floor. She hurled the vase with the dried flowers, she yanked the mosquito netting down from the ceiling and ripped it into ragged lengths. She hated herself. Coward! She pulled the mattress off the bed onto the floor, wadded up the bedding, overturned the bed, the chairs. Failing to overturn the wardrobe, she threw her shoes and books against the wall and stamped on them. She took the gun and fired it into her sea chest, and having done that, she looked around at the shambles of her room.

Only the Madonna and Child that covered the hole uniting her room with Maribel's remained unruffled and serene. Octavia fell onto the tumbled pile of bedding and buried her face.

He was Julian's father, Mother's twin. Once he was dead, the twilight man would fade away and disappear, and in his place (there on the floor) would be . . . the daylight public citizen, the man who smoked cigars and talked with Papi after meals. It was not possible.

Asleep, Maribel is perfect. Look at her hands, her little white hands, with their gentle glowing oval nails—ten tiny transparent seashells. Even the fingertips glow clean and pink. How can hands like that belong to an idiot, an imbecile, a brain-damaged nincompoop? What is wrong with Maribel? An obstruction is lying in the channel of her life force, a valve has failed to open. Octavia understands why her father comes so often to gaze at her while she is sleeping. It is bafflement.

Octavia wants to kick Maribel the way you kick a machine to get it going. Surely the smallest alteration somewhere (the kiss of a prince?) will start up Maribel, set the mechanism working again.

Octavia can remember clearly the time, long ago, when Maribel was much worse than she is now. She used to make her caca on the floor like an animal. She knew she was doing wrong, because she would try to hide it. She would cover it with some article of clothing, or even with a book or a doll, and she trembled when Mother came in. Every day she expected punishment and every day she got it.

"Do I have to train you like a dog?" cried Mother, furious. "Shall I put your nose in it?" Mother locked her in the bathroom to give her the idea, and called the maids, showing them the site of the crime.

"She doesn't understand," said Felipe, in pain.

"Then why is she trying to hide it when I come in?"

"Perhaps because at that moment she remembers it will make you angry. Next time call me."

And she did call him, to find Maribel, embattled, crouched in tears, protecting her treasure in the corner of the room. When she saw her father, she smiled like an angel, and showed it to him. He hugged her, and told her it was fine healthy caca and she had every right to be proud of it, but nevertheless it belonged in the toilet.

His loving patience had no more effect than Mother's tears and anger.

"She's bored," he said, and from the mainland he ordered picture books and toys and dolls and puzzles made of twisted nails. He ordered paints and paper, and had the carpenter make an easel. He himself showed her how to use the paints. He painted the family, beginning with Maribel, who was holding a doll. Then Mother and then Father and then Duncan and Octavia. Maribel was in the center of the paper, bigger than anybody else.

She was interested, and picked up the brush. At first she made nothing but wavy lines and blobs, but one day she took a fresh sheet of paper and made Christ on the cross.

"It can't be," said Mother. "Can it? I swear I think it is."

The cross was red and Christ was green and black.

Papi groaned. "Inescapable," he said. "Christ on the cross. Wouldn't you know." But he was proud all the same.

After that she did not defecate on the floor again. Instead she covered the walls of her room with Christs and animals and trees, and vines and flowers and people. Paint went everywhere, but nobody scolded or complained. Periodically the walls were whitewashed so she could begin anew. Paint was better than caca.

Papi preserved her first Christ on the cross. Octavia found it later on top of a pile of pamphlets as she was nosing through his files.

"It isn't that he loves Maribel more than you," said her mother. "He loves you just as much. But there's no reason to worry about *you*, don't you see? Poor little Maribel—what will happen to her, that's what he's thinking. How to protect her."

"Nobody wants to protect *me*," sniffled Octavia, and her

mother, bored, says, "Oh, Tavvie. You are perfectly able to take care of yourself."

But Maribel has her own bathroom. Maribel has the largest bedroom in the house (perhaps because it is so often her prison). Only Pablo the cat doesn't give a damn for Maribel. He gives her a wide berth. When she comes near, he runs away. Only Pablo loves Octavia and nobody else.

All the same, there is the sun, there is the moon. The sun is Octavia, the moon is Maribel. Octavia is the yellow-haired one, and Maribel the dark. Octavia dominates by day and Maribel by night. Octavia is Cortez and Maribel is the Indian. They need each other.

Father, talking to Uncle Claude, has Maribel in the crook of his arm.

"Brain damage, of course," he says. "But what is perplexing is that sometimes she is so much better than other times. If the brain were damaged, how could this be so?"

His tone of scientific objectivity is fraudulent clear through.

"One sometimes feels—really!—that she is the wisest of us all, and simply holds her peace. That she is God's Favorite." He smiles at her and strokes her hair. He is an atheist who speaks about God a great deal of the time.

When Octavia was little, a bald-headed doctor from Valladolid came to the island and ran his hands over Maribel's head.

"Was it a difficult birth?" he asked.

Father shrugged. "My wife says no."

"You did not deliver?"

"I was away. The child came early. A midwife did the job, one of our local witches. Her fault, I have no doubt."

"Not true," said Mother. "The birth was perfectly normal."

Father started to speak but decided against it. In his mind, Filomena and Mother were both to blame.

"Later on, was there a fall?" asked the visiting doctor.

"Not to my knowledge," said Mother. "The servants say no."

"Reflexes are close to normal limits."

"Exactly!" said Father.

Maribel began making faces, and Mother automatically reached out and slapped her hand. "Stop that," she said.

"Let her alone," said Father.

"Severe illness in infancy?" asked the visiting doctor.

"Yes, with convulsions," said Father. "When she was five years old."

"She appeared normal until that time?"

Father seemed reluctant to answer.

"Yes she did," said Mother.

"It's hard to say," said Father.

"Did she speak?"

"Yes," said Mother.

"No," said Father.

"Felipe, what are you talking about? She talked, she sang. She sang with you, she sang the *Mañanitas*—have you forgotten?—she was a perfectly normal child."

"Normal, was she?" said Father. "Compare her with Octavia at the same age."

And Octavia, noticed, grew tall and proud. But his hand clasping her arm was not loving, it accused her.

"You simply *want* to believe it was Filomena," said Mother. "Why do you insist?"

"I insist? Why do you deny?"

The visiting doctor cleared his throat and turned to Maribel. "Now, señorita," he said. "You're a fine young lady. What is your name?"

Maribel squirmed and did not look at him, but said with perfect clarity, "My name is Maribel."

Both Mother and Father jumped forward, startled. The visiting doctor waved them back.

"And your age, señorita? How old are you?"

Maribel made one of her moaning sounds. Mother and Father leaned forward in excitement.

"How many years have you, señorita?" asked the visiting doctor.

"Thirteen," said Maribel, and it was the truth.

"Oh!" said Mother, astonished. "Incredible!"

"You see? You see?" cried Father to the doctor. "What is one to make of it? Tell me, tell me! What is one to make of it?" He was so excited he stuttered. "I—I—I am a doctor," he said, "but this is beyond me, it is way beyond me."

"She can read, too!" announced Octavia, but they paid no attention. She pulled at her father's shirt. "Papi, she can read. Yesterday she—Papi? Papi, yesterday—"

"Tavvie, run outside and play," he said.

"Yes, run along," said Mother.

The next day Maribel had her first period, and the pattern began. For ten days before her period, Maribel could talk, in her fashion. She could recognize words in a book. Then she clammed up for the rest of the cycle. She would not say one word. It was maddening. It was inexplicable. It was too much.

And it was too much for Octavia, it was all too much, one and the same person to love and hate and be afraid of (yes, she was afraid of her sister sometimes in the dying light, and always afraid that one day she would look at herself in the mirror and see Maribel gazing back). It was too much, plus always feeling wrong and somehow to blame for being smart where Maribel was dumb. She could keep her out of her room by burning incense, but she always knew she was there next door, standing there singing and strange with her dolls, or maybe she had a record playing, ordinary music cha cha cha except in Maribel's room nothing was ordinary, the walls covered with scribbles of crayon and paint, she was always there doing what she shouldn't be doing, thinking heaven knows what, and above all always loving Octavia. That was it, she always loved Octavia, loved her, and nothing Octavia could do would stop it, even burning the incense, hitting her, hurting her, teasing, insulting, stealing her dolls, *nothing* Octavia could do would make her stop this loving, endless loving.

Maribel loved Octavia and Octavia loved Papi and Papi loved Maribel. It went round and round, this love, a round robin of the same dumb love, a helpless, hopeless, hurting kind of love . . . until Octavia got older, and withdrew. She learned about love and withdrew. Once long ago she loved someone too much, someone unworthy, she loved her mother; but she learned better and withdrew.

In Octavia's opinion, hidden on the island somewhere is a voodoo doll responsible for Maribel's strangeness, a voodoo doll with a nail through its head, and a scrap of sanitary napkin tied around its crotch. If this doll could only be found, Maribel would be restored! Maribel would be like everybody else. And the reason Maribel has such an insatiable appetite for dolls is that she hopes, with each new doll: *maybe it's this one, maybe it will be the next.*

Octavia and Julian in the jungle keep their eyes open for the umbilical tree and also for the voodoo doll. They walk through fantastic populations, living and dead, seen and unseen. The coral rock they step on is the remains of a billion billion tiny beings now deceased. Dead bodies everywhere. The sea is a slaughterhouse, creatures eating each other. Even the sand is ground-up shells, skeletons of dead sea creatures. The island is a magic cemetery.

"We have our skeletons inside, they have them outside," says Julian. "Our bones are just to make us stiff so we can walk. But our skulls are shells, to protect our brains."

They walk and feed on death. Their skulls are shells, their bones are sticks. Life is killing, life is eating each other, life is death. Octavia is dizzy, cannot think, feels helpless. What is she? A monster stuffing death into her mouth, trampling life under foot. And everyone pretends this is normal!

What is normal? Here they are, looking for the voodoo doll so Maribel can be free, but how do they know she isn't free right now?

"She could be the normal one," says Julian. "Maybe everybody else has voodoo dolls. Maybe she's the only one who *doesn't* have a voodoo doll."

18

"Mother," says Octavia very faintly.

"Yes." She is in the dining room, embroidering a dress for Maribel.

"I want a lock for my door."

"A lock. Whatever for?"

"Tío Claude comes in . . ."

"Yes?"

"Tío Claude comes in and does this stupid . . . treatment thing."

"This what?"

"He calls it treatments, but it isn't."

"What are you talking about, Octavia? Stop squirming."

"I told you. The purple stick, it's made of glass. And then . . . that other stuff."

"Speak up, Octavia. I can't understand you."

"Everybody has a lock," she wails. "Even Maribel has a lock, why can't I have a lock?"

"Darling, I told you once before. Uncle Clo loves to play games. It's just a game he plays with you."

"It's not a game."

"Of course it is. He's playing with you. If you don't like it, tell him so."

"I did."

"What?"

"I said, I did."

"Are my scissors on the dresser?"

Octavia finds the scissors and holds them for a moment, remembering Duncan and the scissor man, before she hands them to her mother. Is Uncle Clo the scissor man? "I told him," she says.

"Told him what?"

"That I didn't like it."

"He's a tease. He loves to joke and tease. Just take it in good spirit, dear. Lighten up a bit. He likes you. That's why he fusses over you. You should be glad he likes you."

Glad.

Is it somehow her own fault?

"The dreadful scissor man will come," Duncan said, *"to naughty little suck-a-thumb."*

How much does he know, this uncle? Does he magically know about the diapers, the thumb, the way she spies on Maribel? Does he know that Santiago caught her naked making caca in the sand? Does he read her wicked thoughts?

What does he think about? What is going on inside his head?

He stands there in the shadows, in the doorway of the bedroom, looking at her.

"Well, Missy," he says. *"You're a bad girl to be sick."* He pulls up a chair and sits beside her bed. His breathing quickens and she lies there sick, her cotton nightgown a mere wisp of almost-transparent cloth, her chest barely beginning to soften, to fill out, to lose its boyish angularity (all ribs till recently), and her frame still tiny, as tiny as if she were a Mayan Indian, as if stunting were in the air of the island rather than in its heredity and diet. There lies Octavia, feverish and very small, uncovered, but curtained by the hanging

gauze of her mosquito netting. The light is strained, a feeble, help-less light.

"*It's your throat, eh?*

"*Any cough? Pains in the chest?*"

He is moved by her, so tiny, so seductive behind her cascading gauze. He finds the opening and folds the netting back. She is sick, he will treat her. He explains the Electro Tube and plugs it in. He rubs the Electro Tube on her sore throat. Now he moves it along and rubs her shoulders and her skinny arms, he burrows into her closed armpits. He rubs it on her chest, yes on her chest very thor-oughly. Then on her stomach, kneading her stomach.

"*Tummy ache?*

"*Growing pains in the legs and arms? The joints?*

"*This will make you well again.*"

He is getting excited now, but keeps it secret of course and no harm done. He lingers on the tummy. The nightgown, he informs her, cuts down the healing strength of the Electro Tube. "*We have to lift it up,*" he says. "*We'll just go under it.*"

Palm fronds toss restlessly and rub against the window frame. The sounds of wind and breathing fill the room.

"*And now for growing,*" he says. "*Your mama says you need to grow. Grow up to be a big girl. This is what will make you big and strong. Bigger, stronger, every minute.*"

It is not wrong, why should it be wrong? She doesn't even know. She lies there quietly, she likes it. A man can't resist, he can't resist forever, most powerful tug in the world, it will do her good, yes, it will benefit her, she'll grow up strong and healthy, have good instincts, good strong sexual instincts, that's important, sexual down there in that part, like a little purse it is, a purse, my sister, my sister, faster now, oh, Catherine, a child is now—

On his knees beside her bed the light almost gone he feels a whirlwind come over him, a soft black dove enfolds him in its wings. Deep, overpowering. Pause a moment longer now, enjoy, oh, blessed, blessed. Catch it, of course, in the big white handkerchief. A man has needs. All done.

• • •

So! Now! Stand up, be cheerful. An uncle after all. Doing her good, yes, worlds of good. Curing her sore throat. She wasn't aware. Sex is repressed in her. It's there, though, underneath, she's full of sex. Right inside the little purse, where he rubbed it. That woke her up a little bit!

Is he breathing too loud? Cough and clear the throat. Blow the nose. Congested. Find a clean spot. There.

A peck on the cheek, a joke.

"Well now, Missy. Tomorrow you'll be rarin' to go."

She does not respond, she lies very stiffly, can she be aware? Will she tell her mother?

Ridiculous. She's sleepy.

Not as if any harm was done!

A kindness to the child. Pointing the way. Developing her parts, her sexuality. Unconscious benefits to radiate throughout her life. A full woman. Fully alive. Yes, yes, deeply sexy little creature she already is. Seductive little witch. Unconsciously? Don't you believe it! Like her mother once upon a time. How she lies there in that wisp of a nightgown, eyes gleaming. That wanton hair. Pretending to flinch away.

Next time, lead her. Gently. Encourage her. Show it to her. Let her see and touch. Something to see! Her hand on it. Next time. Go slow. She'll love it. Cream inside that little purse.

"Good night now, Missy, you be good. You'll be all well tomorrow."

Refreshed, invigorated. A man, fully sexed. Thank God! And work to do.

19 Today the air is filled with small flying bugs in pairs. They are flying two by two, coupled together. They are small beetles with velvet black wings and a red lacquered dot just behind the head, and they are always linked together. Julian finds them interesting.

Octavia overcomes her embarrassment. "They call them the two-headed bug. There's a head at both ends."

In each pair there is a bigger and a smaller bug. When they crawl, the bigger bug is dominant and the small bug has to walk backward. They put their feet down like Charlie Chaplin.

"That's the male, dragging the female around," says Octavia, with a certain bitterness.

"It's probably the female," says Julian. "With insects, the female is almost always bigger. She uses him to fertilize her eggs and then pft! forgets him. He just dies. Sometimes she eats him. Didn't you have science in school?"

The female, bigger? Remembering scorpions, she realizes it's true, the male is the smaller one. Why is it different with people?

Julian studies the bugs. "They're stuck," he announces. "Have you ever seen dogs get stuck?"

She has, but can't say so.

"It's really funny. Have you got a magnifying glass?"

Even with the magnifying glass they can't make out the connection. They can see only the clean velvet blackness of the twelve little legs. They see that the big bug's head is triangular, and the little bug's head is round. She knows what Julian is hoping to find: a little black penis stuck inside a little black hole.

The double-headed bugs are everywhere and they last for two weeks. Octavia is relieved when they are gone.

Julian has now been on the island for two months, and although he has helped her search, they have not succeeded in finding the voodoo doll or the umbilical tree. One night Octavia dreams that she overturns a rock, quite near the house, and finds—instead of insect eggs or scorpions—a long white curling wormlike thing, repulsive, but her own, her cord. She runs and runs with it, balanced gingerly at the end of a stick, and tries to hurl it up into a tree, a huge cactus tree that bristles with thorns, but it keeps falling down, and she keeps flinging it up until it turns into a huge white snake and comes at her and she screams.

Although she has earned his friendship with the gun, it is clear that Julian is still ashamed to be seen with her in the center of the village. Walking with her (a girl, a little girl) demeans him in the eyes of the boys. She is very depressed. But on the other hand, it is equally clear that at home he likes her more and more. He likes playing cards and chess with her. They play in the cool and quiet of the *sala*. He likes her with him there.

Her spirits rise.

Mother always liked to say that someone special loved me, namely Jesus. Jesus loved children, she said, and suffered them to come unto him. She was certainly not talking about any Jesus that I knew. It was some stateside Jesus from her childhood, the one with the nightgown and the freshly shampooed beard.

The *real* Jesus lived right here on the island, nailed to his cross in the island church, and he was bitter and cadaverous, crowned with a nest of three-inch thorns, blood streaming down his face. His body was speckled with blood, his hair was stringy, his face lined, and he wore a sort of diaper.

Children did not interest such a man. How could they? Torture was his subject. Torture today, torture tomorrow, torture forever.

Jesus the Tortured One.

Mother was not only aware of this Jesus, she was haunted by him. She couldn't forget the night the cross gave way (its footing rotted out by damp) and this gaunt Christ came looming out of the shadows and crashed across the altar face down in the main aisle of the church. On impact, his hands and feet tore loose, and he was free, free of the cross! Word spread through the village like a flame.

Everyone felt it: raw power, unleashed here on our own island, Caracol. Jesus was free! He had escaped, and no one doubted for an instant what he had in mind. After centuries of agony, what else would he want but blood? You could hear him outside howling in the dark. It was a night of swirling wind and clouds that rushed across the moon. A score of black chickens gave their blood that night for Christ, but not in the usual way. This time the magic was *against* him. Let him be our prisoner again. Get him back up on the cross where he belongs. This time we'll nail him down more carefully.

Mother scoffed but she was nervous all the same. Later she told about a recurring dream in which she was pursued through empty moon-washed streets by a flying figure with a crown of thorns and blood running down his face.

Of course he was nailed back in place and the cross was repaired. But now he hung in a side chapel, where anyone could see (I certainly could see) the gleam of hatred in his downcast eyes, the pent-up rage so deep and so implacable the world itself would one day be destroyed by him.

"Octavia, did you know—can you believe—these insane people have actually put a photograph of Maribel in some shrine in the village? Her picture on the altar, can you bear it?"

"I know." Octavia's face becomes masklike.

"You know? How long have you known?"

"Maybe six months."

"Why on earth didn't you tell me? Delila's mother told me."

"I did, Mother."

"Did what?"

"I told you, Mother."

Catherine withstands the full force of twelve-year-old disapproval. "I think you're mistaken, Octavia."

"Well, I did," said Octavia, turning away. "And you said, 'Oh, what nonsense.' "

"I said that?"

Octavia looks stonily at the wall.

"I'm paying attention now, Octavia."

"It's in the shrine of Our Lady of Sorrows. It's the same picture Papi has on his dresser."

"How did they get hold of it? Did *you* have one?"

Fiercely insulted, Octavia says, "Are you blaming me? No, I did not have one."

Octavia does not usually walk with her mother through the town, but today as an escort of bad news she is willing to do it. First, with Delila, they go to the market, and then, sending Delila home with vegetables and fruit and meat, they walk through the central plaza. It's an ugly plaza, desolate and cemented, with a few scraggly bushes, a nondescript fountain where the people can fill their jugs from a faucet, an undersized statue of Peace, a bust of a onetime governor, and a few lampposts.

At the church, her mother says, "Let's step inside."

"It's not in the church, Mother."

"I know. I need to get out of the heat."

Halfway inside the dark interior she stops in alarm and puts her hand on her heart. "He *isn't* gone again—!"

"They moved him to the chapel, Mother. He's right where he belongs."

"Oh," laughs her mother. "So he is. My eyes were dazzled from the sun."

She walks into the chapel and reaching up her hand touches the bloodstained feet.

"There," she says with satisfaction, giving the feet a little pat. "Isn't he the ugliest thing you ever saw?"

Octavia smiles to herself. Her mother is afraid of Christ!

The shrine they've come to visit is next door to the bakery. "We'll buy some rolls and then stop in. Oh, this sun—! And I forgot my hat."

Inside the shrine, when their eyes get used to the dark, they can make out the photograph of Maribel, squint-eyed, propped up against a statue of the Virgin, surrounded by candles and flowers. Catherine gasps, she is outraged. She takes down the photo and makes a scene. In a loud voice she demands to know who is in charge. Two women emerge from behind a curtain and move toward her, their white *huipiles* luminescent in the shadows.

"This is a photograph of my daughter!" says Catherine. "What are you doing with it? Who gave you permission?"

They speak to each other in guttural Mayan. Octavia moves away, separating herself from her mother and her mother's scene, examining the ceiling and the walls.

"You are mistaken," says the older woman. "This is not a photograph of your daughter."

"Of course it's my daughter! I know my daughter. Look at the name of the photographer. He was a patient of my husband and he couldn't pay and so he—"

"No, no," say both women. "It is not your daughter."

Now among the flowers and candles and *milagros,* Catherine sees a saucer of blood, and feels a chill.

"I'll speak to the priest about this," she says, tight-lipped.

The younger woman smiles and shrugs. "The priest has nothing to say. It is not your daughter. It is a señorita who died in child-birth. She makes many miracles. Give us back the photograph."

"I most certainly will not."

"One minute."

The younger woman goes behind the curtain and when she comes back her face is solemn and pious. "I'm told to say if you take that photo bad things will happen. You will have big trouble, many troubles. You will see."

"I'll take that chance," says Catherine, and marches out with Octavia into the blinding sunlight, surprisingly close to tears.

"Suppose," says Julian, "that Time was some kind of creature, a huge enormous creature so big we can't even see that he's a crea-ture, we only see his parts. I mean, we feed chickens and then eat them, right? Well, Time lets *us* grow big and then he eats us. He eats everything. The whole world is his dining room. People getting old? What's really happening is, he's eating them. Sucking them to death."

Octavia gets into it. "And he's so big that the sound of the wind is him, breathing," she says. "And the rain is his peepee, and the ocean is . . . the ocean is . . ." What can the ocean be?

"His eyes," says Julian, inspired.

His eyes!

Moving, splashing eyes!

• • •

A power struggle is going on between Soledad and Filomena, a witches' feud, a duel, *mano a mano.* Domingo won't come right out and say so, but he gives heavy hints.

Greeting Soledad in the kitchen, he slyly says, "I saw Doña Filomena today and she seemed very well."

Soledad glares at him.

"How are *you* feeling today?" Domingo asks Soledad. He winks at Octavia.

"Never better," she snaps. In her apron pocket she carries an arrowhead, a dried-up dog's paw, and a lock of Maribel's hair.

Every morning for a week, as soon as he arrives for work and stops in the kitchen for coffee and a roll, Domingo tells Soledad how well Filomena is doing, and asks how *she* is feeling. And Soledad says *fine,* even when she is pale and gray as a ghost and running to the bathroom every five minutes. Filomena is winning!

But now the word goes round the island: Filomena has fallen and hurt her back. She has to stay in bed. And Soledad has completely recovered. Soledad is winning! Thanks to Maribel, her power source!

But has she really won?

Filomena's brother Tomás has been away on the mainland. Tomorrow he is coming back, and he is very powerful. What will happen next?

Preoccupied, Soledad boils and burns the cream of squash soup and serves it anyway. Papi scolds her. He thinks of Soledad only as the family cook, and has no knowledge of the life-and-death combat that is going on. (If he knew, would Soledad be out of a job?)

Octavia is proud that she can let her cousin Julian in on these secrets their parents know nothing about.

"But can they do that?" Julian says. "Can they make each other sick?"

"Of course they can."

"They're just ordinary Indian women."

"All witches are ordinary," Octavia says. "Until they use their power they're just like anybody else."

"They're ignorant," he says. "I don't believe in them."

But he wonders, and in truth he half believes.

In Octavia's opinion they are fighting over Maribel. Filomena has been muscling in on Soledad's territory, and seeking to use Maribel as *her* power source. Why else would Filomena so casually ask Octavia to bring her Maribel's old hairbrush, saying she had a better one to give her in exchange?

Soledad in her turn is trying to usurp Filomena's position as the most powerful witch in the village. She is growing arrogant, and arrogance is dangerous.

A body is washed up at the *cocal.* It is Eugenio the fisherman. He was out fishing alone. The weather was clear and calm, and his empty boat drifts in to shore unharmed. Why should Eugenio fall overboard in calm weather? Why should he drown, a fine strong man like Eugenio?

Domingo tells Octavia privately that Eugenio was a great favorite of Soledad, he was her cousin. Eugenio has been struck down. Not only that—Eugenio's wife has given birth to a baby with a withered arm.

The war has escalated. As a warning and a punishment, Filomena has killed Eugenio. Octavia is impressed. Killing someone is serious.

● ● ●

Filomena is a serious person. In addition to midwifery, she can bleed, purge, set bones, soften lumps by massage, give herbal medicines, and cure the air, the evil air. She can bring home a philanderer by tying knots in the drawstrings of his underpants. She owns the finger bone of a certain saint and rubbing it over the body she removes disease. With an egg she can cleanse a patient suffering from an evil spell.

Filomena's brother Tomás is a witch who can be bad or good according to how he is feeling. At night he turns into a black burro by rolling in ashes and leaping over a fire twice while crossing himself.

Octavia, in bed, is thinking about Maribel. She is thinking how one day deep in the jungle she and Julian will find a voodoo doll hidden in a shallow cave, wrapped in a piece of cloth from Maribel's yellow dress. Carefully, tenderly they will bear it home, remove the pins, put medicine on the wounds. They will nestle it in a bed of flowers and soft silk, dress it beautifully, surround it with books and fruit, and lo, Maribel will fall into a sleep, a swoon, and from her husk a tall and beauteous stranger will spring up, pale, intelligent . . .

Clad in a long white Grecian dress, she smiles at everyone, at Octavia in particular. Stars sparkle round her head. She opens her arms and her voice is soft as kitten fur.

"*Oh, Tavvie,*" she says. "*All these years! You've been so patient!*"

At her feet lies the silly face of Maribel, baby teeth and all, discarded like a snakeskin. She is so beautiful you have to cry. Not beautiful like Duncan, but mysterious, and dignified, and still a little sad.

"*But, Maribel, I was so mean to you, so mean! I wasn't patient, I wasn't good at all!*"

She strokes Octavia's hair and smiles.

"Don't feel bad, Tavvie, I always understood."

And all the love in Octavia's body bursts open, exploding her heart and all her blood vessels, and she is too happy to live any longer, and she dies and is clapped into heaven instantly.

20 On a rainy afternoon Julian and Octavia are sitting very close together, on the couch in the *sala,* looking at a book. The book is about a sculptor who lived in Brazil long ago and made statues of the saints. He was a mulatto and he had leprosy, so nobody wanted anything to do with him. The whites wouldn't have him and the blacks wouldn't have him. At the end he had to be carried around on a litter. He had no nose and no fingers or toes or even feet, but he kept on working. When he couldn't sculpt any more he painted, with brushes tied to his stumps.

Julian and Octavia, holding the book (a big book full of pictures) half on his lap, half on hers, are overcome by the courage of this man.

Octavia becomes aware that her hip is touching Julian's hip. Her thigh, down all its length, is touching Julian's thigh. The late afternoon sunlight comes slanting in, and the room turns strangely golden, hollow and unreal, like the pictures in the book. Something seems about to happen. What? A quiver of sharp pleasure ripples in her abdomen. She pretends more interest in the book than she is now feeling. She wants to prolong this moment.

But Delila appears in the doorway with mop and broom and bucket. Seeing her, they spring up (casually), and it is over.

• • •

As matters turn out, it is not over. Later, he comes looking for her. He finds her in the gallery and when he says, "Let's read some more, okay?" she knows he felt what she felt, and he wants more of it, and now that she knows that, she is shy and embarrassed.

She follows him slowly down the stairs and into the *sala.* She wants to, and she doesn't want to. She is the monkey and Julian is the lizard and the *sala* is the green line of the jungle. She is walking with him hypnotized, and his jaw is closed on her arm, holding her arm, and she is headed for death, and yet she goes as docilely as if she wanted to go, as if they were lovers walking arm in arm.

They enter. He takes a book, any book, and they sit down. Again the golden hollow light, a tiny buzzing sound, the drifting dust motes of the afternoon.

"Look," he says, and shows her a picture.

"Yes," she whispers, even though the sculpture is Greek this time and the lady is naked.

Their thighs are touching, tight together down all their length. Octavia cannot speak. She does not know what to do. Should she acknowledge this or not? Their thighs tightly touching, his elbow on her lap, holding the book. His elbow. He leans on it so slightly. His hand wants to turn and touch her thigh and her stomach, but he doesn't dare. She knows this. She holds her breath. He turns the page. They have found a fascinating new pursuit. Nothing happens and yet everything happens. They are both hushed as if in church, and they stay there close together on the couch (she has never felt so *alive)* until once again they are interrupted. Octavia's mother, looking for Maribel.

Next time, the third time, perversely, she won't go with him.

"Come on, why not?" he asks in a brand-new private voice that thrills her.

"I just don't feel like it," she says and goes to seek the protection of Soledad in the kitchen. And this is also delightful—knowing he wants it and she won't.

And the fourth time and the fifth she won't, and after that somehow she can't, she has put herself in a bind. Now if she goes, it will be surrender, she will be clearly saying, Yes, I know what you want and I want it too. And she can't do that, not Octavia. She won't be a hypnotized monkey, not even for him. She will kick a soccer ball and fight and play cards and climb a tree, good as a boy in every way save one and better than a boy because she's not so hateful and so mean. She wants respect! Respect and admiration! Monkey-lizard games over picture books are not for her.

Besides, the maids have been teasing her. They say she is turning into a señorita. To prove them wrong, she is more *macha* than ever.

Memories are mosaics. Mine are in bits and pieces. I lay them out before me, like a jigsaw puzzle. Does this piece fit here? Is it the sea, a bit of cloth, a face, a religious image? Perhaps these jagged bits and pieces of my childhood will never make a picture. Perhaps they will make more than one. What then? What if I find a glittering pile left over when I stop?

I am very little and Soledad is fooling me with tricks. She puts the bean under one shell and it turns up under the other.

"There," she tells me, "now you have learned something: whatever you see, it's the opposite. What color is this?"

"It's green."

"And now?"

Silence.

"Well, come on. What color?"

It is blue but I won't say so. I won't give her the satisfaction.

"Green," I say. "Green is green."

She laughs. I can't stand her laughter. How is it possible for green to change to blue before my eyes?

"Well, at least I can read," I meanly say.

She shrugs. "I also, I read."

"Yes? Well, read that."

"Read what?"

"That word."

"That word? That little little word? That one is so little who could read it? I will read this one. This one says MILK. And this great long one, I will read it. It says E-VAP-O-RATED!"

"Yes," I say, "but read that."

"Oh, for that one I would need glasses."

"You see it very well. You don't know what it says!"

"Oh yes, I know," says Soledad.

"You do not."

"I do."

"Then tell me."

"Why should I? Don't you know what it says?"

"Yes, I know."

"Then why ask me?"

And she will not look again. She shows me a giant paper peanut shell and she waves it in front of me and then she claps her hands and says, "Where is it?"

It is gone!

"Look for it," she says. "It is somewhere in this kitchen. I will give you a hint. It is south by southwest."

"It's in your lap," I say. But marvelously it is not. It isn't anywhere. At last I find it, on the windowsill. How did it get there? Soledad's eyes are sparkling, and she sings, mockingly.

> *"I know a secret I won't tell,*
> *Three little peanuts in a peanut shell."*

The peanut shell is a box, and inside, instead of peanuts, are three tiny celluloid baby-dolls. I am sick with mystery.

"How do you do it? Tell me."

"I don't know," says Soledad. "It is a mystery to me. I don't do anything, it just happens."

I inspect the peanut shell. "May I have it?"

"No. It belongs to Porfirio."

"I will buy it!"

But she shakes her head.

I never see the peanut shell again, and Soledad never does tricks again. It is strange.

On the wall of the *sala,* near the couch where Julian and Octavia like to sit, hangs a portrait photograph of Octavia's pudgy grandfather, Don Basilio. Like so many tyrants, he has a comic air. He wears a colonel's uniform, with sword, and brandishes a walrus mustache. One hand rests on the back of a polished, intricately carved black chair. His noble posture is ruined by an inescapable joke: he is cross-eyed.

Don Basilio never saw this photograph. Before it could be developed a band of copra workers (highland Indians enslaved for resisting the theft of their land) chopped his head off with their great bright knives.

Octavia's father escaped death because he was on his honeymoon, on the way home from Texas with a new and pregnant wife, aboard a ship that was anchored that night in the Bay of Campeche.

Afternoon.

Everyone is asleep or has gone out. Julian is playing soccer with the boys. Octavia, waiting for him, sits reading in the portal. Uncle Clo calls her from above, from the gallery, hanging over the rail.

Lately he's been away almost all the time; he's left her alone. Can it last? Every night she dreads going to bed.

"Hey Missy, you, down there," he calls, over the railing. "You better come up, I have something to show you."

(Ha, she says to herself. Not on your life.)

"It's something you'll want to see."

She keeps her nose in her book.

"It's your kitty cat."

She is alarmed.

"Your kitty cat has hurt himself."

"Where is he?"

"He cut his paw. It's bleeding. A bad cut."

Now he has her. She's on her feet. "Where is he?"

"Up here. Under the bed."

And of course Octavia, the fool, goes running, runs past him into his bedroom, and does not hear him shut the door behind her.

And there is nothing wrong with Pablo at all. She examines his paws. They're fine.

"Must have been red ink," he says. He has something in his hands. "Look at these," he says. "Here's something to look at! People just like you." And that is when he shows her photographs of naked children. She looks politely, and draws back. She hates them. Two or three show a naked grown-up man with his back to the camera. A fourth (he turns it over slowly, revealing it little by little, as if to make her curious, to whet her curiosity, as if she is dying to see it) shows the nude man's face, and it is Tío Claude himself.

"I don't like them," says Octavia. "They're stupid." (But ever after, her lovemaking will be haunted by those photos and by him.)

"I can take some photographs of you," he says. "You'll be my model, my artist's model. I'll pay you. Models always get paid. We'll take a walk into the jungle, you and me, ah? We'll find a nice lonely place with nobody around. Absolute privacy. Or we can take a sailboat out to sea, with only the fishes to look at us. Ah? I'll pay you . . . five dollars American for every day you pose! That's a lot of money. You'll be rich."

"No," says Octavia.

"Why not?"

"I don't want to."

She has no idea how to cope with this. She has no weapons against him. He wants to see her naked, he wants to gloat and do the things he does. He wants to take her picture while he does it. He wants to breathe the way he breathes, and fall on his knees and pull at himself, and groan, and make a mess in his handkerchief. Ugh.

"I'm going," she says.

Her cat is in her arms and she marches to the door, which is locked. She tries to open it. There is a pause. He is watching her as he puts the photographs in a small steel box.

"It doesn't open," she says faintly. This man is Julian's father, his *father*.

"It doesn't open? Let's see."

He bounds over, she shrinks back, flinches away from him. And he begins talking the way he talks.

"You'll never grow to be a big girl," he says, trapping her between the wardrobe and the door, breathing the way he breathes. "You want to be a big girl, don't you? You're so little. Look how little you are. Between your legs," he whispers, "you're a nothing. You want to be big and strong and healthy, don't you? Ah? You want to be soft and wet and pink and feel so good. I can make you feel so good you'll think you've gone to heaven."

"I want to open this door," she says.

"What do you love most in the world? This will feel better than that. Hah? What do you love most?"

My cat, she thinks, but doesn't say so.

"I don't love anything," she says.

"Your cat," he says, triumphant. "Your kitty cat. You love to snuggle him, so soft and warm. Hah? This will be better than that. Give him to me."

"No!" cries Octavia.

"I wouldn't hurt your cat."

"No!"

"I tell you what, we'll make a deal. If you're *nice* to me I won't hurt him," says Tío Claude. "If you're nice to me I won't poison him." He is speaking in a very small voice, so she can hardly hear him. "Have you ever seen a poisoned animal?"

The light has faded into black and sticky tar. She cannot breathe.

"Give him to me."

"No!" (Where is help to come from?)

He reaches to take the cat away, and she doubles over, and turns her back, and her cat takes fright and struggles to free himself, digging in his claws in order to spring free, and she can't hold him. Tío Claude (chuckling) grabs him by one leg, and is sorry because her cat explodes and hisses and strikes three times at Tío Claude and runs under the bed.

"Why, that little devil," says Tío, looking at his wrist and forearm. "He ripped me open."

And sure enough, blood stands out along one long and two short lines. Octavia is glad, although it reminds her that this same hated blood runs in her own veins and will forever.

"I better get this washed," he says. "It might infect."

He bends his face down to hers. "You wait right here."

"No."

He squeezes his wound and hesitates. "I'll come see you tonight," he says. "When everyone's in bed and sound asleep. We haven't had a visit for a good long time."

"You can't come in," she says. "I've got a lock on my door."

He smiles and shakes his head. Blood is trickling from the longer scratch and he binds it with his handkerchief. "Your pussycat deserves a spanking, don't you think?"

"No."

"Then you be nice," he says cheerfully. "I've heard of people who burn cats with their cigarettes. I wouldn't do that, would I? Because this pussycat has a little girlfriend who's real nice."

He unlocks the door but still he blocks the way to freedom which lies outlined about his body.

"You'll be asleep when I come in, you won't even know I'm there. Remember, if you tell, I'll tell what you did with your sister. I'll tell how you came in here with me. I'll tell what we did when you were sick, and all those other times."

(We! thinks Octavia. We!) Her face screws up and she begins to cry. He lets her pass.

"Run along, Missy," he says, jovially. "You behave yourself."

She gets out fast. At a safe distance she waits until he goes into the bathroom and shuts the door. Then in a rush she is back in his room burrowing under the bed to comfort and soothe her cat, talking to him gently until he trusts her again and will come out and allow himself to be picked up. When they are outside, she takes him up to the wide flat roof where Uncle Claude would never think to look for them, and soon he is purring and snuggling in her neck.

He is no match for any human being. He cannot understand.

At supper, Mother sees the scratches. "Clo, whatever happened to your arm?"

"Ask Missy," he answers gaily.

Octavia, caught short, appalled, feels herself blush crimson to her ears, and cannot speak. Everyone is listening.

"Her kitty cat misunderstood my intentions," says Tío Claude. "Little Missy thought I was going to gobble him up, and in the rescue attempt, old Tío Claude got his battle wounds. Now you listen here to me, Missy" (he says sternly, right at her), "I do not gobble up kitty cats!"

". . . unless they deserve it," he adds, with a wink.

"Octavia, that cat—!" says her mother.

"It wasn't the cat's fault!" cries Octavia in a passion. And then she faintly mumbles (because to say it right out loud to her doting mother seems an enormity), "It was *his* fault."

"What? Speak *up.*"

"I said it was his fault."

But again she has mumbled, hoping that perhaps someone will hear, or insist, but no one hears and no one insists. Her mother says, "If you can't speak any better than that, Octavia, don't speak at all."

"All right I won't!" cries Octavia, and flinging down her napkin she storms out of the dining room. She will not cry in front of Julian.

In the bathroom she finds her uncle's bloodstained handkerchief fallen on the floor beneath the basin, and (shuddering at the touch of it) she runs into the kitchen. Soledad is washing dishes with Delila. Octavia calls her outside, for privacy.

"Listen," she says. "I'll give you anything I've got except my cat if you will teach me just one thing."

"What thing?"

"To make somebody sick."

Soledad opens her mouth and closes it and rolls her eyes.

"What's this?" she says.

"Come on, I have to make somebody sick!"

"Who?"

"It doesn't matter who. A wicked person."

"Who?"

"Just anyone."

"Well," says Soledad, "I'd need your cat if I'm to teach you that."

"Why?" cries Octavia. "Why would you need my cat?" She realizes that Soledad is only teasing. "It isn't funny." She shows Soledad the bloody handkerchief. "This person. Tell me!"

"Get along with you," says Soledad, spitting in the dirt, eyeing the handkerchief. "Whose is it anyway?"

"I told you, it doesn't matter. Someone bad. I only want him to get sick. Or blind."

"I have to know whose it is."

"All right, it's his. My *tío.*" (She hisses like a snake spitting venom.)

"You don't like him?"

"I hate him. I'll put a nail through this and bury it. I'll cut it in a million pieces. Tell me how, please tell me, Soledad."

But Soledad turns away. "What do I know of all that? What's he done to you?"

"I'll pay you. I've got money."

"What money," scoffs Soledad. Tight-lipped and disapproving, she waves Octavia away and goes back inside. "Go to Filomena for that kind of thing."

To visit Filomena means going to the other side of town, and it is nighttime now. She can't ask Julian to come, she can't ask anyone. If she tells her mother, she'll say exactly what she said before (Octavia can hear her)—that he was joking, that her reactions are childish, that she misunderstood. If she tells her father, he'll only ask if all this fuss has frightened Maribel.

She gathers up her courage and slips outside, runs down the dark street, but lasts only a block before something white and threatening in the moonlight sends her pounding home in fright.

A blind man sitting looking at the sky, his sad eyes full of milk. What is she to do?

• • •

She invents her own ritual in the back garden. Nails, scissors, matches, thorns, a trowel. A dead baby lizard she found yesterday.

Kneeling in an area of moonlit grass, she binds two nails with string to make a cross. With the scissors she cuts and rips and stabs the handkerchief. She sets fire to the sticky parts, the rest she buries, pierced by nails. That is step one. Now she makes a nest of acacia thorns and puts the baby lizard on top of it. The lizard is dead, dried up, its head is cracked, its arms outstretched, its legs straight down by its tail so that it looks almost like a tiny man. Its clean underside is made of tiny scales of blue, pale green, and peach; its mouth is open, its head thrown back in agony.

She carries the thorns and the lizard upstairs and sets them down carefully outside his door.

And for a moment she feels better. But even the most powerful magic takes time, and she has no time. What about tonight? What is she to do tonight? She needs a lock. Her parents have a lock, Maribel has a lock, *he* has a lock, everybody has a door that locks! But she, she has no lock at all. How is she to guard her cat? Where can they hide? Where can they go to sleep?

The grown-ups are still in the *sala,* talking, sipping cognac. "Oh, Claude," her mother sighs. "Does the civilized world still exist? I've been here so long the world outside seems like a myth, an old forgotten story."

Almost casually she asks the question she's waited so long to ask: "When you leave, will you take me with you—the girls and me?"

• • •

And at that very instant, as she listens, an inspiration comes to Octavia. An idea of purest genius. *She could change rooms with Maribel!*

Change rooms, change rooms with Maribel, and lock the door! What a joke, what a marvelous joke!

21 When Octavia pulls Maribel out of bed, leads her next door, and puts her down on her own bed, there is no struggle. Maribel is accustomed to being awakened in the night. She has already been awakened once by Mother, to weewee. With Octavia she is docile, half asleep.

Octavia arranges her sister in the bed, shakes down the mosquito net, waits to make sure she will sleep again, then gathers up her cat, creeps out, and goes into Maribel's room.

Maribel's door has a lock.

The bed has a smell of Maribel, and it is soft and messy, but Octavia climbs in. She is safe. After a while she begins to laugh. She rolls from side to side in silent glee. The joke is this: he will go to her room and find her sister, whom he can't bear! He can't even stand to look at her!

For a long time she listens, thinking she might hear his step, and while she is still listening suddenly it is daylight, sunlight, and the grackles are calling in the garden, and to her surprise she is in Maribel's bed. She remembers why.

In Octavia's own room, Maribel is sleeping peacefully. It worked. It worked! She did it, she has triumphed.

But there is tonight and tomorrow night and all the nights to come. She must be constantly alert.

At breakfast he was not there. He was out in the jungle, Mother said, and wouldn't be back for three days at least. He was a restless man, she said, and had to move around.

Octavia ran into the kitchen boasting. "I did it," she said. "I did it myself and it worked. I got rid of him. Where did he go?"

And Soledad said, "He went off with Manuel into the jungle. Manuel came for him at six and they had breakfast and off they went. He said he was going to look at the houses of the dwarfs, but I think they're going someplace else."

"I hope he falls into a pit and the dwarfs get him." (Octavia closed her eyes.) "I hope his leg drops off. I hope he goes blind. I hope he gets sores all over his body and his bones melt. I hope his back breaks and his arms turn into sticks. I hope his teeth turn into black beetles and he drowns and the sharks eat him."

She opened her eyes. Soledad was watching her with a certain interest.

He came back bitten and exhausted and different. He didn't look at her, not once. Did it actually work?

And from that time on, whenever he was in the house, she exchanged beds with her sister. She had to lie still, listening until Mother roused Maribel to go to the bathroom. It wasn't always easy to stay awake. Once or twice she fell asleep while waiting, but luckily on those nights he did not come.

In the daytime, she stayed out of his way. When she was in her room she pushed the sea chest against the door. It might not keep him out, but the noise would alert her and give her time to roll with her cat into the wardrobe, where he was not likely to find them.

But he let her alone. He was changed. He didn't tease her. He passed her by as if she did not exist. Was it an act?

Once, in her sister's room, she awoke in the night to find someone standing beside the bed. But it was not Uncle Clo, it was her father, key in hand.

"What are you doing here?" he said. "Why is the door locked? Where is your sister?"

She stammered out the lie she had rehearsed. "She wanted to sleep in my bed, so I let her."

Another time she overslept in Maribel's room, and Soledad came in with a tray. Octavia covered up her head, and listened to her moving about. When Soledad came to the bed purposefully, lifted the net, pulled back the covers, Octavia said AAH! to frighten her, but was frightened herself by the expression of horror on Soledad's face. And by the scissors she had in her hand.

"We changed beds," explained Octavia. "She's in my room. What were you going to do with the scissors?"

"*Pues,* what do you think?" said Soledad. "I was going to see if your sister needed a haircut."

"What time is it?"

"It struck eight."

On the floor were beans outlining the shape of a star. In the center of it was a dish. Octavia's cat, hungry Pablito, was lapping up whatever was in it. Soledad looked at him stupefied, started to chase him, but checked herself and turned to Octavia.

"You see? I brought him breakfast," she said.

Pablito sat down to clean his chops and shake his paws. His eyes closed in ecstasy. He washed his whiskers noisily.

Soledad looked at the empty dish. "A little milk," she said.

"That wasn't milk."

Soledad turned into a glaring eagle. "I am keeping your sister safe!" she said. "You think it's easy? It's not so easy."

"Why don't you keep *me* safe?" says Octavia. "Nobody cares if *I* am safe."

• • •

"Your Indian," says Father, "was made by God for suffering. He is the object to be tortured, to be exploited. He is the soft and living flesh upon which all the vilest, most sadistic passions can be vented. The epoch of the conquest was an orgy of the id."

He drains his wineglass and adds *aguardiente.* Having done so, he remembers his manners and offers some to Tío Claude, who declines. Father enjoys having another man in the house. Someone to understand him when he talks.

"The rabbit, the mullet, the Indian!" he exclaims. "Your eternal victims. That is their function in the scheme of things—to be the victims. Your Indian, when he had no white man to torture him, tortured himself. He *requires* torture to fulfill his destiny. He had his butcher priests, all drenched with blood. Did you know they never washed? The Aztec priest never washed the blood from his hair, and our Maya were probably no better. This land—all of it— New Spain—is soaked in blood, in human blood."

He twirls the stem of his glass, his cheeks are faintly flushed. Uncle Claude nods wisely, says nothing. Octavia, staring at him from across the room, curls her lip. For more than a month now she has cleverly escaped him, sleeping in her sister's room when he is home. She sends her evil wishes through the air.

"We who live today, we who were born here," says her father, "we are living monuments to cruelty, greed, deceit. Blood, gold, and lies. Cortez is our god, because he taught us how to lie. We don't mention his name but we worship him all the same. We worship the lie!"

"Hmm, well!" says Tío Claude.

Father offers him a cigar and lights one himself.

"My own family," he continues, puffing at the cigar, looking at it, puffing again, "was slaughtered here on this island. I suppose you've heard of that from Catherine. My parents, two brothers, and a sister. The house was burned to the ground. You've met my assistant in the clinic, young Lenin? Well, his father was the ring-leader. Yes, his father. Young Lenin. That was twenty-five years ago."

"Dreadful," says Tío Claude. "Dreadful shock. I wonder that you stay here."

Father, indulging his habit of speaking for his companions as well as for himself, says, "You will think, you will think they did it because we were aristocrats? Not so! My mother was of the people. And my father's father rose in the ranks from private soldier, having done various favors for his superiors. I have always wondered what those favors were. Women or assassination, almost certainly. What-ever, it was enough to set his feet on the path to wealth and posi-tion. That was after the revolution of 1907, and they were looking for new blood. My father was his eldest son, a stubborn man who offended those in power, and was given the *fincas* here on this island. They wanted him dead, you see, but he was too popular to kill. So they banished him in the guise of political reward! And promptly he fell ill of fever and dysentery—which was what they had in mind. For centuries these islands and the coastal swamps have been the burial ground of political offenders. But he didn't die. He was tough, my father. Today, of course, conditions are a little better, though we still have dysentery and malaria."

"And rats," says Tío Claude.

"And twenty years later the islanders did the job the generals refused to do. They rose up in rage." (He relit his cigar.) "What do you think? Eh? Should we begrudge them their little drink of blood? My father was a tyrant, a brute, a *cabrón*. He treated men like dogs. He whipped them and worked them till they dropped. He raped their wives and starved their children. How can I con-demn those men? If I had been among them, I'd have done the same."

He pauses and a muscle twitches in his jaw.

"They killed my mother, too," he says.

Now once more in Octavia's head (as in her father's) the oily sooty orange flames are leaping. Little brown men, drunk on rage and *aguardiente,* break through the gate, kill the watchmen. Shouting, they overrun the courtyard, burst into the house. They carry ropes, torches, and enormous knives. They drag her grandmother from the house in her nightgown. The flames are reflected in the knives, in her black eyes. She falls on her knees and begs for her life. "My children," she begs. "Spare me for my children." They bind her arms to her sides with fishing line. Her hair, ordinarily so smooth and tight (Octavia has seen photographs) is in a loose braid that is unraveling down her back. Filled with hatred, someone lifts the knife with both hands and brings it down like a cleaver.

Octavia will carry this family melodrama through her life, not knowing where or how to put it down. Where does it fit in Pittsburgh, Pennsylvania? What can she do with it? Whom can she tell? Can she tell her colleagues or her sophomore students at the university: *my grandparents were hacked to death with machetes . . . ?*

Now her father sighs deeply and lifts his glass. "You see, my friend," he tells Tío Claude, "the real true drink for human beings isn't rum or mescal or *aguardiente,* it's blood. Here on this island everyone knows that. When it isn't human blood, it's the blood of chickens that they drink in their religious rituals."

"But they're Catholic," says Tío Claude. "I thought they were Catholic."

Her father stares at him, mildly disconcerted; then laughs to show appreciation of the joke.

Something terrible has happened. Octavia's cat is dead.

Murdered.

She let down her guard, she went swimming with Julian, and in her absence someone murdered her cat, dashed its brains out against the garden wall. She falls on her knees a dozen feet away, holds her face, and begins to scream.

It is Lenin who leads her away, and later buries the two pieces of her cat. In her room she knocks herself against the walls. The pain will kill her. The fault is hers—she left him alone, she failed him. She will never eat again.

Tragically, she tells her father as he stands beside her bed: "I don't want to live."

He strokes his mustache, indulgent, baffled. Love of the weak and helpless he can understand (his pathetic daughter Maribel), but such grief for an animal, a cat—? "Tavia, animals die," he begins. "And people die. You must try to have a sense of proportion."

He stops, not wanting to alienate her. Her pain is real enough, the pain of a child, soon ended. He tries to be patient, to be gentle. The answer of course is another cat. By all means, let her have another cat! He will speak to Catherine.

He stares down at this daughter, moaning, twisting in her bed, and can't help shaking his head. With all the human misery and suffering in the world, these melodramatics over a cat—! He prescribes a gentle sedative.

Pablito, dead. His brains dashed out against the garden wall where on the faded peach-painted plaster, between the blossoms of the passion vine and bougainvillea, they left small stains.

Who did it? Who could do such a thing? There was no question in Octavia's mind. Only one person could have done it. Telling everyone he'd be away for three days, on a shopping expedition to the mainland to purchase diving equipment, to have his photographs developed, he waited until Octavia let down her guard, then he sneaked back.

Mother said it was done by "hateful village boys," but Octavia knew better. He sneaked back, he did it. He came back unannounced and went away again. He was always turning up and vanishing. He was the one. He did it to punish her.

No one could understand the depths of Octavia's grief.

She who had undertaken the care of this special cat, she on whom he solely depended, the only bulwark between his softness and the murderous malevolence all around him—she had failed him. Because of her negligence, he was tortured, hacked in two. She herself was therefore, in effect, his murderer.

She took her hunting knife and plunged it in her left forearm, once, twice, four times. Bleeding, she lay in bed and turned her face to the wall. She was garbage, she was trash, she was rotten meat. She had lost her right to live. She did not pull down the mosquito netting. Let them bite.

She had lost her dearest friend. Whatever sense of worth she had, she owed to that dear friend. She had no parents (they belonged to Maribel), she had no brother, no one to acknowledge her except that cat. Gratitude and love for that cat had flowed from her like blood, and yet she failed him. Over and over she saw the violent act, saw him struggle, try to get away, saw the fear in his eyes. She panted, tossed on her bed, threw herself around her room. She couldn't stand it.

She went to find Julian.

"I want my gun back," she told him.

"No," he said. "It's gone. I lost it in the woods."

"You lost it? My gun?"

And she went back to her room, and wept even for her lost gun, lost with uncaring negligence, now when she needed it.

In the midst of all this she found blood in her underpants, understood its meaning, and sank deeper in despair. Sick unto death, she said to herself. A sickness unto death.

Now she no longer threw herself around her room. She lay in bed unmoving.

Julian came to see her.

"Are you sick?" he said.

"I guess so."

"What have you got?"

"I don't know."

Her uncle returned and she slipped her knife under her pillow, waiting for him. She would not change bedrooms ever again. If he came through that door, she would fight. She hoped he would come —she had nothing to lose. But he didn't. It was her mother who came in.

"What is it, Octavia? What is wrong? Is it still the cat?"

Still the cat. There was no way she could articulate her trouble.

"I understand," said her mother, smoothing Octavia's hair off her forehead. "You're like a mother with her baby. I understand, darling. But a week has passed, and even mothers who have lost their babies don't grieve forever."

Babies. Who could love a *baby* the way she loved that cat? Babies were spoiled, demanding, piglike creatures, loved by all. They did not need more love. Cats needed love, they were rejected and despised. Hungry while others ate. Denied even water, water! because no one cared, no one even thought they might be thirsty. Casual targets of stones and slingshots, tortured, mutilated by boys, their tails chopped off, their eyes blinded, their brains dashed out, their fur set on fire—soft little loving creatures, recipients of all the cruelty of the human race. And still they held no grudge. Behind their fear was love and trust just waiting to be bestowed.

"Uncle Clo did it," she said.

"Octavia," said her mother. "You know that isn't true."

"Mother, he did, I know he did."

"Uncle Clo was on the mainland when it happened."

"He came back."

"He did not come back. He was away for a week. He would never do a thing like that."

"He did it."

They sat in silence for a while. Her mother sighed.

"We'll get you another cat," she said. "A kitten."

"No, no," cried Octavia in a panic. "I don't want another cat. Please, don't bring me a cat!" (Go through all this *again?*)

"All right, all right," said her mother. "Don't make a scene. We certainly won't force you to have another cat."

Soledad scolded her, changing the sheets. "Your cousin lost his mother—his mother!—and he does not carry on as you do. You are behaving very badly. You must come downstairs and eat your food."

Her body was made of stone too heavy to move. The air was stone. Her room, the furniture was stone. She lay for hours turned to icy stone and it became a sought-for state. She did not want it interrupted. It was a sort of death.

Nobody could understand that a person could love a cat. Nobody loved him except her.

She watched a scorpion crawl down the wall and did not care enough to kill it. She hoped it would sting her.

Julian brought her a card in an envelope. It had a picture of a sick rabbit and it said GET WELL.

"I thought you'd be out playing soccer," she said.

"I didn't feel like it. I felt like reading. Those kids . . . you know. They're okay, but . . . I don't know. I can't understand what they're talking about."

He looked at her.

"You've gotten really skinny. You look different. You don't look like a child any more. Of course, you *are* a child."

He was still looking at her, gravely, almost puzzled.

"What have you got?" he asked. "Is it typhoid fever?"

"I don't know." (What is a child? She was never a child.)

He stayed a while longer, fidgeting around the room, looking at her books. Darkness was falling. His face glowed white and anxious in the failing light. She realized again that she loved him, he was the only one she wanted to see, but she was too sick to get up. She was too tired to try to win him. There was no hope.

"Did you know that without gravity the sun and moon would fall apart?" he said.

She did not respond. She did not care about gravity.

"Well, I'll go," he said after a while. "Do you want to play cards or anything?"

"No."

At the door he said, "Get well, okay? It isn't any fun here when you're sick."

Days went by, and in the third week after the death of her cat she came out. She went into the *sala* and played the piano, somberly. It was so out of tune you could hardly guess the notes. She came quietly to the table and ate her food. You can't stay in bed forever. The body needs to move, and here she was where she did not want to be. There was nothing to do but go on drearily living. She would be well again, she would even laugh, she would forget. Tears started but she held them down, for although she might forget *at times,* she would never forget for long. Never. In her heart would always be a tended shrine:

PABLITO, a Loving Cat, Destroyed by Evil.

"You and Julian ought to take advantage of this heavenly day and go to the beach," said her mother, falsely bright.

22

After the murder of her cat, Octavia's daily life continued, on the surface, as before. But underneath there was a change. She was subdued, no longer a tomboy. She wanted to be with her cousin but no longer tried to woo him with her boasting and her derring-do. She was too tired for all that. Instead she walked beside him quietly, and when he played soccer or baseball with the boys she watched him go and made no effort to hold him for herself.

Julian changed too. He sought her out. He treated her with more respect.

She no longer slept in her sister's room, and her uncle did not come. He didn't speak to her, not even in daylight, not even to make his jokes or pat her on the head and offer her a trinket and false sympathy. To Octavia his sudden indifference was in itself a proof of guilt. Despite what her mother said, she knew that he had killed her cat. He was using a seaplane now—he had leased it—and he could have easily flown in that bloody morning, and then flown out again, unseen.

Distracted by his projects, he was the talk of the island. He claimed to have set up a diving station on the southwestern coast of the island, in order to explore the old wrecks known to be there, hoping to find Spanish galleons, hoping to find gold. But everyone said the diving was only a cover and his real work was training irregular soldiers in the southwest interior.

Octavia did not know what irregular soldiers might be, or why he should be training them, but she hoped they hated him and would rise up and slaughter him.

Whatever his occupation, he now came home almost every night, flying in his seaplane.

The sight of him (Pablito's murderer) made her ache with hatred.

How tired I've been, she thought, and just then a possible avenue of revenge came to her. She felt a surge of energy, as though a door had opened.

Now that she walks slowly, like a girl, Julian finds himself looking at Octavia more closely than he ever has before. He is seeing something important he has overlooked. He takes a new interest in their expeditions and even promotes them. He is intensely curious about her body. *She's growing up. She's getting breasts.*

As they walk together in the plaza or along the malecón between the rains, excitement seizes him, like a note, a sustained tone in the background of his thoughts. Before, going through town with her, he always felt a tug of shame. But now their friendship, through some subtle change, has become acceptable. Honorable, even. It does him credit; he is proud. And his own mourning—that dismal damp that has permeated his life—begins slowly to recede.

She's not a child any more. She's growing up. She's definitely getting breasts.

This is her plan: She will search his room, she will find the photographs he showed her. She will take the photographs and present them to her mother as evidence. *I told you and you didn't listen.*

You chose your brother over me. You took his side against me. You were wrong!

Her mother's eyes will be opened. She will cry and hug her and beg her pardon.

Wild with fury, she will *act*.

Octavia tries the door of his room, but it is locked. She tries to climb up the vines to reach his window, but they break and will not hold her.

At the table she can't avoid him. She can't stop up her ears.

"*All* my letters can't have gotten lost," says Catherine. "I don't think you ever read them."

"Remind me," he says. "I've had other matters on my mind."

It is after supper, and they are lingering over coffee. Delila turns on the light, the heavy wood and wrought-iron chandelier that hangs over the table, but Catherine likes the twilight, and has her turn it off again.

"Over the years I must have sent five hundred letters. Did you read them? Did you throw them out?"

"Of course I read them."

"And my stories—at least you read my stories, didn't you?" asks Catherine. "I sent them to you."

"Of course. Those stories that you wrote—excellent! Very clever."

"Well, I *hope* you read them—since they were all about you."

Uncle Clo laughs. "That grubby little boy was me?"

"You know it was."

"What did you call him?"

"Henry."

"Henry . . . why Henry? And which one were you?"

"Gilda. Big sister."

"Gilda the golden girl. And Henry. You made him fall in love. You see, I do remember. What was the name of that one, that story?"

"I called it 'Age Ten.' "

"He fell in love with some awful little girl."

"Netta."

"She wore her hair in a braid."

"She was tongue-tied and homely but Henry adored her."

In the darkening room, he jokes with her: "Why did you make her so homely?"

"You know the answer to that," says Catherine. "Big sister Gilda couldn't bear a rival who was *pretty.*"

Felipe puffs on his cigar, raises his eyebrows. Rival? thinks Felipe, sipping *aguardiente*. Rival? No wonder the father separated them. I'd have done the same.

Octavia, in her bedroom, thinks of poison.

She contemplates the fever thermometer in the drawer of the table beside her bed. The silver line inside is mercury, and mercury is poison.

When she was little she would break thermometers to get at the mercury, shaking it out into her hand, so that it formed a small mysterious quicksilver ball, a liquid pellet in the palm of her left hand. (How could metal be liquid?) She would push it and squash it and worry it. She would put it on the tabletop and divide it in two and three, into dozens of tiny balls, and then she would shove them together until they popped into one again. She would try and try to pick it up until her fingertips were dusted with mercury. Quicksilver.

If mercury is poison, then you could give it to a person in his food and it would kill him. You could give it to a person, put it in his food, and how would anybody know?

Next morning with sleepless heavy eyes she goes down early to the kitchen and insists on being helpful—she will fill the coffeepot, she will carry the cups on a tray to her uncle and her father. Soledad makes a face that indicates surprise, but lets her do it. Poisoning someone appears to be quite easy. If discovered she will innocently say, "It was an accident. I was playing with it and it fell into the cup. How was I to know? I'm just a child."

At the table he is laughing with her father. She has the tray, she has the mercury in a vial in her pocket. She hesitates. She sets down the tray.

What if something went wrong and the mercury got into her father's cup? She is trembling.

Uncle Clo looks at his watch, drains his cup, and leaves the dining room, still talking and laughing, in excellent health.

That afternoon there is a polite knock at her door, and when she opens it, expecting to see Julian, there is her uncle. Squirming in his hands is a frightened white kitten with a red ribbon tied around its neck.

"Well, Missy," he says jovially. "I understand we've lost a cat, and I just happened to find this on my doorstep. And I thought, hey, hey, we've got a perfect little present here to cheer somebody up."

Octavia steps back. "I don't want it," she says. "I don't want a cat."

"Well, you see," he says, "it has no home . . . what shall I do with it?"

"Why did you do that?" she screams at him. "I don't want a cat!"

"Hoo-ee, what a temper!" He puts the kitten on her bed. "Now take good care of it," he says, and goes out the door, closing it behind him, beaming, a virtuous uncle who loves his niece. All he ever wanted was her happiness.

Octavia, unnerved, will not look at the kitten, which is uttering tiny helpless mews. Before she can weaken, she runs to the clinic and finds Lenin.

"You've got to help me," she says.

"But why?" says Lenin. "Why don't you keep it?"

"I'm not interested. I don't want a cat. I can't do it."

"Well then, let it go."

"No!" she cries. "Who would feed it? It will starve. Please, do this for me. I'll do it myself if you won't. Please!"

He can't understand. He thinks she's crazy, but she doesn't care. "Please, Lenin. Come on. Let's do it quick."

She pulls him by the hand to the shed behind the kitchen, and finds the execution box.

Next morning, dripping tears, she buries the small cold body in the garden next to Pablito's grave. It will never suffer now. Its life is over.

"Well, little Missy," says her uncle, after dinner. "How's your fine new kitty cat?"

She hesitates only an instant, and looks for the first time directly in his eyes.

"I killed it," she tells him coldly.

"Why don't you wear a dress?" says Julian. "Fix up. Brush your hair."

Octavia looks at him blankly. Fix up? Brush her hair? What for? She glances in the mirror at her hair. What does he want?

Elizabeth Jane begins to whisper inside her head. He wants a date, that's what he wants. He wants a girlfriend, a *novia.* He wants a *novia* to show off to the boys. Now's your chance!

Elizabeth Jane distinctly says, *He has a crush on you.* Octavia does not believe her. Something is going on, however.

Mystified, she puts on a blue dress embroidered with birds (slips her knife in one of the pockets) and brushes her hair. Out they go through the village, walking together stiffly. She feels like a fool. Everybody looks at them and it is very embarrassing, but much to her surprise nobody laughs, nobody teases, nobody says a word.

Once they get through town and are walking along the sun-dappled jungle paths it is easier, it is the way it used to be. He tells her he found the pistol after all. In fact, he really had it all along, but didn't want to give it to her when she was sick, after the thing that happened to her cat. She was too crazy, he says. He was afraid she would do something crazy. Now he holds out the gun.

She shrugs. "I don't care about it now," she says.

"It belongs to you."

She puts it in the other pocket of her blue dress and walks along, heavily armed. She no longer cares about her weapons, she no longer cares about finding the umbilical tree. She knows the fate of her cord: it was buried.

They skirt around a nesting ground of grackles. She tells him the names of certain trees.

"This is a tree-that-bleeds," she says. "Look." She cuts through its tender peeling bark with the knife and sure enough, it bleeds—white blood pours down its dappled skin like milk.

"Supposing it bleeds to *death,*" says Julian.

"Oh, it heals," she says. "Just like us."

(But her cat did not heal. Her grief will never heal.)

The tree is bleeding badly. It is a stalwart tree, wounded but uncomplaining, arms outstretched. Its blood looks like milk.

Julian takes out his own knife and slashes the tree.

"Stop!" says Octavia, because it seems like murder.

"We could kill this tree," he says. His face is full of emotion. "You and me, just kids, we could kill it." The white blood spills now from a dozen gashes and makes a pool on the ground. The tree says nothing, it does not complain. It is a large thing to be able to kill.

"We could kill a lot of things," says Octavia. "Would you ever kill an animal? I mean, a dog . . . or . . . a cat?"

"No," he says.

They stand watching the lifeblood of the silent tree trickle away.

"I liked your cat, he was a good old cat," says Julian. "I'm really sorry about your cat."

They put moss on the wounds of the tree and walk on.

"Have you ever kissed a boy?" he says.

She doesn't want to sound inexperienced. "Yes," she says.

"Who?"

"I kissed a boy in Valladolid."

"Did he put his tongue in your mouth?"

Her heart constricts. "Sort of," she says. She cannot look at him.

He tries to hold her hand. For a moment she lets him. Then she pulls it away.

"Let's look at each other," he says. "Lift up your dress."

"No."

"Just your legs," he quickly explains. "I only want to look at your legs."

She spends her life in shorts or a bathing suit, her legs in plain view. But today she's wearing a dress, and he wants to look at her legs. That's the way they are, boys and men. What's wrong with them? What are they thinking? Why do they do it?

"No," she says. "That's dumb."

Octavia's mother is planning an all-day picnic to the ruined hacienda at the south end of the island. She has been planning it for weeks. They will go by boat, she and Uncle Clo and the children, to inspect the ruins and the coconut plantation, swim and have a feast of lobsters, grilled by the *cocalero,* on the beach.

"I never see you," she complains to her brother. "You're always going off somewhere. You're off all day, and at night you're so tired out you go to bed. What do you *do* all day? What do you do on the mainland all the time?"

"Supplies," he says.

"Can't we visit you at the diving station? Can't we watch you dive?"

"Of course," he says. "I'll set it up."

"Can't I just come find you?"

He explains. The station is inaccessible by road. A marsh, a mangrove swamp. Not even horses can get there.

"Take me in the airplane."

"I'll do that, Catherine. I'll give you all a ride."

And he does. He gives them all a ride. He takes up Catherine and Lenin. Then he takes up Octavia and Julian. The island is a tuft of green moss on a vast blue plastic skin. The wind makes the airplane toss and buck. It's like riding in a kite.

He even takes up Maribel, over Catherine's objections. The airplane flies out of sight and is gone a long time. Then it returns and lands on the water with its big heavy feet. Maribel climbs out calm as can be, as if she rides in airplanes every day of the week.

Maribel got the longest ride of anyone.

"And the picnic to the old hacienda?" Catherine insists. "It's beautiful there."

"Of course," he says. "We'll go. Just set it up. Some day when it doesn't rain."

He never takes Catherine to the diving station, but the picnic—postponed three times—is still on.

23 Delila and Soledad are huddled together, motionless. They are in the gallery, leaning against the wall near the door to Maribel's room, looking at each other, listening to something, listening for someone ill, someone in pain. Something is wrong. Delila has her hand against her mouth.

"What medicine did you give to Maribel?" asks Octavia. "What's wrong with her?"

"What are you talking about?" says Soledad. "I didn't give her any medicine."

"I saw you."

"You are mistaken."

Octavia is surprised. Soledad is clearly lying.

She finds her mother and asks, "Is Maribel sick?"

"Sick? Why? Does she act sick?"

Soledad is grouchy all day long. In Maribel's room Octavia plays a record but Delila does not dance. She roughly lifts the arm and takes the record off.

"Don't play music now."

"Why not? Is Maribel sick? What has she got? Has she got the typhoid?"

Delila hunches her shoulders, says nothing. Soledad says nothing. Maribel seems all right. Octavia wanders away.

Julian is out playing baseball with the boys.

On her way downstairs Octavia tries the door to her uncle's bedroom as she does every day—and this time it opens. She reaches inside, steals the key, puts it in her pocket.

Her time has come.

The sky is dazzling. Against a carved-out wall of sand a quick restless surf is running back and forth as a wolf would run inside a cage, throwing himself against the bars and turning instantly away. And back again, and quickly turn. All day, all night, no end till death, this restless energy, obsessed.

It will happen like this:

Now that she has the key to his room he can't lock the door. She will find the photographs, show them to her mother, and then (she settles down) she will watch the terrible scene. Shouting, her mother will whip him and drive him from the house. Or perhaps she will kill him. Yes, she will kill him. Not with a machete—with a gun. Of course she will not do it openly. She will do it cleverly so that nobody will know. Only Octavia will know. When his body is found dead, only Octavia will know the truth. And her heart will overflow with gratitude and love and awe. It will be as if her true mother (a giant with black wings as wide as the world) has reappeared at last.

It will happen like this:

There is a fiesta, and Mother takes her brother to see the fireworks, the *castillos*. The gun is in her purse. In the crush of the crowd, as the fireworks are loudest, she presses the gun into his ribs and fires three times. Then she drops the gun, and lies back on the crowd for support. Nobody notices, nobody has heard. The fireworks are too loud, too bright.

Shot three times in the heart, he turns and looks around, not quite at her, just looks around, as if astonished to find himself where he is, in the crowded plaza. Whatever sound he may utter is lost in the explosions. His legs begin to buckle, and the islanders in front of him, absorbed in light, have to shrug him off their shoulders and their freshly ironed shirts. They have to twitch him off so he can fall.

He falls. They trample him.

The gun will not be discovered until later, long after they have carried him away. It will be found by the daughter of the baker, snaggle-toothed Chavela, who steps on it in the sandy plaza. Others in the crush have also stepped on it, without curiosity. But Chavela, curious, looks down, and, pointing, yanks her father's arm. He picks it up, Don Hilario the baker, proprietor of The Coronation of the Virgin, he picks it up and turns it over in his hands. The thought comes to him that this may be the gun that killed the *gringo*. Not certainly, but probably. Who can be sure? It does not occur to Don Hilario to give the gun to a policeman. Policemen are thieves. Instead he brings it to the house of the doctor and hands it to Domingo in a dirty rag. Domingo takes it to the clinic, places it in a basket on the doctor's desk.

No one is sorry the *gringo* is dead. No one! He was training the irregulars, those *malvivientes* who are terrorizing the island. One of his own soldiers killed him, they say. Everyone is glad!

There is a certain fern, the resurrection fern, that lies dormant as a dry brown ball in the dry season, but within hours of a good rain turns green and opens in full leaf. When Octavia is avenged, something inside her will gasp and drink and then expand like a resurrection fern; it will unfold, turn soft, return to life.

• • •

Something is definitely ailing Maribel. Her breasts are bigger than ever. Her slender waist has visibly thickened. Their mother casts an appraising eye.

"Is Maribel having her period?"

Delila is rooted.

"No."

"When is it due?"

"I don't remember."

Mother insists. "Two weeks? One week? Where is the calendar? What has happened to the calendar?"

"I'll ask Soledad," says Delila. "With permission, I'll ask her right now." And she bolts from the room.

Mother waits for Soledad, who does not appear.

Later in the kitchen, Soledad says she too has forgotten Maribel's due date.

"But where is the calendar?" says Mother. "I can't find the calendar."

"Who knows? Perhaps Marifel herself took it?"

"Well, find it please. And let me know when her period begins. Her body looks bloated. She's absorbing fluid. She must be due very soon."

"That could be," says Soledad.

Now that the rainy season has begun in earnest, Julian again proposes to Octavia that they play cards in the *sala*. "Or we could read," he says. "We could look at books, like we did before."

She still won't go. Something holds her back. But oh, she wants to, she wants to.

Today Maribel has painted a brand-new Christ on the cross on her freshly whitewashed wall. This Christ is different from the others.

He is very big, and between his legs (there is no doubt) *he has private parts.*

Yes, this time she has drawn details—hands with bristling fingers, nails, wounds, blood. Not red blood but brown, black, blue, and yellow blood. The cross itself is brown and outlined with small yellow stars. Christ has blue eyes, a black beard, a halo, a belly button. Between his legs is a trinity, complete with pubic hair. And under his feet, across the paper, is a purple scrawl that probably says nothing, but might say, if you look hard enough, (and Octavia for one believes it does say), CRISTO CRUSIBAID.

Mother and Father are acutely unhappy with this mural. Father does not like Maribel's interest in Christ. He is afraid she is going to be religious. Mother would be glad if Maribel were religious and has even spoken of giving her to the nuns. Mother is upset about these private parts.

"Where has she seen such things?" Dutifully she praises Maribel for her mural. "But we must give poor Jesus some clothes. He will be cold without his clothes. He always wears a cloth around his hips."

Maribel takes a brush, stirs it in the jar of water, dips it into yellow. Obediently, she paints yellow around Christ's hips. The private parts strike through, having been drawn in black crayon.

Is she laughing? How can you help but think some small chunk of her mind stands aside as sane and intelligent as anybody else, and watches, watches everything, even her own dumbness, with bright little silent clever eyes, like a mouse.

Today, even though it is raining, Julian has gone over to Santiago's house. He is mad at Octavia because she won't read books with him.

"All right, all right," he said. "I get the message. I'll leave you alone."

What message? She doesn't want to be left alone. Octavia wanders around the house in search of her sister.

Maribel is not in the *sala,* not in the classroom, not in the kitchen or the garden, not in her room. Where is she?

Her room is empty, but charged with her presence. Her dolls, arranged unimaginatively by Delila, sit on the floor in their tiny chairs, sit upon the bed and shelves and chairs, as stupid and vacant as Maribel herself. Octavia is suddenly outraged. How can this sister continue, at age seventeen, to play with these damn dolls?

Dolls of all kinds, from slick commercial beauties with curls and lace petticoats, to stick dolls tied with string. Dolls with real hair, straw hair, yarn hair, plastic hair, painted hair, no hair. Dolls with articulated joints and dolls with armless beanbag bodies, dolls made of corncobs and coconut husks, dolls of straw, of wood, of cloth, of sponge, of leather, of tortoise shell, eggshell, clay, wire, tin, lacquer, plastic, fur, and feathers, dolls with long legs, no legs, dolls with no heads, dolls that are mere blobs, stiff dolls, flabby dolls, every kind, shape, size, texture of doll imaginable, every nationality and race of doll—Octavia despises them all.

When Maribel herself arranges the dolls, the effect is more interesting. The dolls cease simpering and begin to work. They sit in great silent circles, sunbursts, triangles, back to back and face to face, woven, interlocking mandalas of dolls. How many dolls? Scores upon scores. Maribel's appetite for dolls will never be satisfied. It is Papi who keeps the supply coming.

As Maribel's room grows more cluttered, Octavia's becomes more bare and cold. The only luxuries Octavia allows herself are books and one tin painting of a Madonna, which serves to conceal a certain peephole between her room and Maribel's.

And yet, in secret, Octavia loves Maribel's room.

Delila is in charge of cleaning up the mess, washing the brushes, gathering up crayons, providing clean water for the watercolors, scrubbing the floor speckled with poster paints. She is glad to do it because in Maribel's room she can play records and dance while she cleans.

Delila is fifteen and knows all the dances. She teaches Octavia and Maribel and all three surge and sway to Latin rhythms.

Even Catherine, coming to complain, stops at the sight of the three girls dancing in that undersea light that filters through the blood-red blossoms of the bougainvillea, moving to the music in that strange room with dolls arranged in patterns and bright papier-mâché carnival masks (animals and devils) pinned over the bed.

Maribel moves awkwardly, feeling the rhythm but unable to express it. Delila, instinctively expert, wriggles and writhes in front of the mirror. Octavia, tossing her blond mop out of her eyes, copies the steps carefully, frowning, learning, resisting the seduction, holding off, holding off, until at last she can hold off no longer and dances as madly as Delila.

The records are Duncan's, left behind when she went off to boarding school. "Tropical Moon," "Little Blue Shoes," "Watermelon," "Rhumba River," "Kiss Me," "The Stars Are Falling," "Black Dove," "Scream," and "Carioca."

Their favorite is "More, More, More."

Today the room is empty and silent.

Where is Maribel?

As she is about to leave, Octavia hears her uncle's voice in the hall and shrinks down on the far side of the bed to hide.

The door opens and in a businesslike way he thrusts Maribel inside.

"Good girl, very good," says her uncle and shuts the door again. He does not see Octavia.

Maribel's face is red and sweaty. Her arms are folded like chicken wings on each side of her chest. Her yellow cotton blouse is buttoned wrong.

Octavia stands up and stares at her sister, frowning. A brand-new thought is struggling to be born.

24 Rain. It has been raining steadily for a week. Shoes in the closets are exuding green mildew and mushrooms are growing from the beams in the ceiling of the dining room. ("We should put them in the gravy," says Octavia's mother.)

Julian, still restless and cranky, is not to be found. Octavia wants to propose that they go swimming in the rain. You're going to get wet anyway, why worry about rain? But she can't find him and there is nothing to do but read and gossip with the maids. It begins to blow and thunder. Soledad is afraid of thunder. Octavia loves it. She would like to ride on it, as if it were a wild horse galloping across the sky. The house is very dark and the lights don't work. The generator has broken down.

Back upstairs, she observes that the door to Maribel's room is closed. Very slowly, very quietly, she opens it.

Julian is sitting on the bed with Maribel.

He is sitting very close to Maribel and a book is on his lap. He is pointing out pictures and his thigh is pressed tightly against hers.

Octavia steps back into the doorway.

The storm is noisy and Maribel whimpers in fright. "It's all right," Julian tells her. "It's only thunder, it won't hurt you. Look, I'm not afraid."

Octavia watches as his hand comes up and roams all over Maribel's chest, which Mother has wrapped in a special bodice ever since the time she showed herself in the dining room. It's a width of linen laced in back, and it mashes her flat.

"What's this?" says Julian, plucking at the cloth, trying to find a way inside. Octavia sees Maribel's little face first alarmed by thunder and now blankly remote, unable to catch up with these new events. Julian fumbles with her buttons, pulls the blouse off her shoulders, and ponders the linen cloth that is supposed to ensure her modesty. He loosens it, he lifts it up—and there they are. The breasts spring free. Julian catches his breath. Nervously he looks at the door (Octavia moves out of sight) and reaches out his hand. He touches one! She does not scream. She does not react at all. And now he touches the other one, he touches her nipple with his forefinger, he touches both of them, he cups his hands around them, he strokes them, he explores, he feels them everywhere, and still she does not mind. She is docile.

Julian has gone crazy. His teeth are chattering, his hands are shaking as he touches and kneads her breasts. He is trembling, gloating, he is a miser counting gold. He pushes her over on the bed so she is lying on her back and he is lying beside her, half on top of her, feeling her, touching her, exploring her, pulling at her breasts, looking at them, rubbing his face on them, hauling up her skirt. His hands go up her thighs, he is a runner gasping for air. He is all over Maribel. Balancing on an elbow, he humps up his behind and unzips his pants, he opens her legs and . . . oh, he is doing it, doing it to Maribel! His eyes roll up, his body curls, he twitches—

Is that all?

He slides off. He swears. "Oh, shit," he says. For a moment he lies still, face down in the bedclothes.

It is over.

Octavia fades out into the gallery. She goes to her room and stands at the window, looking down into the wet garden.

• • •

When she returns to her sister's room, Maribel is still lying on the bed with her skirt up, her underpants on. Julian has put back the binding on her chest, but it is all awry. One of her thighs (Octavia ascertains) is wet. Octavia touches the stickum, smells it on her fingers, rubs them together. It looks like spit. She tugs at the leg of her shorts, holding it open, and touches the stickum to herself.

Nothing happens.

"Get up," she orders Maribel, and sternly pulls her into the bathroom to clean her leg.

And the very next day, incredibly, Mother asks Octavia, "Have you ever seen anyone touch Maribel, touch her body where he shouldn't?"

"No," says Octavia, her face burning hot.

Her mother paces back and forth, breathing very fast, and looks around the room but does not see it. "What will we do, what will we do?" she mutters. Turning back to Octavia:

"Lenin? Did you ever see Lenin in Maribel's room? Did you ever see him touch her?"

"No." This is not true. Once when they were swimming at the lagoon, Lenin did indeed touch Maribel. Octavia saw him put his hand inside her bathing suit and squeeze her breast. Then his face turned purple and he dove into the water, swimming very fast.

But *everyone* touches Maribel, thinks Octavia, everyone who has a chance.

"What's the matter?" says Octavia, bluntly. "Is she pregnant or something?"

Her mother gasps. "Of course not. How can you think such a thing."

"Don Mauricio touched her," says Octavia. "In the schoolroom once. But listen, if Maribel is pregnant—I know who did it."

"Who?" says her mother.

"Tío Claude."

Her mother opens her mouth and cannot speak.

"That's who did it, I don't care. It was Tío Claude, your stupid brother, I don't care."

Shaking with anger, Catherine slaps Octavia's face, slaps hard. "I've heard enough from you," she cries. "You're a disgusting child! Go to your room."

Octavia, slapped, outraged, glares at her with eyes of hatred and defiance. Holding her cheek, she screams at her mother.

"I'll go, and I'll never speak to you again as long as I live!"

Maribel is pregnant all right. Soledad and Delila are in big trouble. Mother is in hysterics and Papi is shouting at Lenin.

The suspect is Lenin.

Papi is the one who is so certain it was Lenin.

Lenin is nineteen. He began as a houseboy, helping Domingo, and now he is the doctor's aide. Lenin learned doctoring fast; he treats wounds, sets bones. The islanders call him El Doctorcito. At night he is tutored by Don Mauricio, because there is no high school on the island. Papi himself pays Don Mauricio for Lenin's lessons. He has always said Lenin would make an excellent doctor. But how can Lenin go to medical school unless he has graduated from *secundaria* and *preparatoria?* Even if there were such schools on the island, how could he go when his mother depends on his wages?

Papi has done all these favors for the son of his blood enemy— and this (he shouts), this is the thanks he gets!

But it wasn't Lenin, Octavia would stake her life on that. It wasn't Lenin because he loves Papi too much. And it wasn't Julian either. It wasn't Julian because . . . because a person can't get pregnant *overnight.* A person has to miss her period. Octavia's not an ignoramus, she knows *that.*

Lenin weeps and denies it. Over and over he swears that he has not touched Maribel. He is engaged to someone else, the round-faced daughter of Don Carlos the postmaster. Her name is Isabel and they are to be married. Why would Lenin touch Maribel when he has a *novia* of his own?

Octavia knows the simple truth: it wasn't Lenin because it was Tío Claude. And Soledad and Delila are not to blame. Mother herself is to blame, because she wouldn't listen. Octavia told her and told her, and she would not hear.

But what about Octavia? Isn't she to blame?

Who was it put her sleeping sister into her own bed, knowing all the while that somebody would come and find her there, knowing very well (in retrospect, at least) what might happen.

Octavia is to blame.

"Felipe is the one to blame," her mother wails to Uncle Clo. "If he had listened, if he had done what I begged him to do, tie off her tubes . . ."

There's blame enough to go around. There's blame enough for everyone.

Lenin stands in front of the doctor with his fiancée and weeps. "I am innocent," he says. "I have always been loyal to you. You are my father. It is not mine, this child. My life is in ruins."

In private, Mother defends Lenin. "You can't be sure, Felipe. How can you be sure? . . . The problem can be quietly resolved, you know, without this fuss. You yourself can solve it easily."

"What are you saying?"

"An abortion, Felipe. It's so simple."

The doctor won't hear of it. "Never," he roars.

"Why not, in heaven's name?" she says, trying to calm him. "There is no danger. You can take every precaution. The boy is right, you're ruining his life, for what? Some whim? Revenge for those old crimes? What is it, Felipe? There is no reason a child should be born from this unfortunate situation. Come to your senses, please—! For everybody's sake. *Her* sake—"

Papi is adamant. His outrage cannot be contained. The boy must marry Maribel. The boy must give her child a father and a name.

"The child will be normal," he says. "It will be normal and she has a *right* to bear her child. She has a right to motherhood. Who knows what may happen? The hormones . . . pregnancy can bring remarkable changes . . ."

The house echoes with their quarrels.

Soledad and Delila huddle, shrivel in the kitchen. Uncle Clo goes to the mainland. Maribel's waist gets thicker.

Octavia finds the crisis in the household too repulsive for words. She is not speaking to Julian because of what she saw him do. She is not speaking to her mother.

Julian is thin and has dark smudges under his eyes. He is turning pale again and no longer goes out playing soccer with the boys. He doesn't understand why she won't speak to him.

"What's wrong?" he says. "What did I do?"

She loves him, but she can't forget what she saw that rainy afternoon. She has not told him yet that Maribel is pregnant.

The pain in her father's face is unbearable to her. Hanging on his chair, she tries to take the blame, to tell him she switched beds with Maribel. "I'm sorry, Papi," she begins.

He isn't listening.

"Papi—"

Absently he kisses her. His fine drooping mustache is soft as fur. He pats her head but he is grieving for Maribel. Never her whole life long has he touched Octavia without thinking of Maribel. Octavia has all the brains, but what use are they? Her brains give him pain. Always he moves away from her, always he pushes her off.

As if she had gone secretly into Maribel's room one night, drilled a tiny hole above her ear, and sucked her dry. Sucked Maribel's brains up for herself, as you suck eggs to make doves at Christmas.

Octavia doubles up with pains in her abdomen. She hasn't eaten for two days.

"I don't need to eat," she tells her mother. "I'm bigger than I ever was."

Catherine calls in Felipe. "Look how thin she is. Can it be her liver? She's quite yellow. Is it the appendix?"

Felipe, bearded, bruised, with terrible bad breath, comes to her bedside, looks at her eyes, her throat, her ears; he feels the glands in her throat, and reaches to palpate her stomach.

"No!" says Octavia, and twists away from him.

"What's this?" demands her father. "Are you a cloistered nun? Lie on your back."

She obeys, but she begins to cry.

"It's not the appendix," says Felipe. "I don't find a thing. When did you go to the bathroom last?"

"I don't know. Three days ago."

"I'll give you medicine for that," he says, and tells her mother to bring some water.

"What are you crying for?"

"I don't want any medicine, I don't want to go to the bathroom. Don't make me, Papi. Please."

He sits heavily, silently, beside her bed, perplexed. No fever, no symptoms that he can find of any kind except the knotted colon. Perhaps she's in a pout. He stands up.

"You'll feel better, and then you'll eat. We're going to have a wedding in this house—you'll want to go to that, I expect."

Staring out the window he heaves a sigh.

"A wedding—?"

"Your sister's wedding to Lenin."

"Did he say yes?"

"You may be sure that he'll say yes."

"Papi—"

"Yes?"

"It wasn't Lenin."

He gives a short sour laugh. "That's not for you to think about," he says.

"We switched beds. She slept in here and I slept in there."

"Well? You switched beds. What does that mean? You slept in her room. Do you mean—did anyone come in while you were there?"

"No."

"Well then?" He sighs again, almost a groan. "Did you ever see anyone go in?"

"No."

"Did you ever see her with anyone?"

"No."

"Did she ever go out alone, as far as you know? Did she run away?"

"No, Papi. But—"

"But what?"

"It wasn't Lenin."

"Well, it was," he says, harshly. "It was Lenin. We all wish it wasn't but it was. Have you anything else to tell me?"

"No," whispers Octavia.

"When your mother comes back, take these pills. And eat your breakfast. That's an order. I'll send up Soledad with fruit."

"Can a person tell she's pregnant before it shows?" Octavia asks Soledad when she comes in.

"That's nothing for you to be concerned about," says Soledad, setting down a tray. Mango and papaya slices and a glass of orange juice.

Octavia lies in bed poking her stomach, which is hard. "Do they get sick, or what?"

"You'll find out one day."

"Do they feel it move?"

Soledad shifts the foot of the bed slightly to achieve a true alignment east and west. She straightens the sheets, picks up the books that have fallen on the floor, straightens and dusts the table-top and dresser, collects the dirty clothes. While she works, she talks.

"Well," she says, "all this! Your papa throws the blame on me, but I never saw a thing. I watched her like a precious jewel. Ask anyone."

"Do you think it's Lenin?"

"So they say. It never happened while I was watching. I watched her like a little queen, a precious jewel. I never took my eyes off her except when I was cooking. Can you cook and watch at the same time? Yet the doctor throws the blame on me. If Lenin is not to be trusted, then he shouldn't be given the freedom of the house. Isn't that right? Besides, I'll tell you something. There are some women who can get pregnant without any man at all! Yes, it's true. Perhaps your sister is one of these. If you were to ask me, I would say so. The most famous one was the Mother of God herself, *la Santa Madre,* but I have heard of others. Not every hen needs a rooster to lay her egg, *verdad?* Lenin swears it was not he, and to tell the truth, I believe him."

"I do too."

"Well, if that is the case, a very unusual thing is happening, something very strange and marvelous. Perhaps we are fortunate. Right here in this house, right here on Isla Caracol, perhaps we have a virgin birth! Think of it, a saint, a virgin, giving birth! Your father throws the blame on me. 'You didn't watch her,' he says. But I watched her. If there is a man, he came in with the smoke! With the raindrops! Lenin—what a joke. He has his own sweetheart.

Poor girl, she is crying her eyes out. Maybe she's pregnant, I don't know, her mother is furious. Her mother will sue Lenin, she wants a new house. Well, I guess your father will give it to her, no?"

She stops working and holds up her finger. "Everything plays a part," she says. "In this life everything fits together like the thatch in a roof, like the pattern in a blanket. There is nothing left over, nothing. And nothing in the world is unimportant. You are important, because you are her sister. And I, because I take care of her, and Lenin's sweetheart, because she makes a sacrifice, *verdad?* Lenin, also, he's like San José, *verdad?"*

She talks and talks, she can't stop talking. She has never talked so much before.

"I think I'm pregnant too," says Octavia in desperation. "I know I am."

Soledad bursts out laughing, looks at her, and laughs again. "If you're pregnant, I can fly to the moon," she says. "Is *that* what's the matter with you? Pregnant! You're pregnant in the head! What's this?" There on the bedsheet is a stain of blood.

"You can be pregnant and still bleed," says Octavia. "You don't know everything."

"Get up," says Soledad. "Take your medicine. Behave yourself."

Octavia gets up. "I'm feeling better anyway," she says.

Every day now she goes into her uncle's room to search for the photographs, but they are well hidden and she does not dare stay very long. The windows and the shutters are closed. It is hot and dark and scary. Someone who has killed a cat might kill a girl. He is supposed to be away, but she knows how easily he can turn up again. At last, fumbling on the shelf in the wardrobe, reaching behind the packages stored there, she finds something: the steel box. But it is locked, and now she must begin again, begin all over again, going through everything, his luggage, his pockets, his bureau drawers, looking for a key to fit the box.

• • •

Sodden and miserable, Lenin has agreed to marry Maribel and everything has changed. The sun has come out. Mother may be steaming inside, but she manages to smile and hold her tongue. Felipe in his relief becomes a different man. Cheerful, even jovial, he embraces Lenin and shakes his hand. "Now you will be my son in truth," he says with emotion, and embraces him again. "You can live here, and everything will be the same!" His eyes are wet. He is imagining great happiness for Maribel.

"Let them be married right away," he proclaims.

"There is no rush, Felipe," says Mother, mildly. "Wait for Clo to return. It's time for your trip to the other islands. Maribel will keep."

Octavia stares at her mother. Has she capitulated then, so easily? Octavia does not believe it. Her mother's eyes are veiled, preoccupied.

Inside the bottom drawer, in a small leather box with cuff links and a medal and three false teeth in a row with a gold loop at each end, Octavia finds a bunch of keys on a tiny chain. She tries them one by one, the little ones, and finds the key that fits.

Yes. There inside, tucked away beneath two letters from Aunt Jenny and some other papers, are the photos, the ones she has been searching for, a stack of them, bound with rubber bands. She leaves the papers and drops the photos in her pocket.

She is terrified, a thief. To cover her tracks she puts the box back on the shelf exactly as she found it.

At the door she pauses. She is puzzled by those letters, the letters from Aunt Jenny. It strikes her that they were addressed to her mother, not to Uncle Clo. What are they doing in her uncle's strongbox? She hears her mother saying, "Jenny isn't writing me these days. I haven't heard from her in months."

Octavia turns back. Hastily she takes down the box again, unlocks it, removes one of the letters. It has been opened—not torn open in the impatient hungry way of her mother—but neatly slit at the top by something sharp, the way her uncle opens mail. She has seen him do it, using a knife.

She replaces the box, keeping the letter, and tiptoes out, closing the door carefully behind her. If caught, she will be a criminal.

But nobody catches her, and retreating to her room she drops the photos in her sea chest and puts the letter in her pocket. She does not feel triumphant, she feels sick. Her stomach and her heart are jumping. Her room is contaminated.

To breathe again she runs up the ladder-steps that lead to the roof. From the wide lonely roof she can see everything—town, church, jungle, sweep of sky, white beach like a crust, like a fingernail. For once there is no wind. The sea, though wrinkled, seems to have stiffened into immobility, its tidal movements stilled, even its waves halted in mid-surge as though caught in a photograph, or seen from a great height, from outer space.

As she opens the letter, Uncle Clo's sea plane with its two big feet roars overhead, approaching from the south. Guiltily she springs up, hiding the letter against her chest, and watches the plane settle lower and lower, circle and disappear behind the mangroves to touch down on the tidal river. He is returning from the diving station, or the camp of the irregulars, or wherever it is he goes. She urges the evil-air to make him crash, and squats down again, hands shaking.

Aunt Jenny's writing is impossible, illegible. What does it say? "Dear Catherine . . . I am waiting . . ." No, "I am *writing* . . ." Now and then a phrase jumps out amidst the ripples and lumps. "I am writing because I must warm you . . ." No, *"warn you."* Warn you of what? Octavia cannot make it out.

But on the second page quite clearly Octavia reads "this family tragedy" and "apparently for years" and then "forgive my silence—

I couldn't bear to . . ." Bear to what? To bind your hand—? To *break* your hand—? To break, to break your . . .

Down below her mother is calling. "Octavia!" She has been out all day, in the village, but now she's home, acting as if there were no problems anywhere, busy preparing for her long-delayed picnic excursion by boat to the south end of the island, to visit the ruins of the old hacienda. Papi is away. The picnic is for Uncle Clo and Julian. Never mind Lenin. Never mind poor Maribel.

"Octavia, are you up there?" calls her mother up the ladder-steps. "Come down, I need your help."

Octavia does not answer. She puts the letter in her pocket and looks out at the horizon line. She has understood enough to know the picnic will not take place. The picnic will be canceled. Because tonight, after supper, while her mother and Uncle Clo are still in the dining room, she will spread the photos and the letter on her mother's bed where she cannot possibly avoid them or their meaning.

I should have told you long ago, Aunt Jenny wrote. *I couldn't bear to break your heart.*

25

When Cortez landed in the new world (Don Mauricio has told Octavia), the Indians literally *could not see* the ships or the horses. They saw *something,* but not ships or horses. They saw . . . enormous birds, floating islands, clouds, gigantic dogs, four-legged men. What was actually there—ships and horses—had to be forced into known shapes before their eyes could see.

And when Octavia shows her mother the pack of snapshots she has found hidden away in Uncle Claude's room, in the strongbox on his wardrobe shelf, her mother is as blind as the Indians. She sees something, all right, she sees photographs, but not *those* photographs.

Octavia has laid them out on her mother's bed, you see, without a word, unable to come right out and admit that she's been snooping in her uncle's room. (If her mother hangs up on *that,* they'll never get beyond it.) Octavia hopes to catch her unawares, to watch her reaction. She spreads the photographs in rows across her mother's bed and waits outside the door.

At last her mother comes, as she always does after supper, to straighten her hair and examine her face in the mirror. She walks inside, sees what is on her bed, and stops.

"What's this?" she says.

In mild surprise, she bends over to look.

There are the photos neatly spread in front of her. Her eyes fall on them, and—nothing. Blank. She glances at them idly, one after another; absently she picks them up and sets them on the bureau all without a word. She doesn't see them. She can't see them. In fact, even Octavia couldn't see one of them. What was it? A girl's face in a tube? looking out of a receptacle? a bucket? looking calmly up through all that curly hair, and something wrong with her? Catherine's eyes brush over it and move along.

Octavia cannot believe her mother's indifference. She wants to shout and protest. Shaking in the doorway, she manages to say: "They belong to Uncle Clo."

Her mother fingers them again, looks without looking. She lingers for a moment on the one that seems to be a girl in a barrel and then she sets them all aside as if she is bored, and says, "Uh-huh."

That's all. "Uh-huh."

What does she think she has seen? Does she think an artist has posed those girls in order to paint them? Does she think they are illustrations for a book on depravities in far-off lands?

To Catherine's eyes the "models" are certainly not children—children don't engage in acts like these. What she sees are strangely shaped adults. And that man, that unclothed man who looks a bit like Clo, is certainly not Clo, not her brother Clo; he is someone else, lord knows who, she has no idea, nor does she care to find out.

Because at that very moment jovial Uncle Clo is waiting for her downstairs, smoking one of Felipe's cigars, sipping *aguardiente*. There are worlds that cannot coexist.

She shakes a pill from a bottle into the palm of her hand and swallows it without water. She looks at herself in the mirror of her dressing table, bending her knees, sinking down a bit in order to see herself without sitting down. She wipes a smut off her cheek and smooths her hair. She grimaces to check her teeth. She does not question or reproach Octavia. Instead she sighs, and vaguely says, "Octavia, did you check your sister?"

"Yes," Octavia says in a tight voice.

"Is she asleep?"

"Yes."

And nothing more. She goes downstairs, goes back to Uncle Clo.

Octavia stands a minute. She closes her eyes and leans her head against the door. Then, leaving the letter behind, she gathers up the photographs (what else is there to do?) and puts them back where she found them. Bitterly, she slips into her uncle's room and restores them to the small locked box on the wardrobe shelf.

What Uncle Clo has done is evidently something grown-ups overlook. And her own crimes—snooping, stealing other people's private things—may well be worse than any act of his.

She goes back to her room and stares at the wall. She thinks of her cat Pablito and begins to cry, remembering how he purred on her shoulder, remembering the weight of him, and how she used to hold him to the mirror to admire him twice.

The next morning Catherine has a headache and complains of lack of sleep. Her face is grim and pale and she moves as in a trance. But the picnic is not canceled.

It does not occur to Octavia that her mother may be in transition, trying to understand, trying to take in what she has seen.

On the forty-five-foot fishing boat *Amor Fatal,* the family sets out for the *cocal,* the coconut plantation on the south end of the island, where the old hacienda lies in ruins, half buried in sand. Catherine, Tío Claude, Julian, and Octavia are the picnickers. Maribel does not come. Papi is on his monthly trip to the other islands. Lenin, in shock, is attending to the patients in the *clínica.*

The sky is blue, the wind is light, it is a perfect day. However, once aboard, nobody talks to anybody. Each one might as well be all alone. Uncle Clo is frowning and moody, Octavia, bitter and abandoned, and Catherine is nursing her headache; she has brought a book along and tries to read, but her eyes are too painful. She shields them with her hand.

Octavia makes a discovery. In her mother's book, marking her place, is the letter from Aunt Jenny. What does that mean? Is something going to happen?

Nothing happens. Everything is peaceful.

Julian throws chunks of bread in the air for the seagulls that come crowding around from everywhere, fighting and making a great racket, catching bread in the air. He looks at Octavia. She turns her head away and puts her nose in the air, but in her heart she has already relented. She is still angry at what he did to Maribel, but she is feeling all alone in the world and needs a friend. When they arrive at the *cocal,* she will graciously consent to speak to him. They will make up and she will show him the ruins of the old hacienda.

Manuel the deckhand dives with sack and spear and scuba tank through crystal water to gather the lobsters they will eat for lunch. The water is so clear it is like air. They are hanging in air looking over the side at the swimming form of Manuel, forty feet below.

After a two-hour trip they splash ashore onto a beach littered with coconut husks and brown fronds. Catherine walks sedately across the sand. Her face is masklike. She does not speak to Uncle Clo. She is not excited by this picnic after all. Octavia keeps an eye on her.

They are greeted by the *cocalero,* Don Luis, who has been told to expect them and prepare the cooking fire. He is a squat brown man in his fifties who used to gather chicle on the mainland, and cut mahogany in Chetumal and Belize. Running diagonally across his bare chest is an appalling scar some twenty inches long. A *chiclero* cannot escape the machete, it would seem. He was lucky to survive. *Chicleros* kill each other every day, says Don Luis. It's just the way *chicleros* are. Deep in the rain forests of the mainland, rival gangs raid each other's camps, steal the chicle, and kill each other. Killing is for profit, sport, and recreation. Even on Saturday night, when *chicleros* dance and get drunk, bodies pile up outside the door.

Don Luis reports that a *chiclero* was washed up on this very beach last month with thirty dagger wounds in his body. He was still alive, swept here from the mainland, twelve miles across the treacherous channel, bleeding from thirty holes.

"He took six hours to die," Don Luis says. "Ai, *chicleros.* They are tough." He himself quit the chicle business "for personal reasons." He spits in the sand.

Listening to Don Luis, Octavia and Julian relax and begin talking to each other again. Uncle Clo, wearing a loose blue shirt and khaki shorts, looks out to sea. He seems preoccupied. Catherine arranges dishes on the picnic table. Her face is stiff but there are no signs of a quarrel. Nothing has changed. Octavia feels sick.

Sudden excitement down the beach. Men's voices shouting for Don Luis, and he goes running. Manuel has spotted a sea turtle! This is the season when the huge clumsy beasts come up on the beaches to lay their eggs.

Julian and Octavia run too. Tío Claude is following them. Catherine says, "No, thanks."

The first thing they see are the deep tracks from the sea, two parallel furrows more than three feet apart. Then they spot the turtle. What a giant! She has already started to burrow into the sand so that only her head and the dome of her shell are showing. As they come up, she is at bay, hissing and shaking her great head, trying to frighten off the men who surround her.

She is aware now of her terrible mistake, coming onto the beach by daylight. The time for turtles to lay their eggs is dawn or brightest moonlight.

The men move behind her, careful of the jaws. "If a turtle gets you in her beak, good-bye leg," says Don Luis cheerfully. They are also wary of the flippers. The hind flippers are used to bury eggs but can throw sand in the eyes of an enemy.

Quickly they grab her before she can free her flippers. They hoist up her rear and she falls forward on her neck. The hind flippers, now free, are beating against the men, but in one big thrust they heave her over onto her back. She is helpless now, hissing and rubbing her neck in the sand, beating the air with her flippers, waving her flippers the way a baby on its back will wave its arms and legs. She weighs a hundred and eighty kilos, says Don Luis. All four men were needed to turn her over—Manuel and the captain, Don Luis and Tío Claude. They stand around her now and laugh.

Octavia knows the futility of protest.

"Vamonos," says Don Luis. "We have our lunch."

"No, turn her back again," says Octavia. "So she can lay her eggs."

They laugh, and leave the turtle struggling.

Lunch is lobsters split and broiled over a fire of coconut husks. The drink is coconut milk. Don Luis selects the coconuts carefully. Choosing your coconut is an art, he explains. Each tree has a different taste according to its proximity to the sea. Each nut has a different taste according to its age. Fallen, brown nuts are too salty. Small green ones are jelly-like and make some people sick. Best are the large green ones that are beginning to turn brown.

He picks a nut and with two strokes of his machete the ends of the nut are cut off. One more flip and a small hole is chopped into the hard shell for drinking.

Catherine has brought potato salad, fruit, pie, and wine. She helps the plates and silently, dutifully, sits down to eat. Octavia is mildly gratified. At least her mother is behaving with a proper dignity. At least she isn't capering around, gushing over Tío Claude, showing him everything, the way she usually does.

And later, over the pecan pie, Octavia catches her mother staring at Uncle Clo in a strange way. She is staring at him as he eats his pie, staring sadly but intently, absorbed, with her mouth slightly open, the way a person looks at a movie.

But all the same, nothing happens. Octavia grinds her teeth.

After lunch, Octavia and Julian explore the ruins. Parts of the old wall are still standing, and Don Luis has stretched a sail and slung a hammock there to make his house.

"My grandmother died right here," she tells Julian and stamps her foot in the sand.

Her father had shown her the very spot when she was little. He was not angry at the people who did it. He said they were oppressed and confused, and it was not their fault. Something drove them. "Would they have killed you too, if you'd been there?" asked Octavia. "Perhaps," he said. "In times of trouble, mistakes are made." "But if you'd been killed, none of us would ever have been born." "That's right," her father said. She clung to his hand and did not care to look at the old hacienda. Ruined walls. Flowers. Bees. Silence. The sea.

Octavia's other grandparents lived a different life in Washington, D.C., a peaceful placid life, said Mother. Nobody killing anyone. But Father challenged her. He said in Washington, D.C., many people were black and oppressed, the descendants of slaves. He said her parents were exploiters like his own, and one day the blacks would rise up like the islanders and bring a revolution. He said her father was a military man whose life was dedicated to oppression, and there was not a pin's worth of difference between her father and his father, except that his father was more open about it.

"It's not like that at all," protested Catherine.

• • •

To be important in Julian's eyes, Octavia builds the drama, and is carried away herself. "It was like the movies. I mean they dragged her out of the house by her hair, and cut her head off, and just joked and laughed. Right here. It really happened."

Julian stares at the spot, and after a while, he says, "How do you know they joked and laughed?"

"Everybody knows," she says. "And then they raped her."

"With her head cut off?"

Octavia nods.

"That really happened?"

"Yeah. Right here."

"If my father had been here, he'd have been killed too, and I would never have existed," says Octavia.

In a mood of pleasant horror they walk in privacy through the rows of coconut palms. They are wearing their bathing suits. They walk together side by side without talking. She is glad they are friends again, but can't forget what happened in Maribel's room.

"I saw you," she tells him. "The day of the thunderstorm, I saw you with Maribel. I saw everything, I saw it all. I know what you did."

He turns so pale she thinks he may faint or even die. He breathes out loud and leans against the trunk of a coco palm with his head down on his chest.

"I haven't told anyone," she quickly says, to relieve him. "I'm not going to tell. Nobody knows but me."

Julian has trouble speaking. Stammering, he says Maribel will not have a baby because he didn't—he didn't do anything inside of her, he did it outside. He says fooling around with Maribel was a rotten awful thing, the worst thing he has ever done in all his life. He says he doesn't know why he did it, he is a rat, and he can't sleep at night. He hates himself. He is ashamed. He says his uncle Felipe would kill him if he knew, and he would be right to kill him, because he deserves to die. He says he will never do it again, he swears he never will, he will never touch her, he takes his oath.

Octavia has news for him.

"She's pregnant already," she says. "Maribel is pregnant. Didn't you know that?"

He looks at her with tragic eyes. "You're only saying that. You're kidding me."

"I am not," says Octavia.

And now sweat stands out on his forehead. He looks green. "It can't be," he says. "I only did it once. I didn't go inside, I swear. I swear! Look," he says desperately, "her underpants were on! She can't be—what you said."

"Didn't you hear them fighting, my mother and father? They think it was Lenin. They're going to make him marry her."

"Oh, my god," says Julian. He sits down. "Oh, god."

She takes pity on him at last, and says, "Maybe it wasn't you." He looks up at her.

"You only did it that one time? You swear?"

"I swear. Octavia, I swear."

"Well, she's been pregnant for two months, they say. So if you're telling the truth, it couldn't be you. It was somebody else."

"It wasn't me, it wasn't me. I swear it wasn't me."

He goes on and on about what a rat he is, and when he can't think of anything else bad to say about himself, he looks at her mournfully and shakes his head.

"The funny part is that you're the one I really like," he says.

"What?"

"You," he says. "You're the one I like. I really like you. A lot. I don't know why I did it. I did it because I didn't think . . . you'd ever like me . . . the same way."

Does she dare believe this? Did he really say it? She is confused, lapped in white flames that don't burn.

"And now you hate me," he says. "No wonder you hate me. I don't blame you. I've wrecked everything."

"I don't hate you." (The truth is that in one cool, objective part of herself, she found what he did to Maribel very interesting.)

"You're too young," he laments. "That's the trouble. You're still a child."

"I'm not," she says. "I'm not a child."

"That's what you *say*. But you'd never let me do anything, you're too young."

"I'm not too young."

"Would you let me?"

Now that the weather has broken, the sun is shining in a damp blue sky, the island is drying out and the buzzards are soaring again, high up on the currents of air. Octavia can't answer.

"I don't know," she says.

"Would you?"

She wants to say, "Do I have to?"

"Would you?"

"No."

"There," he says. "You see?"

"I'm not too young! I just don't feel like it. I could if I wanted to. Sometime I might."

"Boys are different from girls," he says. "A boy really needs it. He *has* to, it's like a pain. You know? If he can't get it from somebody he really likes, he has to, you know, go someplace else. Girls are different, girls don't need it, not like boys."

"I don't know," she says. (She thinks of her cat, crying for it, moaning in the street. Do Julian and his father go crying in the street? Are girls like that? Did Elizabeth Jane go crying in the street?)

"We could never get married," Julian says, "because we're first cousins. If we got married, then when you had a baby it could be a monster."

"I'm never going to have a baby anyway," she says. "I hate babies."

"When you're grown up you won't say that."

Already he is acting superior again. A minute ago he was sui-
cidal. Amazing how quickly he has recovered.

"You're afraid to have a baby," he says. "Like I'm afraid to go to
war."

"I'm not," she says.

"Well then, I'm not either."

They continue their walk through the rows of coco palms.

Julian now says in a certain voice, a tight and private voice that
she has come to recognize, "Hey, let's roll down our suits."

"No," she says. "What for?"

"Roll yours way down like mine."

"No."

"Why not?"

"I don't feel like it."

"We could be *novios*. I'd like us to be *novios.*"

He has said *novios!* He has come right out and said it.

Octavia, charged with adrenaline, turns away and fiddles with
her stringy salty hair. Octavia and Julian, *novios.* If they are *novios,*
he will stay with her and never go off with the boys. *Novios!* Does
that mean he gets to look at her?

"Come on," he says. "Roll down your suit. Like mine."

He has folded down his trunks until they are just a rope around
his groin. In back you can see the cleft of his behind. "Come on,"
he says in that special little throaty voice. "I won't do anything."

"I can't," she says.

"Why not?"

"I don't know why, I just can't."

"Are you having your period?"

Octavia is staggered. It is the most important conversation she
has ever had.

"I won't do anything, I swear. Put your stomach against mine."

And slowly she comes closer, and their stomachs touch. She can
hardly breathe.

"Roll down your suit."

She pulls the straps off the shoulders, and then stops.

"I can't."

"Yes, you can. If you do, it means we're *novios.*"

She hates it and she wants it, she is paralyzed, she is a hypnotized monkey in the jaws of a lizard. She loves him, she wants him for her own, and this is what she must do. She has to do it. Life demands that she do it. Move forward, dare! In anguish she closes her eyes and drops the suit to her waist. It is like exposing herself to the executioner's knife. She waits for death. Nothing happens. She opens her eyes. He is looking at her with his father's face.

"I don't like it," she cries, and pulls the suit up. She has demeaned herself! Her spirit-torso has become disgusting flesh and blood. She will never do it again. He is her enemy.

"Wait, don't go," cries Julian, "don't go away. Let's stay here for a while."

But she stamps off and he comes running after.

"Where are you going?"

She won't answer him.

"Are you going to see the turtle?"

She strides along ahead of him.

"All right," he says. "Then I'll come too."

Circling around the grown-ups, who are lying on blankets in the tossing palm-frond shade, apparently asleep, they find the turtle still flapping on her back. For all her efforts, the heavy shell has only sunk down deeper in the sand. Overhead in the blue sky a few *zopilotes* are attracted by the struggle and float in circles.

Octavia and Julian stand and look at her.

"I'm going to turn her over," says Octavia at last. "She wants to lay her eggs."

"You can't turn her, she's too heavy."

"We can dig a trench. One side of her slides down into a trench, and then we shove her over."

But the sand falls back into their trench, they can't get deep enough, they need shovels. The churning flippers of the turtle are a constant danger.

As they are digging there like dogs, Don Luis turns up with his machete in his hand and a sack over his shoulder. He laughs at them. Octavia gets an ominous feeling about the machete.

"Don't hurt her," she says. "Let her lay her eggs. Why won't you let her lay her eggs?"

"You watch me now," says Don Luis, "and you'll see something interesting."

With his machete, he cuts the soft undershell of the turtle, loosens its fastenings, and raises it like a lid. He cuts into the body of the turtle. She is still alive. He slashes at the heart and the flippers slow down, stop and start and stop again. The beak is open, mucus in gooey strings is coming from her eyes. The turtle is dying.

Octavia stands close to Julian, then moves away.

Now the turtle is motionless, lying on her back with her stomach open and exposed. The shell is a bowl, a slimy bowl, full of blood and yellow oil. A horrible smell is coming from her. *Zopilotes* are landing on the beach.

Don Luis sticks his arm into the mess, up to the elbow in blood and liquid fat. He grins at them, searching around for the eggs. One by one he pulls them out, ten, twenty, thirty eggs, on and on, so many eggs, one hundred and forty eggs.

Next he reaches in and finds a bag, the ovary skin, with still more eggs, tiny eggs, the ones she would have laid next time. They have no skins and are only yellow pellets.

Don Luis pats at his stomach with a bloody dripping hand. "Good to eat," he says, waving the bag of tiny eggs. "Hang them in the sun. *Muy rico!*" He puts the little eggs on top of the big ones, and pulls some empty bottles from his sack that he has dropped on the sand.

He fills eight bottles with putrid orange turtle fat.

"Very good, a cure for colds," he says. "You rub it on your nose and chest."

• • •

It is over. Don Luis is finished, for now. Later he will cut the meat into strips and dry it in the sun. The shell and the skull he will leave for the *zopilotes* to clean up. He kicks off his sandals and walks into the sea to clean himself.

Octavia goes off in the other direction, into the dark orderly grove of palms. She feels herself trembling violently. Even her teeth are out of control, chattering. Julian follows her.

"Are you okay?"

"Go away," she screams. "Leave me alone."

She goes off alone as far as she can, and then crouches down on her hands and knees to cry out in a high thin voice she doesn't recognize. Nothing is right. Nothing will ever be right again.

On the way home, even with Aunt Jenny's letter open in her hand, Catherine is still on excellent terms with her brother. The sea is smooth, like pale blue satin. Octavia, morose and silent, watches Julian fool around. He climbs over the railing of the *Amor Fatal* and hangs on outside.

"Climb over," he says.

"No."

"You're scared."

Wearily, obeying her childish self, she climbs over. They both stand outside the rail, holding on. Julian, showing off, lets go the rail and catches it, lets go and catches it. And now Octavia, quick as a snake—without warning, without intention or knowledge of what she is about to do (but timing it carefully all the same)—puts one foot against his side and shoves with all her strength. She hates him. He is to blame for the turtle. He is to blame for Maribel. All men, all boys, they are to blame.

His hands tear loose, and he goes down splash into the sea. He is under water a long time, but at last his head bobs up and he looks at her and lifts his arm. He has swallowed water and can't speak. The boat churns on. No one is looking, no one is aware of what has happened, even though he gasped on the way down, and the splash was plainly audible.

The boat moves on, he falls astern. Still standing there outside the rail, remote and unconcerned, Octavia watches him.

She waits and waits, in a dream. Five minutes go by before she climbs back over the rail and tells the captain. Julian is overboard! Quickly he swings the boat around in a great arc and advances the throttle. They go speeding back to look for him.

"What is it, what is it?" say the grown-ups, opening their eyes, feeling the motion of the boat.

Only five minutes, but they have trouble finding him. Already the tide and the currents have carried him farther out. They have a hard time spotting his little brown head like a coconut in the great wide sea.

They pull up beside him and fish him out. He has swallowed water and is coughing. He is worried about his sneakers. He has lost his sneakers.

On deck he bends over, coughing and dripping. The grown-ups make a fuss. He is *persona non grata.* Uncle Claude shakes him, cuffs him, chews him out. Catherine says he has frightened everyone to death.

Octavia waits for him to tell on her, but he does not.

Gasping, dripping on the deck, he says, "I just fell, that's all. My hands let go."

His eyes flick past Octavia. She stands at a little distance, and does not speak. He could have drowned. A shark could have eaten him. Her mother's binoculars are in her hand and she looks through the wrong end. She looks out to sea, she looks at the wake, at the birds. Everything is very tiny. What has she done?

She is so dazed by her own violent act that she almost misses the quarrel when it begins. Mother and Uncle Clo, in whispers, at the rail. She hears him say, "Don't do it, Catherine. At least hold up a while." And Catherine, her nostrils flaring like Duncan's, says, "You sicken me."

Bewildered Octavia hardly takes it in. Her beloved cousin, soaking wet, missing his sneakers, is curled up in the bow—lonely, out of reach, perhaps forever. He could have died. He could have had a cramp . . . he will never forgive her. He is angry, he is deeply hurt.

"I was sick all night," says her mother bitterly to Uncle Clo. "Vomiting."

Octavia now lifts her head.

Uncle Clo is sarcastic, rubbing his neck. "Sorry about that," he says. "The fact that *I've* been sick my whole life through hardly matters, does it."

Her mother makes a sound of disgust.

For once he looks directly in her eyes. "It's not a choice, you know," he says. "I've never had a choice."

She waves her hand as if to wipe him away. "Nonsense," she says. "You married. You had a wife."

He is silent for a while and then says, "Yes, I married."

"You have a son."

"Correction," says Uncle Clo. "She had a son."

That makes Catherine look up sharply, in surprise.

He shrugs.

What are they talking about? It is Octavia's turn to be like the Indians who couldn't see the Spanish ships.

"I've said I'll make it right," says Uncle Clo. "I'm perfectly willing. Good God, I *want* to make it right."

Her mother grimaces like Duncan and blots the perspiration from her forehead and her lip.

"It's done throughout the world," he says. "Done every day . . . a priest who doesn't know the family . . . It's not illegal. Uncle and niece—it's commonplace."

"Hideous," she says. "Unbelievable."

"I have a right to some fulfillment in my life."

She turns on him. "Fulfillment! Is this your fulfillment? To use my daughter as—"

She sees Octavia listening and lowers her voice. For a time she hushes him every time he speaks. But little by little they forget, and Octavia catches more of it.

He is saying again, "Don't do it, Catherine."

Do what? thinks Octavia. What is her mother going to do?

"In my book, it's murder," he says.

Are they going to murder Maribel?

Her mother throws back her head laughing, but her face flushes red with anger. "Oh wonderful," she says. "Your exquisite moral sense. I understand. Of course we mustn't offend you."

Uncle Clo is more vehement than Octavia has ever seen him. "Why won't you listen?" he says. "I'll take her off your hands. Be honest, Catherine, once in your life. You're dying to be rid of her."

Ahead of the boat brown pelicans plunge in the sea, gulping fish. An escort of seagulls flaps and divebombs the pelicans, hoping to steal their catch.

"That's a vicious lie."

The argument goes on and on. The wind is picking up.

"I can't take it in," she says. "My brother, my own brother. Did I deserve this, Clo?"

"Possibly," he says.

Her mouth comes open.

"If you'll look back, I think you'll recognize your contribution," he says.

"My contribution—"

"Even Jenny in her letter speaks of it. Or did you skip that part?" He snatches the letter from her hand and reads. " 'More provocative than you realized, perhaps, in your innocence . . .' " He laughs, crumples the letter and tosses it overboard. "Your innocence."

"I see," she says at last. "The blame is mine. Of course. You are a marvel, Clo."

Two dolphins chasing the boat break water not twenty feet away but her mother and her uncle take no notice.

He changes his tone. "Catherine, listen to me. It's plain to see that you're not happy here. You belong in the States. I can finance your trip. I can carry you a year or two until you settle in. You and Octavia. How's that?"

Catherine looks at the sky, at the sea, and tears roll down her face. "Rescue," she says in a choked voice. "Rescue." She closes her eyes and moves away from him, turning her back. With her handkerchief she blots the tears as they come out.

"Fairytale wisdom, Clo," she says huskily. "Never make a wish —it might come true. I can't talk any more. Not with the children here."

The rest of the trip Catherine sits in the bow not far from Julian, her body bent over, her arms wrapped around her straw bag as if it were a precious child. She doesn't say another word until late afternoon as the *Amor Fatal* approaches the pier. The sun is setting against the angular blue-black clouds that appear on the horizon in late afternoon. To Octavia these grotesque misshapen clouds are dwarfs and goblins creeping up and posing all along the wide horizon line.

By now her mother seems perfectly calm. She sits beside her brother and even puts her hand on his arm.

"I was remembering the boy we saw through the ice," she says. "Remember, Clo? We all went skating on the canal, and I was trying to teach you—because you were never any good at skating—and the bigger children were ahead of us and we heard them screaming, do you remember? We saw them all gathered round, and we kept skating, and the ice was so black and transparent you could see right through it, you could see dead leaves and twigs floating by, and we saw that boy, right beneath our feet. We saw him under the ice, and his hair was floating back and forth and his eyes were open, and he put his hand—his fingertips—against the ice, right where we stood, he put his fingertips against the ice and looked at us and then he sank away."

Uncle Clo clears his throat.

"I remember very well," he says. "His name was Blake McCall. He lived two blocks from us."

They sit together quietly.

"The last time I saw you, in Washington," she says, "was in Union Station. You and Papa were on the train, and the train was pulling out, and I was running on the platform, beside your window, trying to keep up, and you were inside and you put your fingers on the glass. Like that boy. I remember so clearly. You looked at me and put your fingertips against the glass. Five little pale green circles on the glass."

Uncle Clo makes no comment. The boat pulls in at the pier and ties up. Everyone is tired and disheveled. They gather up their clothes and picnic things.

"One final question, Clo," her mother says. Her smile is crooked but her voice is calm enough. She is using the false bright tone she uses for the benefit of guests. "Just idle curiosity," she says. "I get the impression that you're *glad* Maribel is pregnant. Tell me, is that true?"

He looks down at his hands and chuckles. "Dear sister, I do feel a certain modest pride," he says. "I never thought it could happen. That's why I don't propose to give her up."

He takes her elbow and guides her to the landing plank. "Here," he says politely, "you're carrying too much. Let me have that basket. Julian—!" he calls. "Come help your aunt."

26 If ever I return to Caracol, I'll go by sea. Air travel is destructive, it forecloses memory, it tampers with the damp soft inner clocks of time. It would never do for such a trip, a trip back, to find old walls old flowers old dolls old stains of blood, old stones and trees, to find again the stunted pyramids and timeless tide pools in the coral rock warm as a womb for all the tiny mysteries that grow in them, and the blighted banana trees that cannot flourish in the sad poisoned ground, ruins, moons, seas, and stars (have I ever seen such stars?), dark faces and the odd guttural glottal-stopped tongue I never learned to speak, the dying and unwritten Mayan of the islanders.

Only one Mayan phrase has stayed with me. I don't know how to spell it, but it sounds like *Bish u bel akeek*. My father said it. Anguished, raging, he threw it in my face.

It was very late, the middle of the night, the starlit night after the picnic. Father had been away on Isla Maria but he came home unexpectedly, two days early, hitching a ride on a fishing boat. Perhaps he was suddenly suspicious, haunted by my mother's veiled, blank smile as she deferred to his wishes that Lenin and Maribel be married and that the child be born.

There was a fiesta in town that night, with fireworks and music and drinking. The house was dark when my father returned, and he went immediately to my sister's room.

It was empty. The bedsheets were drenched with blood.

• • •

He ran calling for my mother, calling for Soledad, but no one answered. He raced through the house to find someone, anyone. In the *sala* he switched on the light and called again, for Catherine, for Maribel, but neither one was there.

I was the one he found, sitting alone on the couch.

I remember his face in the sudden light. I remember what he said. He spoke Mayan, that's how distraught he was. He took me by the shoulders and put his twisted face right into mine. *"Bish u bel akeek?"* he said, and shook me. I knew what it meant.

Where is your sister? was what it meant.

"Bish u bel akeek?" he roared at me, his face discolored and his eyes frantic. He never spoke in Mayan, and I knew only a few words, but I understood him.

"I don't know," I said.

"Why don't you know?" he shouted. I stood in front of him with my mouth open. Was I her keeper? Evidently he thought so, and instantly I thought so too. I *was* her keeper, and I had failed.

Quickly he scanned the *sala* and the schoolroom beyond and went out. I sat there, blinking, feeling nothing.

Later I went to find him, because it came to me that I did know where she was. I knew with certainty, and I could lead him to her. But he had gone, and Mother had gone, everybody had gone into town, toward the church, everyone looking for her among the drunken crowds at the fireworks, attracted to light like moths.

They were wrong, they had gone the wrong way. They should have gone into the dark, toward the beach. Maribel was always drawn to the sea.

So I went after her myself.

I thought, *I'll take my pistol,* and saw in surprise I already had it in my hand.

It won't be easy to go back by sea. They'll tell me it's impossible, no ship goes there. But I know better. It's true the telephone will never help me, nor letters of inquiry, nor travel agencies—I must go down to the waterfront myself on my own two legs to the filthy piers where the filthy water laps against the rotten pilings and ask the sullen arrogant men who have worked there all their lives. And they won't want to answer me, they'll be hostile and suspicious and they'll give me the wrong answers, they'll despise me, not knowing me, not being willing to know me, but I'll persist, persist. I'll find a way.

New York to Baltimore to Charleston to Tampa. New Orleans to Progreso. Progreso to Puerto Juárez, to Chetumal to Cuidad de las Flores, Puerto Nuevo, and home. No use denying, the journey must be done by stages. No single ship will take me there. I could begin in cleanliness and comfort if I wish. A cruise ship running down the coast, West Indies bound, why not? Enjoy myself. A romance, a conquest, a tiny drop of blood . . . No matter how my trip begins, sooner or later I'll have to find a small rusty freighter, barely seaworthy, listing wretchedly to port, its mahogany cargo shifted in a storm, confined, stinking, dirty, peppered with rats, commanded by a stubble-faced gap-toothed tyrant. I saw those vessels often enough, limping up to the pier at Caracol. I'll find one somewhere and I'll get on board.

I was the one who let her out of the house. Unlocked the door and let her out. I don't know why I did it. I was in the vestibule, rooted like a plant, just standing there among the leaves and vines in almost total darkness leaning against the wall.

I was looking inside my head at what I had seen that night: Mother and Filomena bending over Maribel under the light of two standing lamps, Maribel with her eyes wide, her knees forced open, her mouth taped shut, stark naked on a *petate* mat on the floor of her room.

Instruments, cotton, blood.

Mother and Filomena doing something unspeakable to Maribel, stabbing her deep between her legs.

Pale and murderous, my mother screamed at me to leave the room. "What are you doing here?" she cried. "Get out! This isn't what you think. Go back to bed. I'll explain it to you later. Now get out!"

They were putting her to death. My sister Maribel was being put to death, like cats and dogs.

"Get out!" screeched Filomena, lifting her black beak, the beak of a hawk. "Out!"

The smell of antiseptic. I backed away. The smell of chloroform.

Hours later I was standing in the entry in the dark, and suddenly she was there, Maribel, with her face as white as moonlight and we looked at each other. We looked at each other in silence like a pair of animals. There was equality between us and we communicated in a way we never had before.

In the dark I couldn't see the blood.

Mother had said she was all right. Mother had explained to me that it was best for Maribel. It was not like the animals, she said. Not like the pregnant cats and dogs. A simple operation, ending the pregnancy, nothing of importance. Maribel was sleeping soundly, she was fine.

But she wasn't sleeping. She was awake and on her feet and she wanted to leave the house. She wanted to go out that door. It seemed to me she had the right, that's all. It seemed to me that she'd been bullied and tortured long enough. Without saying a word she asked to go out, and without saying a word I let her go.

I didn't throw open the door for her. I didn't push her out. It wasn't that bad. What I did was barely unlatch the door, and having done that I turned once more to look at her and once more we stood without moving, drawn together but not touching or speaking, just standing there, and then I went away. The door was heavy but she managed it. I didn't watch her go. I went and sat down in the dark *sala.* I sat there waiting in the dark a long long time, before they came to look for her. They came right past me, calling.

Delila said that Maribel went out "to find the place God wanted her to die."

That was Delila's opinion, not mine. She wanted to go out and she'd been denied enough. That was my opinion. She knew very well what she would find outside. She chose to go. For once she was going to get what she wanted, she was going to be free. But I never told anybody what I'd done: unlocked the door. They would say I killed her, and I didn't kill her. I never killed her. Mother was the one who killed her, if anybody did. Mother and Uncle Clo.

In the dark, in the night, Octavia runs out to find her sister. To her right the beach ends abruptly in mangroves and the tidal river where Uncle Clo tethers his seaplane. Maribel will not be there.

To the left the beach extends into town toward the pier. Octavia runs to the left. She stumbles along in the sand as fast as she can. At a certain point the seawall begins. The beach narrows and sinks gradually farther and farther below the wall, which protects the waterfront street and stores and houses. There is less sand, more coral. A smell of drains. A distant sound of drunken singing. The sky is full of stars and the flickering glow of fireworks, like heat lightning.

At last Octavia sees something white and shining down the

beach, below the wall. A pile of white, like a sheet. She runs faster. She is right—it's Maribel. On a narrow strip of sand and coral, no more than six feet wide, Maribel is lying down.

Her nightgown is stained and wet and heavy with sand. It clings to her legs. The black stains are how blood looks in starlight. The surf runs up to her and back, with a hissing hushing sound of bursting bubbles. Silver lines are moving, changing, disappearing all over the black sea. (Ever after, drifting into sleep, Octavia will see those silver lines.)

"Come on, Marifel," says Octavia. "Get up."

But she won't get up.

Octavia pulls her, shakes her. The black stain is wide and sticky.

"*Vamonos,* Marifel."

She is too limp, too heavy, too slippery and wet. She won't get up. Octavia tries and tries again to lift her, drag her, make her walk, and finally gives up. She slides her own legs under Maribel's head and shoulders, cradling them. There is nothing else to do. She puts one hand on Maribel's cheek. In the other she has the gun, in case of drunken boys. She waits.

The night, the stars, go on and on.

On the pier the day they arrived, he stared at Octavia and said to her mother, "Why, Catherine, she looks like you."

"Does she?" said Catherine doubtfully. "All that hair?"

"She does. She looks like you at that age."

"Me in a wig then!"

"All right. You in a wig."

"I wish we were twelve years old again. I wish I had my life to live over."

"That's silly."

"I know, but oh I do wish it with all my heart."

And Octavia standing there embarrassed.

• • •

The night, the surf. Roman candles in the sky. The coral is bruising Octavia's thigh. It's cold. Maribel is cold.

"I'd go to war," she boasts to her cousin. "Would you?" They're in the schoolroom, spinning the globe.

"I guess," he says. "I'm not afraid, I just don't want to kill anybody. I don't hate anybody. Do you hate anybody?"

Yes, she wants to say. Yes.

"I mean, enough to kill them?"

And Octavia can't meet his gaze.

Don Mauricio comes in and catches them together. "July and October," he snickers. "I've heard of May and December, but never July and October. What a love affair!"

And with his tongue he slips out his two false front teeth and broadly grins, to make them laugh.

Mother says to Uncle Clo: "There are times, I admit it, when I'm tempted just to let her go, let her walk into the sea. It's what she wants. I get downhearted and it seems to me her life has just one purpose—to blight our own."

(Octavia, on the starlit beach, cries out, "That isn't true!")

"Once I did it," her mother says. "I let her go. I opened the front door and said 'Go ahead.' And I stood there watching to see what she'd do, bumbling along. And do you know what happened? Octavia came racing around from the back like a little watchdog, and grabbed her hands and pulled her inside. She was just a tiny thing then, maybe five or six, but she did that."

("I did?" says Octavia. "I did that?")

• • •

The night goes on, the surf is cold, the stars have moved.

It's like a week, two weeks, a month. Octavia and Maribel are tangled up together. Chilled and wet, Octavia weaves in and out of consciousness, sleeping in fragments of moments. Maribel is heavy and cold. She is clutching Octavia's hips with iron elbows. Something has happened, Maribel has turned to iron, she is holding fast to Octavia. The tide is running over them. The surf wants Maribel, it is running, lapping, asking, begging, over and over. Tugging, pulling, it wants to take her out to sea. The surf is rolling Maribel, nagging at her legs.

"Look at her, Octavia, look. You'd never know. Would you? Would you know?"

Octavia, curled up on the couch with her red cat, reluctantly looks up.

Catherine Sandoval, exile, stands with her hand on the back of a carved wooden chair. She wears a pale green blouse and a white skirt with a border of green leaves. Her amber hair is pulled into a bun. She watches Maribel parade across the dark tile, across the oriental carpet, to touch the wall and back again.

"Very good, Maribel!" she calls.

But Maribel, passing the open door, glimpsing the seductive flowers, the sun and dense green shade of the patio beyond, wavers, yearns toward freedom. Already she is forgetting, drifting off.

"No, no," says Catherine sharply. "Keep going. Lift your head." She crosses to the door, puts her shoulder against it, heaves it shut. Maribel, lifting her dark and enigmatic head, keeps going, patient as a donkey.

She is wearing her new red dress and does not look ugly at all, looks almost beautiful, civilized, fashionable, all dressed up as if she were going to a party, carrying an embroidered purse over her arm, her hair curled and shining, her feet in shoes with heels, walking patiently through sun and shadow. Amazing.

Octavia, her knees up, her feet on the couch, her eyes hidden behind the cascade of stringy, almost kinky yellow hair, contemplates her sister and searches for something cruel to say.

"Why does she have to move like that?"

"Like what?"

"Move her behind like that."

Catherine looks. "Good heavens," she says. "That simply happens when a person walks. Everyone does it. You do it."

"Me!" says Octavia. "I do that? I do not!"

"Well, you will, when you get older."

"Men don't do it."

"Men are formed differently. Women have wider hips. Maribel is seventeen now, she's a woman. Don't slow down, Maribel," she calls. "Step, step. Head up."

"Why should women have wider hips?"

"Because they give birth. Nature has made women's bodies for bearing children."

Octavia finds her arrow, shoots it in her mother's heart.

"Is Maribel going to bear children?"

Catherine's face changes, darkens in anger. She manages to smile.

"No," she says carefully. "Maribel is never going to bear children. Of course not. But her body doesn't know that, don't you see." She reaches out to pat Octavia's knee.

"What about the time she ran away?" says Octavia, and snatches her knees away. "You thought she was pregnant, didn't you!"

Maribel, aged thirteen, has been missing all day long.

"Who left the gate unlocked?" says her father in a fury.

"Well I didn't do it, Felipe. It certainly was not me."

They carry Maribel upstairs to her room and she lies bedraggled on her bed. Papi, clenching his fists, can't bear to look at her, can't bear to examine her. He is struggling.

"Filomena can examine her, Felipe. Let me send for Filomena."

"No," he says, "I'll do it."

He closes his eyes and holds his breath as if he is plunging in the sea. Mother gives Maribel a doll to distract her, and in a rush he spreads her legs apart and spreads that part of her, her underneath, wide open with his fingers, shines the flashlight into her so fast she is scarcely aware of it. Grimly he puts his finger there, and whatever he sees or feels it is enough. He closes her legs and covers her, and his face is shrunken and black with pain.

"Bathe her. Irrigate her. Throw her clothes away, and watch the calendar." And he goes striding out of the room.

After that, his nightmares come back. They start up again as bad as ever. Every blessed night, the flames. He tries to rescue something from a house in flames. Something urgently important. Night after night he risks his life in the raging fire for some small infinitely precious object—which turns out in his hands to be of little value. Some ridiculous object—a playing card, a fever thermometer, an empty test tube.

And then he stares at it in the palm of his hand, perplexed, trying to understand.

"Let Papi alone, Octavia. He isn't feeling well."

"What's wrong with him?"

"He doesn't sleep."

Octavia wakes up with a start. Someone is coming toward them, shouting, splashing through the surf, someone who means harm, an enemy, a swelling darkness outlined in stars. Octavia, half in dream, prepares her gun. No one will carve up Maribel while she's on guard, no one will take her eggs and use her as a toilet, not while Octavia is standing by.

In her ears she still can hear her father shouting in Mayan. *Bish u bel akeek!* he shouts. *Where is your sister?* She's here, she's here, she's bleeding on the beach. But it is not her father coming toward her. Is it her uncle with a pack of drunken boys?

In the surf, her sister won't get up, she won't, she won't, she is stubbornly dying.

They're closer now, they're twenty feet away. There are no boys. It's Christ dragging his grave clothes, eyes like silver jelly, dull and shimmering, nothing behind them, the eyes of a shark. It's Don Luis with his machete, Filomena with her knives, it's Cortez the conqueror, and someone . . . someone else.

Octavia lifts her gun. She aims, she fires. The stars whirl off, they scatter baying like a pack of dogs.

She fires again, and hears a cry.

Someone calls her name, and she is knocked into the sand.

It is not clear what is happening. She fights for her life and for her sister's life ferociously. A fountain of light bursts in her head. Ambiguous figures with spears and shields and cotton armor surround her and try to capture Maribel. Chanting unintelligible syllables in deep bass voices, they pull and tug and grab at her. They force her down into the water and wet sand, they hit her and tear her gun away. Concealed behind them on a portable throne is a giant bloodstained figure whom they serve. Their queen. Or Xtabai. Octavia can't be sure because of seagulls winging at her eyes, trying to eat her eyes, to drink them, peck them out.

Through all of it, someone keeps distracting her and shaking her. A voice, shouting and pushing.

She fights to hold on to consciousness as darkness flowers in her head. She lies pinned down, defeated, hurt. Someone bends over her sister. In iron stillness, someone says, "She's dead." And someone else (a man) says, "Take the gun."

Now for the first time Octavia sees her mother there, with stars behind her, and something else—a great black bird or cloud of smoke. Octavia sees it, and knows immediately what it is. Her real, true mother, the original, is swooping down in a whirlwind, entering the body of the other.

The two are one again.

Through darkening mist she sees her mother reach out for the gun and take it. She sees the gun now in her mother's hand, raised up to shoot. She sees her mother's face. She can let go now, she can rest.

<table>
<tr><td>

27
</td><td>

When she wakes up in her own bed, Octavia finds her head is bandaged and her teeth won't open. Delila tells her what is wrong: her jaw is fractured. Mother is nursing a gunshot wound in the left hand, and Maribel is missing.
</td></tr>
</table>

"Oh, Marifel is gone," Delila sobs. "She went into the sea, she was carried out to sea, what will we do?"

It was Lenin who X-rayed Octavia's jaw and wired it, Lenin who X-rayed, cleaned, and bandaged Mother's hand. Felipe is in no condition to help anyone—he is raging roaring weeping drunk, knocking around in the clinic. His eyes are blurred. He falls down and rises, crashing against his desk.

Around noon of the next day Maribel's body, carried out to sea by the tide, is washed in again, toward shore. The sea like a good dog returns her. Julian is the first to spot the floating bundle which is Maribel. He wades out in clear warm water up to his neck and struggles with her in the waves, dragging her toward the coral beach. Her long black hair full of sea creatures sticks to his face, enters his eyes. She fights him and clings to him all the way to shore, as cold and heavy as a nest of eels.

Her face is slate-blue, she is dead.

There is no bullet wound, she died from loss of blood. Surprisingly, the sharks have left her intact. Delila calls it a miracle.

Nobody mentions Uncle Clo, and Octavia does not ask. She doesn't need to ask. She knows what happened to Uncle Clo. He too is dead. Mother shot him on the beach. If there is no body to bury, that's because, like Maribel, he was washed out to sea, and the sharks that left her unharmed had their feast on him.

Octavia remembers her mother standing with the gun in her hand. She remembers her face, a terrible god-ridden face, and she is certain.

No one is concerned about his absence. His comings and goings have always been unpredictable. Everyone assumes he is back at the training camp with the irregulars. His airplane is still moored in the tidal river, but that is not remarkable. No doubt he left by boat.

Dumbly, like an animal, Octavia grieves for Maribel. Over and over she has to learn afresh: *she's dead.* It's as though Maribel had lived inside Octavia's body, and now that she's gone, there is this pain, this wound, a void that must be filled. Inside her head she's working day and night to understand, and somehow to prevent her sister's death. Over and over, she blames herself for changing rooms with her sister, she tries not to do that, not to change rooms. It doesn't work. She tries to believe that she found a lock, she buys the lock, she installs it herself on her bedroom door, and Maribel is still alive and well. . . . It doesn't work. Over and over she tries not to let Maribel out of the house. Instead, she runs to call someone—her mother, Lenin, anyone, even Uncle Clo. This does not work either, but the effort goes on and on, she can't stop, she's laboring, there's no relief, it's like giving birth. All day, all night she labors, trying to find relief—but all that happens is this death, her sister's death. It's death she's giving birth to, not life. No matter what she does, the death can never be aborted, nothing can be changed. Maribel is bleeding on the beach, she dies, she dies, she dies again.

All day, all night Octavia sees the silver lines of the surf on the black sea, feels it swirl against her legs, she feels the wet cold body of her sister lying on her lap that endless night.

She is dreaming, she can't hold on to reality. She has her sister and can't leave her, she can't call out—the streets are full of drunken boys. She can only guard and wait. The surf is foaming, surging, lapping at their legs. With a hushing sound it comes seducing, and falls back with a sigh. It hurries in, surrounds, caresses, falls away. Octavia huddles beneath the seawall with her sister and her gun. Her body aches. She sleeps, awakes, and fights off sleep. Her sister's skin is cold and rubbery.

Breaking into a dream, her mother and her Uncle Clo come running, calling, hurrying down the beach, splashing in the surf—but they are not coming to rescue her, they are enemies. Exhausted, half in dream, Octavia sees them as a darkness approaching, a darkness obsessed with Maribel. Something about her, something she can't help, arouses them. It's because she is pregnant, because she is weak, because of her eggs, because she is female! Outlined in stars the enemy is very near. Octavia prepares for an attack.

She hears a shout. They have seen her and are running faster. Octavia will stop them. She will defend her sister. No one will touch her sister. Let them die. She fires her gun.

For the first time in her life she points a gun at human beings and pulls the trigger.

Convulsively she pulls the trigger, hears a cry.

The cry comes from her mother. The bullet has passed through her left hand. Octavia has shot and wounded her own mother—who cries out, looks at her hand, wraps a scarf around it. In shock, she scarcely feels the pain. She gasps and whimpers, wraps a scarf around her hand, and keeps on coming.

Her uncle, racing forward, hurls himself at Octavia and grabs her hand, but she screams and fights him off. Her sister rolls over, face down in the surf, and Octavia butts her uncle, she attacks in a paroxysm of rage, screaming, flailing, kicking, biting, striking, butting, trying to use her gun again. He cannot hold her, his hands slip, her arms and legs are everywhere. At last he hits her in the face with all his strength, an awkward, backhanded blow that breaks her jaw and knocks her, crumpled, into the wet sand. He tears her gun away.

He tears her gun away, hands it to her mother, and bends down to pick up Maribel.

Octavia will never forget what she saw next, in the fraction of a second before she lost consciousness: her mother in a clear white flash, her mother entered by a god, her mother fresh and new in her transformation, her real true mother with the gun in her hand.

There is no doubt in Octavia's mind that she saw her mother rise at last in vengeance. There is no doubt whatever in her mind: she heard two shots and saw her uncle fall.

And then her mother carried her home. Leaving behind the two who were dead, the two who were lovers, leaving them for the tide to lift and tumble and carry out to sea, ignoring her wound, her mother picked up the one who was living, picked up Octavia, and carried her home.

Soledad, overcome with grief, accuses Filomena.

"You killed her, you!"

Raging, she launches herself at Filomena with Domingo's machete in both hands like an ax, but her husband and her brothers grab her arms before she can hurt anyone. She shouts. She has proof, clear proof, that Filomena did it on purpose. The proof is there, there in the room, in the bedroom of Marifel. Not bloody rags or instruments—the bed! Go look, she screams. Anyone, go look. The bed has been moved. The head of the bed is purposefully pointed to the west! Who would do that but Filomena?

For the last time, Soledad and Delila bathe Maribel. They dress her in her new red dress and comb her hair. Domingo and Lenin carry her down and lay her in her coffin in the *sala*.

Mother gives permission for the villagers to come and say good-bye.

"They loved her so much," she says.

But when they came, the villagers, bits of Maribel began to disappear. First the hair went, then the fingers and the toes. Sneaking past my door, they crept into her bedroom and stole her clothes, her paints, her menstrual napkins (carefully preserved by Soledad), and with shears and machetes they were working on the rest of her when Lenin and Domingo drove them away. What finally went into the grave was nothing much.

My mother and my father in their sorrow never knew about these things, but I did.

To keep my sister company in her wooden box, I had heaped her dolls around her, but when I came to look for the last time, they were gone. Not just her fingers and her hair but all the dolls were gone.

Lenin, little wiry Lenin, coughing, dripping tears on the coffin boards, was driving the first nails when I couldn't stand it and said, *Wait,* because I remembered two more dolls. They were dolls she gave me once and although I didn't want them at the time I didn't know how to refuse. They were hidden away in the drawer of my sea chest.

Lenin and Domingo knew how badly she needed a doll to take with her, and they pried the lid open, clawed out the nails, while I ran to my room and back again.

Two dolls, two sister dolls.

One I laid very gently in the trough between her bosom and her arm. The other I kept, I had to keep it, I couldn't let it go. Lenin covered her chopped-off hair with his handkerchief. She smelled of the tide, not of death. Then blam blam blam they nailed her down again, with ninety-nine nails.

Lenin drove the first twenty nails. And Domingo (mottled and scarred, the color of tree trunks) did the rest of it. They nailed the coffin shut and on the lid they set a dish of *copal* to burn, but it was too late. Even her womb was gone. They had sliced her belly open, found the womb, and carried it away.

Filomena said that there were two, two foetuses; it had been twins that she was carrying. My family has a history of twins.

In her room, surrounded by dolls, I asked her once: "Which one is Tavvie, Maribel?" And she picked the doll she thought was prettiest. She held it out to me. She put it in my hands. Smooth golden hair, pink cheeks, vapid blue eyes and rosebud mouth, a ruffled dress of yellow and white, and Mary Janes on its little white feet. I hated it, but she insisted.

"And which is Maribel?"

She hesitated, looked them over, all the dolls, and finally picked one. A stick—a twig—with patches of bark, with a black pod for its head and wadded straw for hair and skirt. A rattle doll from one of the black islands. Magic, very likely. Juju.

"That's Maribel?"

She nodded her head.

She was always cleverer than we thought.

• • •

There is now an official story about Uncle Clo: he has been called away. There is also an official story about Octavia's broken jaw and her mother's injured hand: drunken revelers at the fiesta were to blame.

And Julian, what of Julian? What was he told about his father? It is a question Octavia never has courage enough to ask of anyone. Presumably he's been told the official story. His father has been called away.

At Maribel's funeral Octavia sees Julian for the first time since the picnic. Mother has an arm around him, and the other (with the bandaged hand) around Octavia. They stand and watch the mason brick in Maribel forever. Papi is not there. Delila is the only one who cries.

On the way back to the house, Julian falls in beside Octavia and asks, "What happened to you?"

She can talk through her unmoving teeth, but it sounds strange.

"I fell," she says. She will not be the one to tell what happened to his father. How could she tell him? How can she speak of it, to anyone, ever?

After that she doesn't see him for days. She eats in her room. Lenin says her fracture is very small. Drink lots of milk, he says. She stays in her room eating flan, caramel custard salted by Delila's tears. Flan is full of milk, Octavia tells Lenin, and it slips between her teeth.

Of the next few weeks, up to the day of our departure, I remember almost nothing, I draw a blank—except for my mother's visits in the night.

Almost every night after I went to bed she came into my room and sat beside me in the dark and cried. She watched beside my bed

with tears running down her face, the way Papi used to watch over
Maribel. We didn't speak. I remember her teeth, how they glistened
in the moonlight when she cried—especially that one incisor
slightly twisted on its axis, a sharp tooth, a hand-me-down from
some ancestral hunting animal, a reminder that those were teeth,
not jewelry. They tore flesh. That was their mission, don't forget it.

In the darkness I was in awe of her, almost afraid. But what she
had done on the beach . . . For me, it was the balance of the
world that she set right.

We left the island one morning at dawn as the green parrots flew
overhead. My father was not there to wave and say good-bye. After
Maribel's death, he left us, walked out of the house and went off to
the other islands. A week later he sent word from Isla Maria that
Lenin should take over the clinic. He wasn't coming back.

Domingo and Delila helped us with our things. Soledad, gray
and haggard, came to the pier and embraced us one by one, my
mother, Julian and me.

"You must grow up now," she said to me. "Your mother needs
you."

One unlikely person hanging around the pier to watch us leave
was Santiago, my old enemy. I assumed he had come to say good-
bye to Julian, but it turned out to be me he wanted to see. He
walked right up to me and solemnly held out his hand, like a
grown-up. In astonishment I took it.

"I'm sorry you're leaving," he said. "Everything will be changed
here now. You're going to the United States?"

"Yes."

"Will you come back?"

"I don't know."

As I climbed on board he handed me a farewell present and a
letter. "Open it later," he said.

I still have that letter, and I keep it in my desk. It is written on lined school composition paper in a big awkward hand. The letters all run together but with some labor you can decipher it because wherever a word ended he squeezed in a big dot. It knocked the breath out of me, that letter.

> I am sorry about your sister. I know you are very sad. And I am sorry about the death of your cat. It was I, Santiago, who killed your cat. I did it for base reasons. I was jealous of everything you liked because I wanted you to like me instead. I always liked to look at you and you never looked at me. I killed your cat because I was angry and also to get rid of it. I have learned from this that jealousy is an ugly passion and people should not give way. I wish I had never done it, because it made you fall sick. I wish now you had many cats rather than I have killed this one large cat. I would give food to these cats. I will never forget you. May you go well.
>
> Your friend,
> Santiago Lopez Romero

When we left the island, Mother and Julian and I, the *Camilio Canto* took us to Puerto Nuevo on the mainland. In Puerto Nuevo the freighter *Commercial Enterprise* with a cargo of mahogany was bound for the States and took us aboard. For seven sun-filled days we wallowed sluggishly through tropical seas on our way to New Orleans. The cabins were unbearably hot, and we stayed on deck in the breeze all day. Julian and I explored the ship while Mother stood on the fantail, cradling her bandaged hand, staring at the wake. Seagulls were all around her, dipping and crying, but she never looked at them.

We stayed outside at night as well, trying to sleep in the sagging canvas deck chairs, until we were so sick with the need to lie down that we were willing to brave the steaming heat below.

Every morning I would wake up tired out from searching for my father all night long. I wanted to say good-bye. In my sleep I knew I'd never see him again.

"Is Papi coming to the States?" I asked her.

"I don't think so, Tavvie."

"When will we see him?"

"Oh, one day."

But I knew the truth. Now that Maribel was gone, he didn't want us any more.

• • •

The fourth day out, in the Bay of Campeche, lying off Veracruz, my mother came out of her dream and put her hand on my shoulder.

"Come, Octavia, I'll show you something."

She led me below, down the passageway to the bathroom in the center of the ship. She took me inside the bathroom into the heat and turned off the light. What was I supposed to look at?

In the dark she flushed the toilet.

"Look."

"At what?"

"The water."

Then I saw: the surging water in the bowl was alive with phosphorescence, sparks of light, spiraling and flashing as the water leaped and sank.

That night in our shared cabin we lay in double-decker bunks in the dark with the door ajar to catch whatever breath of air was stirring. I went to sleep but something woke me up again, a sound. It was Mother, talking in the dark. I think she was delirious with heat and sorrow. Her voice, a kind of disembodied monotone, was talking about the past, about her honeymoon, and how on shipboard, as they were traveling south to meet my father's family, a cable came with word of the massacre on Caracol. And then (while the ship was anchored in the Bay of Campeche, where we were now, this minute), how she miscarried in the toilet bowl and flushed it away amid the glittering swirl I had just seen.

"I was seventeen," she said, "a child, like Maribel. It was too much to understand."

Was she talking to herself or me? In the dark her voice droned on, a pitiless flow of words: the pain, the heat, the small white form, the spiral universe, and Maribel presiding at the center of her story just as she presided in the center of our house. A vacuum in the eye of a storm. A spider in its web.

I said nothing, what could I say? As I listened, Mother, Father,

Maribel, the Bay of Campeche, became confused. I faded back into sleep and dreamed that it was Maribel she flushed away, or me, and we whirled down and round in blackness filled with little lights.

Next morning in the cabin, while Catherine is sewing a button on her blue striped skirt, Octavia makes a discovery about herself: her hair is changing.

She wants to show it to her mother but feels shy.

"Well, my hair," says Octavia.

Catherine looks up. It's not that she doesn't listen, there's just a slight delay.

"Your hair?"

"It's turning straight."

Catherine puts down the skirt and examines the top of Octavia's head, peering over her glasses, lifting and touching the hair with her fingers. "How strange," she says in her new faint voice, "it's true. You can see exactly where it's getting smooth. And I think it's darker. Do you suppose . . . the shock . . ."

She gives a verdict: "It's shiny and pretty. I think you'll be pleased with it."

"I am. I'm pleased with it."

For a moment they hold these positions, Octavia motionless with bent head, Catherine with her fingers in Octavia's hair. Octavia holds her breath. Her ears are ringing, her blood is rushing. She wants to kiss her mother's hand and cry, *I'll make it up to you, Mother, I'll be so good, you'll see.*

The moment passes. Catherine sighs, picks up her sewing, and goes back on deck.

Octavia, staying behind, brushes her hair and feels an impulse new to her, a certain curiosity. She thinks about it for a minute, then shuts the door, pulls off her dress and cotton underpants (darned by Delila, hand-me-downs from Duncan), and steps before the full-length mirror on the closet door. She is a gambler risking all.

And there it is. Octavia's naked body, not at all as she supposed. She always thought, she just assumed, that she still had the body of a child, a bony chest, short sturdy legs, no waist or hips worth mentioning . . . she never looked below her chin, she never *cared* to look, not really look. And all the while this new and different body like an alien force was working in the dark—shifting, changing, stretching upward, swelling here and shrinking there, secretly forming itself. Octavia stares. It isn't Maribel, but it isn't Octavia either. The waist goes in, the hips emerge. The thighs are long and full, and between them (in her heart she knew it, all the time), a shadow: dark blond curling pubic hair. On the chest two rounded swellings. Breasts. She never had breasts. Nipples bulge out soft and barely formed. She never had nipples; she had flat pink smudges. Twisting around she discovers that viewed from behind the waist seems even smaller and twin buttocks stand out round and firm. A female body.

She gazes from every angle at her new possession. Can she accept it? Does she like it? Does she hate it? Is Maribel inside her trying to get out?

All in all, she can't help feeling gratified. In fact, she's proud. She feels like a *bruja* with a brand-new power source.

Octavia is moving forward. She has taken a full step. Not only does she dress herself carefully every morning to show off her new body, but she has found a brand-new occupation. On the sunny deck of the *Commercial Enterprise,* speechless, sweaty, flushed, thrilled as a wire in the wind, Octavia holds hands with Julian at the rail.

July and October, holding hands!

Having once begun, they do it all day long, their hands are insatiable. They stand close together and he tells her everything she needs to know about the United States. About traffic jams and ski slopes, football games, the YMCA. Although he is mindful of where he stands when she is near, he has forgiven her for pushing him overboard. He doesn't even ask her why she did it—which is lucky since she wouldn't be able to answer. She couldn't say, *I did it because of your father, I did it because you are a boy.*

While her mother, her real and suffering mother, stands on the fantail staring at the boiling green wake, Octavia and Julian kiss. They step into a corner, out of sight of the deckhands. They are in love. The landmark kiss, her first, is not overwhelming. It is dry and warm, an experiment, a trial run. The next one gets better, interesting but still a strange thing to be doing. Between kisses they walk around or lean on the rail, breathing lightly, looking out to sea. They hold hands. Their shoulders touch.

Standing with Julian she has no space inside her head for thoughts of Maribel or of her father. Power leaps and plays around her like St. Elmo's fire.

All the same, one step is enough, for Octavia. Holding hands and kissing are enough. The rest of it, the *sex* part, she disdains. Sex is for dogs. Sex is what her father did that morning to her mother and she cried. It's what her uncle did and made her do, and made her feel. Sex is shame and infection, it is nothing she will ever ever do.

Holding hands with Julian is as far as she can go.

When he whispers, "Let's go to my cabin," she giggles as Elizabeth Jane might have giggled, and pushes him away.

Not for ten years will she take the next step, when she gathers up her courage and marries. On her wedding night in the Skytop Motel she will tremble and hide herself, frigid as ice cream. She will dream of mutilations, seeing her Uncle Claude as a vile old man with a withered leg and a tin cup, the bones of his leg all brown and dry and twisted, like the wild grapevines you find hanging in deep woods.

• • •

The gift that Santiago gave me on the pier the day we left the island was a deer's eye seed. An *ojo de venado,* a hard oval seed with a light brown skin marked with a dark brown line.

I still have it. Today at the bedroom window in Pittsburgh, looking at the rain, remembering my cousin and the *Commercial Enterprise,* I think of Santiago too, and turn the *ojo de venado* over and over in my hand.

They come from far away, these seeds, from Venezuela it is said, where they drift down the rivers into the sea. Most are lost but every now and then a rare one can wash up on any beach throughout the world. Santiago found one and polished it himself. It was all he had to give, the only thing he prized. He gave me what he had, a jewel.

My father was always drawn to Santiago. He was angry and frustrated when he learned that against all his advice Santiago had stopped school to work full time for his family.

"Santiago is a bright boy," Father said. "Now he'll never escape the island. You, Tavita, are free in a way Santiago never will be free. You will escape, you will have an education."

"And you, Papi? Will you escape the island?"

"No, Tavita."

And he never did. Six months after we arrived in the United States, letters came from Soledad and from Lenin telling us that he was dead. They said he died of meningitis on Isla Maria, but I know he died of grief.

For me, the violence on the beach, the death of Uncle Clo, had somehow realigned the forces of the world. For my poor father, nothing would ever be put right.

He couldn't forget Maribel. He couldn't forgive my mother, or himself, or a world where such things happen.

• • •

I set these memories down in bits and scraps, pawing through my childhood, looking for a clue, asking Filomena, asking Domingo and El Veinte, Soledad and Maribel and Santiago. *Shall I end this pregnancy? Why am I afraid to have a child?*

Like tracks of seabirds in wet sand, the signs and messages point everywhere.

I'm on a sunlit beach, alone with Uncle Clo. He's deformed and hairless, four feet high. Obscenely ugly, he does not belong in life.

Shuddering, I kill him with a karate chop to the Adam's apple. I feel unclean, as if I've mashed a huge repellent bug that's come inside the house. To make sure he's dead, I use the edge of my hand as a saw, and saw at his neck until there's no longer any doubt.

He's dead. He lies there, definitely dead, and I'm the one who had the nerve to do it. I'm a hero.

To dispose of him, I drag the body across the sand. I pick it up and heave it into the tropical sea.

Splash. He floats face up below the surface of the sea, plainly visible, rocking gently with the swells. I look at him and celebrate. *You slimebag, Uncle Clo, you pitiful old creep. With my bare hand I sawed your lizard's neck, ha ha! I heaved you over the sand, you're floating there, you're dead!*

His face under the clear green water begins to change.

It transforms itself—another face is forming, a different face. I see in horror that it isn't Uncle Clo at all! I've made a terrible mistake, I've killed somebody dear to me, not Uncle Clo, somebody innocent and trusting, a cousin, a cat, a child! Who is it? Someone who needs me, someone I desperately love. What have I done?

It is 4 A.M. I turn to Justin in a sweat. My blood has all drained out, I'm having an anxiety attack.

"Wake up, Justin, wake up please."

Justin wakes up. He listens attentively but does not empathize. Nightmares, like enlightenment, are nontransferable, it seems. I want him to say, Oh my god, Octavia, how horrible, how unbearable. I want him to gasp and share the horror. The face, how it changed before my eyes . . . He cuts me off.

The subtext of my dream is clear to him.

"Throwing someone into the sea reverses birth," he says. "It's a dream about abortion. You deserve it."

He turns his back. Laughing bitterly, I go into the bathroom to throw up. Morning sickness in the middle of the night. I look at my swelling breasts and belly and it's clear to me this body now belongs to Maribel, 100 percent. It's not Octavia, it's Maribel, and the worst of it is, she wants to bear her child. Wants to, needs to. God, I'm trapped.

The dream is torturing me. Who did I kill? Someone that I dearly loved. With alka-seltzer fizzing in a glass, I get back in bed and Justin twists the knife:

"Giving birth is the sole act that gives a woman moral intelligence," he says. "Baudelaire."

I drink the alka-seltzer.

This is the man I have allowed past the lock on my door, into my bedroom, into my bed. Sometimes I think I love him only for his name. *Justin* was as close as I could come to *Julian*.

On the table beside my chair stands a photograph in a silver frame, a studio photograph of my grandmother with the twins, the tender twins, about age six. Grandmother (she of the snow and the enlightenment) is wearing a velvet vest laced with ribbon and trimmed with lace. She has a thin velvet band around her head. Her hair is light but her eyes are dark and gentle, and she holds a book on her lap.

I study the children. Self-satisfied Catherine, a bow in her long hair, sits on the left looking demurely at the book. And on the right the scissor man, angelic Claude in a sailor suit, leans against his mother's knee and gazes in her face. His lips are parted. His hair grows sweetly on his neck. His eyebrows are so light they hardly show.

How does one thing become another thing?

I look again at Catherine and shake my head. Something does not ring true.

This little girl, could she have grown into a woman who would shoot and kill her brother? Could she have done it? Could Catherine my mother have fired that gun? Even under such extreme circumstances (the pistol in her hand, the betrayer bending down to pick up the body of her daughter, the rush of truth sweeping over her), could Catherine my mother have killed her twin? The sin of Cain?

Do I really *know* she killed him? All these years I've never doubted for an instant. It was an article of faith. How was I so sure?

I'm on the beach with Maribel. I've been struck, I'm losing consciousness. I see my mother's face . . . the gun in her hand . . .

Did I really hear those shots?

My world is cracking, all around me.

Is it possible? Is Uncle Clo unpunished?

She never said outright, *"I killed him,"* but she let me believe it. I finally came out and asked her, you see. I asked her point-blank. Not because I doubted, but because I longed to hear it from her lips, to savor it again. On the fantail of the *Commercial Enterprise,* I came right out with it:

"Mother, where is Uncle Clo?"

Her body went rigid, and she took a while before she answered. One of the crew threw garbage into the wake, and I watched the seagulls scream and fight.

"Uncle Clo won't ever bother us again," she said at last, and put her arm around me.

Uncle Clo won't bother us again. It could mean anything.

To me, shaking with awe and gratitude, it was confirmation. I said to her: "I know what you did, Mother. I saw it."

She looked at me.

"I was still conscious," I said. "On the beach. I saw you with the gun. I saw you kill him."

She started to speak but I broke in.

"You were so brave to do it, Mother. It was for us, for Maribel and me. That's right, isn't it, Mother?"

"Octavia—"

"I'll never tell," I said. "I'll never tell anybody, not one soul in all my life. No matter how old I get, I'll never tell. No matter if they torture me, I'll never tell. You can trust me. And nobody knows but me. They think he went away. They don't care about him, even if they knew they wouldn't care. They'll never follow you to Washington. You did it for us, didn't you, Mother? It was for Maribel and me."

I was begging for an answer. I put the words into her mouth once more: "You did it for us. For Maribel and me."

She looked into my face for a long time, and looking at me hurt her in some way. Finally, in a thick, strained voice, she said:

"Tavvie, of course. For you."

Tavvie, of course. For you.

After that, we never mentioned him again, either one of us. We never said his name.

Tavvie, for you.

What did she mean, exactly? Could she have meant, *Tavvie, I see your need and I'll give you what you want—?*

Did Mother lie to me?

• • •

My husband Justin can't understand why I'm upset.

"Good God," he says in the morning, as we dress for work. "Why do you need to know? Is murder the only proof of love you can accept? If she lied, the lie itself was an act of love. If she actually shot him, she did it from rage and jealousy, not love of you. Don't kid yourself."

I think again of the night when I conceived this child, the night I heard her voice as if from a ship at sea, with seagulls crying and the breezes flickering on my skin like feathers.

Maybe she *was* calling from a ship at sea. Maybe standing on the fantail with the seagulls overhead, she was calling into the future, beaming a message across twenty-two years.

Maybe she was saying, *"Forgive me."*

Cortez, father of lies, with four hundred men held off fifty thousand and conquered America. He conquered, and in exchange he taught his crucial art. "The art of deception," said my father. "The art of the lie."

Until he came, in the springtime when the fires were burning, the clever lying *gringo* with four hundred men (who, lacking antibiotics, treated their wounds with grease, the grease not of turtles but of fat dead Indians)—until he came the Indians did not know how to lie. They did not understand (my father said) that a person could deliberately, persuasively, charmingly, reasonably, say for his own advantage what he knew to be untrue. The practice was not part of their culture or experience. That's why he bewildered them so. It never occurred to the Indians that you could lie.

They finally got the hang of it, of course; too late.

Mother was pearly white like Cortez, and she knew how to lie. To smile and lie, to stroke your head and lie.

• • •

Why would she lie?

What purpose would it serve, this lie? She could just as easily have told the truth, whatever it might have been. *Tavvie, I drove him away.* I'd have been content with that. Why lie? Why shoulder a crime she didn't commit? Was it for her own convenience? To bind me to her in a spiderweb of awe and guilt?

While we lived in Washington I was as good to her as I knew how. Whatever she told me to do, I did, without complaint. Sometimes I slipped, but I never forgot for one minute the sacrifice she made, the terrible gift she gave me. I tried to make it up to her. I studied hard. While she taught Spanish at Miss Hooten's School (where Duncan once had boarded), I took my degree at George Washington. To please her. Then I kept going and took my master's. Pleasing my poor mother was number one on the priority list. Her deformed left hand just broke my heart. Day in, day out, I blamed myself.

Tavvie, of course. For you.

Who would know the truth of it? Aunt Jenny?

When we left the island we lived with Aunt Jenny for ten long years. She fed us and housed us, she more or less supported us. Mother wanted to pay for our keep, but Aunt Jenny wouldn't take it, since she was the one who inherited the house and everything else my grandfather left behind him.

Aunt Jenny is a happy, homely old lady with buck teeth and crinkled gentle eyes. When I asked her once the secret of her happiness (humming and smiling all day long), she told me that her dead mother comes into her bedroom every night of the world, just before she goes to sleep. All she does is stroke Aunt Jenny's hair, very lightly, touch her cheek, pat the blanket, and go away, but she leaves behind a sense of marvelous comfort. Aunt Jenny never sees her, just feels that gentle touch, and it makes her happy. Even though she's deaf and losing her grip, even though she doesn't know who's living and who's dead, she's a really happy old lady.

I'm glad my mother doesn't visit me at night, not every night; I wouldn't care for it.

I place a call to Washington.

"Why hey-o, dear," she says in her gentle voice.

"Aunt Jenny, I'm calling to ask you about Uncle Claude."

"Who?"

"Your brother, Claude. My mother's twin. Claude? Little Clo? You remember him."

"Of course, dear. Clo and Cata, those little twins. Oh my, they were a handful, I can tell you."

"Aunt Jenny, when did he die? Can you tell me when and where he died? Try to remember."

"What-say?"

"Uncle Claude, Aunt Jenny. How did he die?"

"Little Claude?"

This is going to be harder than I thought. "Not *little* Claude, Aunt Jenny, *big* Claude. He grew up. He became a man, remember?"

"That's what generally happens, dear, with little boys."

"Tell me about his death, Aunt Jenny. Please tell me. Please remember."

"Is this Octavia?"

"Yes, Aunt Jenny. It's Octavia." She's drifting, poor thing. A mistake to call.

"I was supposed to tell you something, but I can't think what it was," she says. "How are you feeling, dear?"

"Fine. Aunt Jenny, just tell me when and how he died. My Uncle Claude."

"My goodness, dear, he didn't die. What a terrible thought. He's far from well, but he hasn't left us yet."

I take a breath or two.

"Aunt Jenny? Are you telling me my Uncle Clo is still alive?"

"Are you in Pittsburgh, dear?"

"Aunt Jenny, all my life I've thought he died on the island. Uncle Claude. I thought he died when I was twelve years old."

"Well, yes, he did. I mean we thought he did. But he turned up again, you know, was it four years ago? Claude's very tough, you know. He doesn't blow out like a candle. No indeed he didn't die. What a thought! Let's see . . . in Japan, there was an accident, the train . . . was it a car wreck or a train? . . . and someone died . . . the driver died . . . or else . . . not Claude, the driver. Claude broke his kneecap and his hip, that's it. And he came back. He's in Virginia. No, no, he's in the old men's home—a nursing home—in that town, that chocolate town. You know. Hershey. Or else . . ."

"Aunt Jenny?"

"What-say, dear?"

"Do you know what you're saying?"

"What-say, dear?"

"Are you sure it's not a dream? Are you absolutely certain that he's still alive?"

"Those little twins were motherless—I had to be their mother, don't you know," says Aunt Jenny. "But, lord, they were a handful. I couldn't control them, either one. Is this Octavia? Have you heard from your mother, dear?"

Mother has been dead two years. Aunt Jenny is clearly out of touch. She's in another world living on faulty memories. But all the same, train wreck, car wreck, old men's home—what if it's true?

It occurs to me that Hershey, Pennsylvania, is not so far away from here. I could check out Hershey with my own two eyes, track down the nursing home and find . . .

What will I find? A wreck of a man, in a wheelchair. Rheumy

eyes and shaking hands. Pinching the nurses as they pass. Pipes and whistles in his sound. Time about to do him in—not Mother, not me, nobody but Time.

No punishment? The bastard got away with it?

Raging, fuming, I run amok in the old men's home. I run amok with a pair of barber shears. I stab and kill the lot of them. Nurses toss the bloody bodies out the door. They pile up one atop another, elderly *chicleros* on a Saturday night.

Uncle Clo, alive?

I wander around the apartment in shock. It's very dark. *Palm fronds are rustling, the mosquito net is down. I'm feverish, my throat is sore. I'm twelve years old and small for my* . . . Hold on a minute. Times have changed. I'm married. I'm in Pittsburgh now, grown up.

If my uncle's still alive, he could be anywhere. A nursing home in Hershey, or a taxicab in Pittsburgh. He could be downstairs right now, on the doorstep, his finger lifting toward my bell.

If he's alive, one day he'll surely come. Next week, next month, next year, five years from now, he'll come. I see him smiling at the door, an elderly relative, affectionate, reformed, bringing gifts. I feed him. Yes, polite and dutiful, for Mother's sake, I feed him lamb chops, peas, and baked potato. On his lap he holds my little daughter (daughter, yes, for it's a girl I'm carrying, I know that it's a girl). He calls her Missy, strokes her silky hair, his hand rides up her leg. I take her off his lap, send her to bed. Over coffee, we reminisce about old times. Can he really think I don't remember?

Now I pretend I'm called away or else distracted by the phone, and he is free. Quietly he stalks the hallway, stops outside the bedroom of my child. I see him in the darkness, standing, breathing, lifting up his hand. He doesn't know I'm waiting near the window. Nude.

Come in, old man, don't change your mind. Come look at me. I'm half in shadow, half in light . . . half woman and half beast

. . . I'm calling you. I'm beautiful and nude and in my hand, the barber shears. I'm Xtabai.

"Come in, old man," I call so sweetly. "Come close, come over here."

Would my sister Duncan know?

I phone her in Virginia, first time in years. As always, she's away. In the south of France this time, "traveling." She'll be gone six months. The obsequious male voice that answers the phone gives me a mailing address in Biarritz.

Night comes. Justin corrects his papers, stretches, heads for bed.

"All these years—have I deluded myself?" I ask him.

"If you did, it was because you needed to."

I take a pill and find myself at Duncan's door. She answers the bell herself, wearing baggy white shorts and an old brown cardigan sweater speckled with tiny tacky balls of acrylic fuzz. She is dumpy and looks sick, with red-rimmed eyes and her stomach sticking out. She is sucking her thumb! Duncan? A surprise, but then I haven't seen her for ages. People change.

Inside the house I see tin cans on the table and linoleum on the floor.

"Duncan, I've come about Uncle Clo. I need to know about him. Is he dead?"

In answer to my question she pops her slimy thumb out of her mouth and begins capering around, shouting at me, hitting her fists on her thighs, saying the names of colors, over and over.

"Black, white, yellow, red!" she shouts. "Yellow, red, green, brown!" Her white shorts have a brown and yellow bubbly stain in back.

She shat herself. Duncan!

• • •

All day at work I go through the motions. I laugh and joke with my students, I try to concentrate on Borges. Jorge Luis and his dream-tigers. I am thinking, Borges would know what really happened on the beach. He'd dream it, he'd read about it in an ancient musty book.

After my last class I keep an appointment at the doctor's office in a heavy foursquare house of grimy brick. I lie on the table waiting to see him, and nurse Martha Kelly full of good cheer pulls down the sheet and presses a stethoscope to my belly. She fiddles with the dials on a machine nearby. There is a tiny sound in the air, a ticking sound.

"What's that?" I say in alarm.

Very fast and very small. A pulsing sound.

"Turn it off," I say. "I don't want to hear it. That's not my pulse, that's too fast. Oh god, turn it off, what is it?"

Martha, beaming, turns the volume high. "You know very well what it is."

A heart, a beating heart. Louder, louder. Volume going up. It fills the room, this rushing, beating heart. It pulses down the corridor. It beats against the walls. Louder, louder, from the void, un-beatable, sheer energy, it fills the room, the house, the street, it spreads out over the city, it beats in radio waves over the oceans and the mountains, over my island, Caracol, it penetrates the graves, the sea, the whole wide world.

The foetal heart. Primitive, demanding.

The ancient drumbeat I've been yearning for and dreading all my life.

If ever I go back to Caracol, I'll pay my respect to El Veinte in his pale blue playhouse with the red wasps in the eaves, and I'll visit

Maribel. She is just bones by now, a skeleton with a doll in its arms, the Tavvie doll she gave me once, a baby doll with yellow Dacron hair and eyes that opened and closed. She called it Tavvie and she gave it to me, and I laid it in her coffin long ago to keep her company.

Time builds a frame for horrors, so they say.

I'll go to our house, and touch the kitchen-garden wall where the life's blood of my cat made an ugly cascade. Only a stucco wall, after all, with massed bougainvillea, grasshoppers, and little lizards hiding in the leaves. The stain will still be there, but faded, smaller than I thought, and dusty, hidden under blossoms. A poison-truth long swallowed and assimilated.

I'll put flowers on my father's grave, if I can find it. Did the islands erupt in celebration when my father died? Were the villagers glad to be rid of him, his pills, his injections, his obsession with clean water? Did they celebrate with a shout of joy and drunkenness as they did when the *gringos* of the fruit company left, and never mind that the children were sick and the soil poisoned? Back to the *curanderos,* back to the old ways: clear the jungle, plant the corn with sticks?

By now they'll have other problems. By now they'll be overrun by tourists, overbuilt with great hotels. Swimming pools, golf course. Will I find anything I know? At least the sunsets will be the same. The sky can't have changed. At night the planet Venus (lover of the moon) will cast a golden track across the sea. The swirl of luminous transparent cloud will wash across the sky from horizon to horizon.

Actually she gave me two dolls, my sister did. The Tavvie doll and the Maribel doll—the one she said was Maribel—a rattle doll from the black islands, with a stick for a body, a pod for a head, and dried straw for a skirt. I've kept that doll. I store it in the box of Christmas ornaments.

Every year while Tavvie molders in the grave, Maribel crowns the tree.

In bright sunlight Octavia, nearly thirteen, eagerly leans forward in the bow of the *Commercial Enterprise,* sniffing the wind, squinting in the sun, straining for her first glimpse of the new world of television, snow, and traffic jams. She is not thinking about Maribel. Unlike her mother, who is drawn to the fantail, looking back, Octavia faces forward, into the wind. She is looking for New Orleans, gazing at the horizon line where soon the snow will rise up from the sea.

She stands in the windy bow at a moment of beautiful balance. Loved by Julian, acknowledged by her mother, she is growing, she is strong. She has no inkling of her future life. She does not foresee that Julian's aunt will be waiting for the boat in New Orleans to take him away from her, nor that within six years, having just turned twenty, he will be dead in Vietnam.

She does not foresee her wedding night in the Skytop Motel, or her father's death, or her mother's, or the frantic terror she will feel (at age thirty-four) when her waist thickens and her breasts enlarge, and she learns—as if it is a death sentence, as if she is doomed to chloroform and the execution box—that she is now as pregnant as a cat or dog, as pregnant as her sister Maribel.

On the deck of the *Commercial Enterprise,* Octavia dances to the music of a radio. Delila is her model. Timidly at first, then with increasing confidence, she wriggles and parades herself. The deck-hands laugh and cheer, they gather round and clap.

Julian glowers. He is jealous!

How can she doubt her command of the future?

It is true that every night in the sweltering cabin, trying to sleep, she hears the sound of rushing water. Every night the turmoil tosses her about, the suction pulls her down and flings her out—she sinks into glitter, flies off into the universe. The danger takes her breath away.

But it's not unpleasant. In fact, it's a thrill. Balanced in the moment of her greatest happiness, Octavia is now asleep.

Luminous, a billion stars. The winds of space, the whirling galaxies. Below the ship, in dark sea water, a tiny form goes drifting, dreaming, turning. Wisps of paper cling to it like chiffon veils.

Scribners